P9-APX-311

Matthew Oliver was enthusiastic when he received the invitation to work at the Colindale Institute. The Institute's computer resources had been set up to correlate research findings throughout the whole European Community—a huge forward step for Western science, and a fascinating project to work on.

But then a member of the underground CLC asked him to serve as a spy for them, to uncover the secret they were sure was hidden behind the Colindale's quiet academic exterior. One day later, that man was dead, murdered. And when Oliver got to the Colindale, he found that his predecessor too had been killed.

Something very important and very deadly was going on at the Institute, that was obvious. But Matthew could never have guessed just how awesome the project was . . . and how chilling.

DAVID G. COMPTON was born in London in 1930; both his parents were in the theatre, and he was brought up by his grandmother. After eighteen months' National Service, he tried a variety of jobs—as a stage manager, salesman, dock worker, shop display manager, jobbing builder—before turning to writing.

Mr. Compton lives in London; his hobbies are music, sailing and vintage cars. He is the author of several radio, stage and television plays, and of a recent mainstream novel, *THE PALACE*. He has published two previous novels in the Ace Science Fiction Specials series, *SYNTHAJOY* and *THE SILENT MULTITUDE*.

THE STEEL CROCODILE is an original novel for the SF Specials, never published anywhere previously.

THE STEEL CROCODILE
by D.G. COMPTON

AN ACE BOOK

Ace Publishing Corporation
1120 Avenue of the Americas
New York, N.Y. 10036

THE STEEL CROCODILE

Copyright ©, 1970, by D. G. Compton

An Ace Book. All Rights Reserved.

Printed in U.S.A.

ONE

GRYPHON TURNED on the high-frequency jammer. Before being taken over by the university, his office had been used by an insurance company, and therefore had been fully wired. Gryphon had ripped out the equipment as soon as he'd moved in, and bought himself a bug jammer. It stood on his desk now, neither obtrusive nor in any way concealed. Matthew recognized it from the advertisements, and also because it was the model recommended in the previous month's bulletin from the Civil Liberties Committee. Matthew wasn't himself a member of the C.L.C., but he was on their mailing list on account of his work.

"Were you followed on your way here?" Matthew nodded. "So?"

"So I did what you said." Matthew felt grubby. He'd never had a tail before. He was a sociologist, an ethnologist, not an alienee. Not that he had anything against alienees—some of his best friends were . . . But if working at the Colindale meant that he was no longer to be trusted, then he'd refuse the job while there was still time.

"It worked?"

"Not at first. I didn't believe in your radio homer, so I did a lot of running up and down stairs and hiding in doorways. I might have saved my energy."

"Where was it?"

"In my coat collar. Silly little thing on a pin. I expect it was stuck there while I was in the washroom at the Ministry."

"They must have thought you very innocent, Matthew. They have much craftier ways with the old hands."

"Innocent? Don't you mean naïve?"

Of course he was naïve. He needed naïveté in his work; it helped him to remain outside, separate from the problems he studied. Abigail didn't agree with him, of course—her tutor had preached total commitment, the discovery of truths-from-within: far truer truths, Abigail said, than his overall ones. Abigail . . . even to remember her name comforted him. He wished she were with him at that moment. He functioned so much better with her around.

"And this pin," Gryphon was saying. "When you found it, did you do what I suggested?"

"I did not. What about the feelings of the next man—being followed all across London for no reason at all?"

"He'd probably be used to it. Most people are."

"It's all wrong, Gryphon. The very fact of being followed—it made me feel guilty at once."

"Isn't that one of the points? Besides, with my letter in your pocket they'd have said you *were* guilty."

"That's what I mean. I'd rather you left me out."

Gryphon's room was cool, with reversible wall panels in green and black, white bookshelves and racks for microfilm. The picture on the back wall was responding to the harsh city sunlight with a range of metallic yellows and grays. The window overlooked St. Paul's, the dome below them sharply striped with the shadow of the narrow Senate House. The University had come there as part of the European Save-the-Cities campaign, populating the voided towers with thirty thousand undergraduates. Matthew looked down at them, not ant-like, too still, too controlled by their fear and by an awareness of its potential. He wondered irrelevantly if Paul, Abigail's brother, was among them. He remembered his own College years, his and Gryphon's, in the days before the students had really tried their strength. Even then he had avoided the tear gas and the batons, and so had Gryphon. They had pretended to be apolitical, too absorbed in their studies. Perhaps they had been wise beyond their age after all.

"Well?" said Gryphon. "What did you do with it then?"

"The pin? I'd gone into a gents to search for it, so I flushed it down the pan." Matthew shivered. "There you are. Being watched. Scuttling. Hiding in lavatories. Looking for electronic pins. It's ridiculous—and slightly disgusting."

"I wonder what its range was. Amusing if your tail is running after it along the course of some sewer."

Gryphon wasn't answering him. Matthew turned back from the window.

"You're not answering me."

"Don't let's be too naïve. You're here, therefore—"

"I'm here to tell you I've decided to turn down the job at the Colindale Institute."

"You made that decision thirty seconds ago. I watched you make it."

Always so right. Always the harder, clearer mind. So

why still a junior lecturer? Matthew, on the other hand, had been consultant on half a dozen major resettlements, was author of as many books, retained by three of the nine industrial giants. . . . It seemed an impressive record.

"And I hope to watch you unmake it." Gryphon pinched the bridge of his nose as if he still wore glasses. "Why did you come, Matthew? And why did you throw your tail as I asked you to?"

"It's the moral duty of"—Gryphon was laughing at him but he battled on—"of everybody to make tailing as difficult as possible. Or we'd be back where evasion on its own was proof of guilt. And you know how the Public Prosecutor—"

"That battle's been won, Matthew. We can thank the student body for that, if not much else." He sorted through his papers and found a booklet which Matthew recognized: *Physical Surveillance and the Free Citizen,* issued by the C.L.C. "There's another one coming out next week on Audio Surveillance," Gryphon said, "and there's nothing the Public Prosecutor can do about it. The citizen has a right to protect himself. I want you to become a spy, Matthew."

No pause, no change of tone. Was it a compliment, considering him too intelligent to be softened up first? Or an insult, knowing him too stupid to need any finesse at all . . . ? Gryphon wasn't smiling.

"Matthew, I want you to accept the job at the Colindale Institute, and I want you to tell me what work is really being done there."

"You want me in jail for life?"

"Reformative custody . . . and it might be worth it"—

8

Gryphon sounded tired—"if you got the information out to me first."

Matthew wondered what Gryphon's first name was. Five years at University, twelve years since, and he was still Gryphon. Matthew decided it was a mannerism, and became irritated.

"Your paranoia shows, Gryphon. That's why you're still a junior lecturer."

"Your wife, Matthew, is a remarkable woman."

It was a remark that Matthew couldn't resent, for its implication was correct. He had never spoken like that to Gryphon before in his life, and he should have. Abigail was making him grow up.

"She'll agree with me about the Colindale. Surveillance, distrust, secrecy . . . there's plenty of useful work I can do without all that. If being head of the Social Study Department means being watched and having my letters monitored, then I don't want it."

"You could write in code. There are plenty of good coders on the market."

Gryphon wasn't missing his point. Indeed, he was making it even more forcibly.

"I don't need the money."

"None of us does. We're vocationalists—sorry, dirty word."

"And I'm not interested in the status."

"You are, but not very. Probably not enough."

"So I shall find another job. Take some time off even. Cultivate my own garden. Abigail would like that."

They had a cottage in Wales. Abigail would like that. Their chance to discover if their better life was no more than a Thoreau fantasy. Gryphon sighed.

"When I heard they'd offered you a job at the Colindale I thought they'd made a mistake. I still do." He was rolling a microfilm to and fro on his desk, watching it closely. "Their first, their only mistake in a very long time. Which is why we must, must, must take advantage of it."

"We?"

"You and I. This isn't a C.L.C. matter. Far too indefinite. I need first-hand evidence before I can put it to the Committee."

"I'm not a member."

"Nobody ever is."

"But I'm really not."

Matthew knew he was being willed to involve himself, to ask the question. Once he did so he was past halfway to accepting the answer, accepting its intellectual necessity. Gryphon wouldn't be bothering otherwise. A cloud covered the sun, and the picture on the back wall shifted to orange and blue.

"You'll have to tell me what's going on." Done for. "After all, what possible erosion could come from the Colindale? It's one of the most enlightened projects ever thought of."

"I look for pattern, Matthew, and when I don't find one I get suspicious. You believe in pattern, and so do I. It's possible, of course, that my sample just isn't big enough."

"Computers?"

"I've tried, of course. Not even remote associations emerge. Nothing. Just a list of isolated facts."

"Tell me." Putting himself up to his neck, and beyond.

Gryphon clipped the microfilm into his desk viewer. It contained a list of names, with symbols beside each.

He spun the reel, letters flicking shapelessly by. The striking of the Cathedral clock passed unnoticed.

"Ten thousand students over the last four years," Gryphon said, "analyzed by age, sex, race, income, political, religious and integrative criteria. The four years of the Colindale Institute. Ten thousand examination results, ten thousand theses, ten thousand decisions on further education, ten thousand first year grant appropriations, ten thousand second year appropriations. And no pattern." He spun the reel back again. "Examination results, thesis subject, social relevance, political bias, even sex—nothing makes a discernible pattern." He stopped the reel, enlarged a single name, translated the code for Matthew. "Danderson, female, twenty-three, unmarried, Nordic, fifth degree affluent, Communist, Buddhist, integrative index 01. Examination results, par for her year, disappointing on previous record. Thesis subject, virus caging in the S.17 group. Rating, 90—that's very good. Further education, naturally. First year appropriation, five hundred marks. Second year appropriation, nil." He sat back. "Which makes Miss Danderson an excellent example of what is worrying me."

Matthew stared at the row of Astran coordinates. In view of the rating, five hundred a year was niggardly. And why the sudden cutoff?

"Any explanation given? Subject duplication?"

"I expect so. It's a usual one. No way of checking, of course."

"What makes you think the decision came from the Colindale? Why not the Appropriations Board?"

"The Board exists on a political basis. A sample as big as this ought to reflect that fact, even allowing for overcompensations."

"So you want me to find out why Miss Danderson was discouraged."

"And four thousand like her, Matthew. A forty percent cutoff, and no pattern."

Matthew frowned. To make the issue one of academic freedom was unfair, attacking him where he was least protected.

"I gather your figures deal only with the physical sciences."

"Three months' work. Not possible to include Arts or Social Sciences, even if the information were available to me. But I'm confident from what members of the staff have told me that there's the same lack of pattern."

Of course there was a pattern. There must be. Group decisions threw up patterns. A lot depended on the subtlety of the scanning.

"I've been using the Friedmann 5000," Gryphon said. "Loops, parallel scanning, the lot."

"I still don't see why you think the decisions are originating in the Colindale."

"Perhaps they don't. Perhaps it's just coincidence that the pre-Colindale appropriations were quite childishly predictable. . . . Somebody has to make the decisions, Matthew. Whether they are right or wrong depends on the criteria."

"And you want me to find out the criteria as well."

"You'll probably be working on them."

Gryphon was a member of the central C.L.C.—Matthew knew this and had always tried not to know it. Not to act upon such knowledge was an explicit admission of approval. And Matthew neither approved nor disapproved. He was a sociologist. He hunched his shoulders against the choices being forced on him.

"If we decide to use anything you tell us, Matthew, the leak will immediately become obvious. You'll be the first one to come under suspicion."

"You're only saying that to make the whole thing a point of honor to me."

"Intellectual honor."

At first Matthew had been keen to go to the Colindale. It was a considerable honor to have been invited there. The computer resources of the Institute had been set up to coordinate and interrelate research findings throughout the whole European Community. By pooling the scientific resources of the member nations it minimized waste and moved competition out onto the larger, inter-powerbloc scale. Also it made its data stores and cross-referencing capability available to thousands of universities, research groups, and individual scientists. In the terms of its charter it was not a decision-making organization. If it was being used as such, then people should be told. Centers of power needed watching.

"I must talk it over with Abigail."

"I wouldn't. She'll only push you even further than you want to go." Gryphon paused. "One other thing. I hear there are other people interested in the Colindale. People even less constitutional than we. I should like us to get in first, simply as a matter of saving lives."

"Other people?"

"A group. Bombs, guns, the usual paraphernalia of militancy. So don't dawdle, there's a good fellow."

Abigail was in the garden. A city garden, a Kensington garden, not a very large garden, not even very beautiful. Nevertheless, only money brought such things. The garden was money. Claiming to be uninterested in money, Matthew stood at the top of the iron steps down to the lawn and watched his wife playing with the cat. The sunlight made her dress very yellow against the green grass. The room behind him was high and cool, with elegant plaster work and old-fashioned calm. Had the day-long leisure of the pre-industrial rich really been as desperate as people said today, perhaps in order to excuse their present desperation?

Abigail existed to disprove them all. She was not in the least afraid of inactivity, of the small preoccupation, and she felt no moral qualms. She was filled by whatever she did. Now, playing with the cat, she shared its rightness, its energy, its precise adjustments. . . . He went down the staircase to her, his hand trailing in the honeysuckle that had grown up around the cast-iron supports of the rail.

"Tell me what you think of Gryphon," he said.

"Come and sit down and get grass stains on your trousers."

The cat crouched, glaring at Matthew's feet as they approached, then was off through the bushes and over the wall.

"You're very beautiful this evening."

"So are you."

She looked up at him and he kissed her, stooping, his hands on her breasts.

"No—"

"Whyever not?"

Her bright brown eyes looked up over his shoulder, at the upstairs windows of the house next door, just showing above the garden wall. He moved his hands up and held the curves of her skull in them, containing her thoughts in them, her mind.

14

"You once said you'd gladly keep house for me in a bus shelter even."

"So I would."

"Fat lot of cuddling we'd get in a bus shelter."

But he loved her unfashionable modesty.

She was silent. He knew, not through his fingers, that her thoughts were on the material wealth surrounding them. She disliked it, used it, disliked herself for using it, enjoyed it, feared it so that sometimes it almost stood between them. They'd never come anywhere near to the bus shelter, the shack that she obscurely felt would have ennobled them, and she blamed him for this easy success, this cheerful failure to be poor. A Roman Catholic, her attitudes were strangely puritanical. Yet she knew about poverty. All her life till she had met him she had been poor. He moved his fingers through her hair, close against the hard white bone.

"I love you more than yesterday," he said.

They lay on the grass, just their hands touching. The sun was lowering, and Matthew half-closed his eyes against its brilliance on the white stucco of the house behind them. There was a recent cherry tree, its stippled, shining bark exuding reddish anemones of resin. The garden itself was old and tired, with dusty figs growing against the south wall, nectarines, and a pear tree long barren. The woodwork of the greenhouse sagged: if Matthew repaired it technology would dictate extruded aluminum and anti-filter sheeting. So he left the dulled white paint to gather mold, and the glass to cloud over. The garden might have been claustrophobic, preserved falsely, feeding on itself. Instead it formed a starting point and a safe return.

15

"I'm taking the Colindale job. It'll mean moving house in a few days."

"Is that all it'll mean?" She leaned up on one elbow. "The work sounds so abstract. Your hold on reality is flimsy enough at the best of times."

"Plenty of studies have been done on closed academic communities. I'm sure they'll be watching out."

"I feel uneasy, Matthew. That's all."

"Besides, it looks as if I shall be having a strong outside interest." He stood up. "Let's go indoors so that I can kiss you."

They went up the curving staircase and in at the French windows. He kissed her. They stood together for so long that their shadow had time to move on the soft carpet within the room. He told her about what Gryphon had asked him to do. He repeated the question he had asked earlier.

"Tell me what you think of Gryphon."

"I'd rather tell him to his face. He's a bore." She smiled. "I suppose what I have most against him are the short cuts in his conversation. The more right they are, the more insulting. People should be allowed to progress at their own tempo."

"That's funny. I find his assumptions of my intelligence flattering."

"They're not meant to be. He only makes them to prove how even more intelligent he himself must be."

"That's very uncharitable of you, love."

"He's arrogant, Matthew. I can't stand arrogance." She turned away from him. He thought how small she looked. "But you must do what he wants you to."

"If I'm found out it'll finish me."

"Good." She turned back to him. "Finish you for

what? For all this?" She indicated the room, the garden, the town car, the long-haul car, the holidays, the space. "For all this?"

"It might mean jail."

"I'd wait for you."

"You romanticize."

"God loves me. We're never tested beyond our strength."

Matthew thought of the millions in mental hospitals. God loved them too. Unfathomably.

"I'll take you out to see our new house in the morning," he said.

She walked away, went downstairs to prepare his dinner. It wasn't that he needed to guard her faith. Years ago he'd lost the conceit that it depended on his protection, on the things he said or left unsaid. It existed in spite of, or perhaps because of . . . The front doorbell rang and he went to see who was there.

"Police." Two men in slacks and bright shirts. "We're looking for a Dr. Oliver. Matthew Oliver."

Matthew was wary. "I am he," he said.

"Will you hear that?" said the fatter of the two men. "The verb *to be* governing the dear old nominative after all these years."

"You wanted to speak to me?"

"Detective Inspector Kahn, that's I. Sergeant Wilson, that's he too. I reckon."

Matthew had obviously started badly. The guilt he already felt had made for a bad beginning. He tried to do better.

"Please come in, Inspector."

"That's nice. If you don't ask, we push—so where are you?"

The two policemen entered. They stared at the staircase curving up under a glass cupola. Matthew knew he should ask them for their identification warrants. He wanted to avoid being difficult.

"They tell me you write books. Get all this writing books?"

"It helps." He refused to sound apologetic. "I also work for a government planning agency. And for one or two business corporations."

"The man, Sergeant Wilson, is a vocationalist. Holy, holy . . ."

"Perhaps he can't help it."

They walked, trailing Matthew, through into the living room. Kahn lit a cigarette and threw the match on the carpet.

"Name of Edmund Gryphon mean anything to you?"

"I know him very well. We were at College together."

"You were at College with ten thousand, but you know Edmund Gryphon."

"We shared a room. We had a lot in common."

"Had . . . ?"

"Have. We still have a lot in common."

"You said *had*."

"He's a physicist. We work in different fields. I haven't seen so much of him latety."

"Then have you a lot in common or haven't you?"

"We think with similar techniques." He was pleased to have avoided saying they thought in similar ways. Words could be dangerous. "It's a question of minds, Inspector."

"Which I wouldn't know about."

Matthew decided he was wasting his time. "What's Dr. Gryphon supposed to have done?"

The police sergeant had been looking along the bookshelves. He flipped out a C.L.C. pamphlet, *Aspects of Censorship,* and held it up for Kahn to see. The inspector sat down, made himself offensively comfortable.

"And you haven't seen so much of him lately."

"Not for a month or two. I was with him this afternoon, though."

"Wise man. University porter, half a dozen students, they all saw you."

"I'm not surprised. My visit wasn't secret in any way."

"Yet you threw your tail."

"Of course."

"He knows his rights, Sergeant. You and me must watch ourselves."

Naturally the interview was being recorded, probably from the sergeant's shirt pocket. The balance between legality and intimidation was very nice. Matthew asked for the policemen's warrant cards and was shown them. His wife came up from the ground floor.

"Visitors, Matthew? I thought I heard the doorbell."

He made the introductions.

"Shall I go or stay?"

"You can please yourself." Kahn had not risen. Abigail led Matthew over to the couch and sat him down beside her. The sergeant was still prowling, looking now in the music chest beside the harpsichord.

"I asked you what Dr. Gryphon was supposed to have done," Matthew said.

"Illegal, you mean? Nothing, as far as I know. Perhaps you know better." Kahn tossed cigarette ash in the direction of the fireplace. In that room his shirt was the greater offense. "This visit of yours—tell us why you made it."

"I'm leaving Central London in a few days . . ." Matthew had had time to work this one out. "Taking up a new job out in Colindale. I thought I'd have a chat with him before I went."

"A chat. . . . What about?"

"Nothing in particular." He saw he'd never get away with just that. "We talked about"—improvising—"some of his students' results. They were sociologically interesting."

"Tell me."

"It's the relation of background to performance, Inspector. Plus variants such as leisure activities, ethical positions, integration/alienation quotients, and so on. There seems to be a clear connection between these and—"

"You could keep that up all day, Dr. Oliver."

"I don't understand you."

"True or not, you could keep that spiel up all day. It's your field. You could keep it up all day."

Abigail's hand tightened on his, her anger like an electric current. He felt none himself, only an intense depression. For her sake he defended himself.

"You asked me a question, Inspector Kahn. I was doing my best to answer it."

"So you talked about whatever it is you vocationalists talk about."

"There's no need to sneer. Isn't the police force classed as a vocation, in view of the hours you work?"

"The police force, Dr. Oliver, provides a legitimate outlet for men with a warped or immoderate need to excercise power. Warped or immoderate, the words were."

Matthew's words, the words he had written. A tag

like that would have gone the rounds. Theory at the time of writing: now observable fact.

"You don't like the police force, Dr. Oliver."

"Would you want to be liked?"

Inspector Kahn was amused. He showed his amusement loudly, for a long time, longer than was credible. At last he subsided.

"So you talked about students' records. On a visit to tell him goodbye."

"We have a common interest in techniques of statistical analysis."

"And then you shot him."

Even Sergeant Wilson was still, caught at the window, etched into by the sun behind him. Matthew could hear the sound of the house around him. His perception altered, narrowed to a policeman's colored shirt collar, driving Abigail away, denying her hand in his, leaving him alone with Gryphon's death.

"Shot Gryphon?"

"Records show you with a license for a laser pistol, Dr. Oliver."

"That's right. I . . . In case there was any more civil unrest I thought—"

"No bullet, no ballistics. No ballistics, no proof. And you the last person to see Dr. Gryphon alive."

"Except the murderer." Abigail was on her feet. "I shall issue a formal complaint. You have no right to interrogate my husband without—"

"Emergency regulations have a way of lingering on, Mrs. Oliver. If parliaments are frightened enough."

She faltered, looked back at Matthew. Her vulnerability restored him. The policeman had spoken the truth; for her sake if for nothing else he wished it were not so.

"Don't worry, love. They still need to be able to prove more than just the opportunity. . . . I have a laser, Inspector, because they can be tuned down till they only burn. I'm not good with guns and I didn't want to kill anybody."

"They can also be tuned up till they go straight through and take a piece out of the chair behind."

"I know that."

Matthew wouldn't be shocked again, refused the picture of Gryphon held up in his seat by flesh welded to the chairback.

"But not by me."

He and Abigail stood in the open doorway and watched the police car till it turned the corner at the end of the tall street. Shadow from the low sun lay in a precise roofline across the houses opposite. There were plane trees with heavy, summer-dark leaves. And aching pavements. The rich were very silent, and kept safely within walls.

"Do you still want me to go to the Colindale?"

Abigail didn't answer. He felt that, without outward sign, she was crying. Her grief was always like this, an inward bleeding. He put one arm around her and let her rest her head on his chest. He looked out above her at the street.

"That was a silly question. I'm sorry." He pressed his chin down into her hair. "There have always been bullying policemen, and suspicion, and hiding around corners. I suppose they're necessary. We've just got spoiled, and let our sensitivities become unbalanced."

He heard himself trying to sound wise. But she didn't move away from him in disgust. Perhaps she didn't mind. Or hadn't been listening. Or had even found what he said true. . . . If his protection was to be worth anything she needed to respect him. But to retain that respect he must now expose her to the Kahn and the Wilson, and expose her again. For they were what Gryphon's job for him at the Colindale was about. He drew her gently into the house and closed the front door.

"Poor old Gryphon." He did not grieve for Gryphon, only for the idea of someone dying. "I wonder what he did to get himself killed."

"Been right on one level and wrong on every possible other."

So casual?

"It's funny how you never liked him."

"I'm sorry he's dead. Desperately, desperately sorry. I feel—"

"You'll ask for prayers to be said for him at Mass?" He looked at her, sensed something he did not understand, perhaps anger. "That's not sarcasm, Abigail. I just wasn't sure that prayers could be said for non-Catholics. Officially, I mean."

"I expect the truth is that he was killed for his moderation." She smiled brightly. "It's the usual reason nowadays. I doubt if the authorities would want him dead."

She was describing the entire failure of the C.L.C. Its sanity had made it acceptable, had made its reactions able to be predicted, able to be absorbed. Matthew walked away, back into the living room. Society evolved. Perhaps man was too multifold ever to control its direction.

"We'd better eat," he said.

Inspector Kahn had never seriously suspected him of killing Gryphon. The visit had been purely routine, to be cheered up in the only way Kahn knew. If he'd needed a target, the space of Matthew's life supplied him with one. He earned five hundred a month; he had never known to the slightest degree what had once been called hardship; above the basic twenty he only worked the hours he cared to work. But he felt deprived. Possibly he bucked social pressures and worked forty hours or even fifty. Possibly his wife thought he was crazy. Possibly his flat was forty up. Possibly there was no Wide Open Door Group working in his housing unit. Possibly there was and he hated it, being a born recluse. . . . Whatever the causes, he could never win. Matthew went over to the harpsichord and sat down at it, sliding his knees under the keyboard.

He struggled with Scarlatti while Abigail finished getting the dinner ready. He wondered if he liked the music, or only his own dexterity. Whichever it was, it overlaid the evening's unpleasantness, made him excited and happy. He chose the stamping, more rowdy sonatas, torrents that he tried to catch at as they flowed past him. When Abigail came up with the food he was wide open.

"Abigail love, what can I ever do to deserve you?"

"Just love me."

Such replies were hard to credit. It would be easy to attribute them to fear, or false naïveté. But her presence took away from him his nagging need to analyze. He put his arms around her thighs as she stood beside him holding plates.

"I do."

"Then we're all right."

24

But as he hugged her he knew perfectly well that things were never as simple as that.

During the meal they talked about the Colindale, and the people Matthew would be working with. He knew most of them only from the work they had done, always of particular distinction. Even his future assistant, Margaret Pelham, had been unavailable on his previous visits. But he knew her work very well, and admired the habits of mind it showed. He had met the principal, of course, a psychiatrist called Chester Billon. The interviews had been long and detailed and very tiring.

"It's an odd name, Matthew. Is he American? And what's a psychiatrist doing in charge of the Colindale?"

"I'm not quite sure. He's one of these physiological psychiatrists. Got there via chemistry and microbiology. And I doubt if he's American. He doesn't sound like one."

"I don't like physiological psychiatrists. They use large hammers for very small nails."

"They get more done than the analysts."

"Perhaps that's why I don't like them."

They laughed, spinning a shield around themselves, secure in the love they would make later.

TWO

FOR ABIGAIL the police car was unimportant, and the policemen—but for the news they brought—hardly real. Edmund was dead. Incomplete, years too soon. The moment she had recognized the nature of Kahn's bullying it had ceased to bother her. The questions had gone on and on, around and around, offering no threat in the face of Matthew's innocence. Now they had stopped.

She stood beside Matthew and watched the car out of sight. She had loved Edmund. Not as she had loved him once—not any more in love with him—but with a sad love, as for a cripple. It was through him that she had met Matthew, in the years when Edmund was coldly denying her everything but hope. Loving her from behind bars, chopping at her hands if she put them through, but never sending her away. And through him she had met Matthew.

"Do you still want me to go to the Colindale?"

She found it hard to connect Matthew's words and discover their meaning. Edmund was dead, his soul already judged. Over the last few years she had seen him infrequently—at University functions when she had gone with her brother, a few dinner parties, a sailing

weekend arranged by Matthew among the Greek Islands. On these occasions the echoing coldness in him
had repelled her, remembering how it had once hurt.
He shouldn't have died so. He should have been given
time.

"That was a silly question. I'm sorry."

Long ago she had told Matthew what she had once
felt for Edmund. He couldn't have forgotten. It must
be that he didn't know what to say, was embarrassed,
jealous even. She couldn't go on listening. Edmund,
whom she had failed to get through to, was dead. And
God was merciful. . . . Then the front door was closed
and she was alone in the hall with Matthew.

"Poor old Gryphon. I wonder what he did to get
himself killed."

"Been right on one level and wrong on every possible
other."

"It's funny how you never liked him."

She had been willing to discuss the subject in a way
that Matthew found easiest. But not at the price of
denying the past, denying her responsibility.

"I'm sorry he's dead, Matthew. Desperately, desperately sorry. I feel—"

"You'll ask for prayers to be said for him at Mass?"
So he didn't want to know He always moved off into
the mechanics of her faith when he needed distance.
"That's not sarcasm, Abigail. I just wasn't sure that
prayers could be said for non-Catholics. Officially, I
mean."

Sarcasm? Perhaps there was something she hadn't
heard. . . . She felt so far from Matthew that it frightened her. If he was jealous without cause he must battle
with it by himself. They knew too much about each

other: reassurances would be insulting. She chose a remark completely neutral.

"I expect the truth is that he was killed for his moderation. It's the usual reason nowadays. I doubt if the authorities would want him dead."

She turned away in the direction of the staircase down to the kitchen. Behind her Matthew said, "We'd better eat," not having noticed.

She went downstairs and chopped onions angrily. Above her Matthew began to play Scarlatti, also with anger. His clatter made the ceiling buzz. She concentrated on what she was doing, the texture of the onions, the way the rings separated, the rim of each circle sharp against the next, each crisp squeak of her knife. The bitter, milky vapor stung her eyes. Actuality. There, at that moment, physical actuality. The onions browned, and the pizza dough rose among olives and peppers and slivers of anchovy. And Matthew's body, folded over the harpsichord when she took plates up, lived and breathed and moved. She loved him. It was so lucid, so simple. And through him she experienced the other half, the man-ness of God.

As she stood beside him where he sat at the harpsichord he asked her what he could do to deserve her, offered her phrases, formal thought.

"Just love me." She said the words, feeling their inadequacy to be their strength. He put his arm around her thighs. Mind stopped getting in the way between spirit and body. And the love they made after the evening had shaped to it, was a unification.

Dear Saint Joseph and Saint Anne,
Find me a husband as quick as you can.

It was a childish prayer, but she was grateful to have had it answered in Matthew.

The coffee bar was austere yet vivid, Vasarely out of Bauhaus. She had walked there, even run a little, humming with the excitement of sunshine and coming change. Always she climbed out of sleep slowly, not really in the day till ten thirty or eleven. Matthew had long been up and away, snatching moments, submerging them, she thought, with devoted activity. Even when she was dressed and out of the house the streets came to her only gradually, the bookstalls, the exhibitions, the students, the occasional town cars. The thrill of living could only be accommodated bit by bit. And now the smoky coffee bar, eleven fifteen.

"Abby, you're early. Come and sit down."

"I ran."

"Ran? It's the over-forties who run. What the hell are you proving?"

Her brother pushed back a chair with his foot and she sat down. He was soberly dressed, carefully shaved, pale as if from sleeplessness. He wouldn't welcome being fussed.

"Give us a cigarette." He offered the packet. "Thrown any good bombs lately?"

"That was in your day. Students don't throw bombs any more. They're too intelligent, too afraid of chaos."

"Oh Paul, not one of your gloom mornings. What's wrong with being afraid of chaos?"

"Nothing." He lit her cigarette, then poured coffee for both of them while the machine checked his student's card against the account. "I thought we might talk about the summer vac," he said.

"Matthew's just taking up this new appointment. I don't expect we'll be having one."

"Don't vocationalists ever rest?"

Abigail wondered what was wrong, why he wanted to spoil her morning.

"You're not stupid, Paul. That sort of sneering doesn't suit you."

"I mean it. A man should exist in himself, not only through his work."

"I'm not going to justify Matthew to you. If—"

"Drink your coffee, sis." He was seven years younger than she. Far enough away for them to get on well together. "I know I'm being runtish. It's because I want something."

She would have liked to take his hands, it was that sort of morning, to offer him anything she had. He wouldn't appreciate it.

"I don't know what I can give you except money, Paul. You know there's always plenty of that."

"Bless you, Abby."

"Then it is money?"

"There's a summer project a group of us wants to do in the African Federation." He pushed an ashtray across for her. "We're avoiding Student Council backing in order to have a freer hand. Travel's cheap enough and food's no problem. It's the beads we'll have to give the natives that'll come expensive."

There was no need for him to tell her all this. And if he was driven to give explanations they ought to be good ones. She knew from her own training that there were bribery allocations—called fieldwork easement funds—available from many organizations other than the

Student Council. If he wanted to have a good time while in Africa he should say so.

"What is this project?" she asked.

"The uses made of superstition in regional merchandizing." He laughed. "It's red hot. The Student Council are the only people who would touch it; they're not afraid of the merchandisers. But they'd pin us down in a dozen ways."

"Like making you hand over your findings to the C.L.C.?"

"I don't think that would worry us."

"Wouldn't it? I thought the C.L.C. was impotent, wishy-washy liberal—a tool in the hands of the authorities."

"It exists." He shrugged his shoulders. "It must do some good, I suppose."

Even this guarded admission was new. For years he had done nothing but shout militancy; if he had at last recognized the realities of student power she was delighted. The lesson of the last disorders was that such immense power frightened not only its victims but its possessors. European society had come near to collapse. Now the student body as a whole was wiser, with a longer perspective, concerned to work as a leaven through their whole lives rather than only during their years at University. If Paul had come around to this view she could forgive him anything. She got out her check book.

"Ten thousand do you?"

"The group will be very grateful." Again a wrong note.

"Paul—something's not going on, is it?"

"Of course something's going on. We're going to split the whole racket wide open, the obscene, religio-sexual

31

confidence trick that's being played on unsophisticated millions, stroking their pitiful new wealth away from them. We're going to mount the same investigation as the merchandisers mounted, analyzing folk myths, fetishes, tribal symbolisms. And we're going to show the direct relationship, the disgusting relationship between these and each successful merchandising operation. We're going to expose the European merchandising ethic for what it really is. And that of the other power-blocs as well."

She knew that this tirade was an evasion of her question. But at least his anger was genuine. She made the check out for fifteen thousand and handed it across. He read her neat, left-handed writing.

"Getting a little vulgar with our riches, aren't we?" But he took the check and put it in his shirt pocket. "So the old man's got a new job . . . and I use the term affectionately. I know he's not really old—only forty to your twenty-nine. And what's eleven years?"

"Now you've got your money, can't you be a bit nicer? These digs at Matthew are so tedious."

"Of course. It's how young you feel that counts. And Matthew feels like a ten-year-old." She wondered if he was meaning to be obscene. He laughed, lit two more cigarettes and passed one across. "I'm sorry, sis. You married him, so perhaps he isn't the dead weight he seems to be. Just don't be bent into his shape, Abby. That's all."

"I'm my own shape, Paul. You know that."

He laughed again, embarrassed. In the pause that followed Abigail looked away, around the coffee bar. There were a few students, but it was filled mainly with older men and women, presumably lecturers. She guessed that Paul had chosen it as the most respectable of the University bars. On another day Edmund might have been among them. She drew on her cigarette, coping with the recollection that Edmund was dead.

"Sad about Edmund Gryphon," she said abruptly.

"You might not have heard. Frankly I funked telling you."

"Funked telling me? But—"

"Do me a favor. I may have been only a child, but I wasn't blind." To her surprise he took her hand and squeezed it. "Who told you? On the tell, was it?"

She decided this was a question she could get away with not answering. She was suddenly angry with herself for having remembered, angry with Edmund for having got himself killed, angry with herself again for minding so much. And Paul, it was surprising that he should concern himself for her. So little that Paul did seemed to add up.

"All a long time ago," she said. "You mustn't worry."

"Who's worrying? I'd say I was sorry, only what good's being sorry? Most sorts of being sorry."

The reference to confession lay between them like a sword on the table. Neither of them dared take it up. It was only lately that conversation with Paul had become like this, with so much they didn't talk about.

"Heard from Mum and Dad recently?" he said.

"Mum phoned last week. She was full of Dad's Retirement Counselor. Plans for this and plans for that. It may be good sociology, but it sounded pretty horrible to me."

"That's it. Horrible. The application of mechanical techniques when everything else has broken down. That we have a science of sociology at all is an open

33

admission that the world we have made for ourselves is basically rotten."

He was talking nonsense. Such nonsense that she hardly thought about it. She had wanted to talk about how they could help, not wallow in slick nihilism.

"You should change courses," she said sharply, "if you really feel that way about it."

The house was still empty when she got back. Matthew would be collecting her at two, so there might be time to wash her hair. She leaned at the top of the stairs overlooking the garden and decided that the walk home deserved a cigarette. Her talk with Paul had dragged on pointlessly: she had learned that he was leaving for Africa on Saturday by the eleven o'clock plane and that he'd be away six weeks or more. In return she had told him unimportant things about the Colindale. . . . Yet he was her brother, and they had once understood each other.

The cigarette took her whole attention. The feel of the stub, the cupping of the smoke behind her tongue, the different ways to inhale and exhale, the steady, delicate erosion of the white paper, the gray droppings that crumbled hygienically to dust. She stubbed out fifteen full minutes of her life on the underside of the iron handrail.

If Matthew was coming for her at two, then she'd better go and change into clothes more suitable for the Colindale. She founded all her mental pictures of the place on the name of its director, Chester Billon. Vaguely she imagined a dusty street with tethering posts, cowboy country with the uneasy addition of laboratory blocks and computer centers. Matthew would have a broad-brimmed hat and be magnificent in his bearded six foot two. And she . . . Somehow, although in these imaginings she was always there, she never really existed. Then she realized what was wrong: the cowboy's name had been Dillon anyway, not Billon. Something came into her mind from the linguistics course: d/b transfers were very common . . . or wasn't that d/th? *Bad* in German, *bath* in English. *Pfad* in German, *path* in English . . .

What a lot people had tried to teach her. And then given her a degree. In spite of that she still had a good mind when she cared to use it. Matthew would arrive soon, so she'd better wash her face. This she did, drying it vigorously on a *genuine* towel Mum had sent her for her birthday. *Genuine* was the latest trade word for *old-fashioned*. A few years ago *traditional* had been more common. . . . One could see the progression and ought, with luck, to be able to predict the next step. She heard Matthew calling from just inside the front door.

"I must just put on some lipstick. And brush my hair."

"It's two o'clock. Have you eaten?"

"Coffee with Paul. And I'd better change my skirt."

"Abigail, it's two o'clock."

But she heard him go into the kitchen and she knew he'd be getting her something that she'd have to eat. And suddenly she was hungry.

She took off her skirt and went downstairs with several other skirts over her arm. Matthew was frying bacon and reconstituting bread for a sandwich. She laid the skirts out on the kitchen table.

"Which one shall I wear, Matthew?"

She could see him make an effort.

"The red one's very pretty."

"For the Colindale Institute? Not too saucy?"

"Please, Abigail—it's five past two."

She held the red skirt up against herself, refusing to be hurried.

"When did you tell them we'd be there?"

"It's myself I told, not them. And I told you too, days ago. I told you I wanted to leave sharp at two."

"Don't be so pettish."

"Pettish?"

"Pettish, pettish, pettish."

Matthew suddenly put down the slice mold, and the bowl of breadmix. He took the skirts, scrumpled them into a large ball, and threw them down the waste chute. It was, for him, an incredible gesture. After that, anything might happen. Afraid and penitent, she retreated from him, holding the one remaining skirt tightly behind her. He advanced.

"There are," he said, "many more things in life than self-imposed punctuality."

Behind them the bacon smoked in the pan, and eventually they turned to move it.

As always, sleep was a natural part of their love-making. And the slow return at his side, the warmth of him, the smell of sexuality, the bony hardness of his chest. He moved, and looked down the sides of his nose at her.

"I'm sorry I threw your skirts away, love. Doing a thing like that . . . it's—"

"It was funny really." He mustn't make a drama out of it. She stretched. "What's the time?"

"Who cares?"

But she knew he did care. There was suppressed tension in his arm under her head. She craned up to see the clock.

"Matthew—it's half past three."

"Like the gentleman said, who cares?"

"We can't spend our whole lives in bed, Matthew."

The suburb of Colindale had tried to come to terms with the motorway by throwing up huge blocks of flats. There was a heliport as well, and a big new Catholic church. Quick-growing elms had been planted, now ten years old. But below the striding motorway too much old building remained, ribbon development along meaningless roads. The roundabout at ground level had a thatched motel, a bowling alley and a covered swimming pool, their neon flickering even in the brilliant June sunlight. A small factory was being torn down and a larger one put up in its place. The road was constricted, undergoing reconstruction. Abigail realized how much the stasis of Central London was untypical of life.

She felt warm and full. She had spent much of the journey praying, as always, for a baby. For the four years of their marriage they had shied away from the mechanisms that might help them, the implants, the impregnations. She had even avoided the indignity of being properly examined. She preferred to trust in God and Matthew.

He moved the town car smoothly across the traffic lanes and headed out past a hypnotic succession of maisonettes, their black and white frontages flicking past almost audibly. They represented the poverty that Abigail had been brought up in, and she felt as if she were coming home. Her parents still lived like that, as boisterous as their surroundings. But if this was home, then what was the Kensington house she shared with Matthew? And the Colindale Institute that must now be so near, what would that be?

Matthew drove on past a shopping complex and a self-service battery station. A hundred or so batteries were on charge in open-fronted racks. She glanced across at their own charge gauge—the car had been in all night, had a good thirty hours left. Matthew sat silently beside her, all his attention on the crowded traffic lanes. She edged closer to him, put her hand between his legs, looked out of the car windows with new courage.

The Colindale Institute was dark blue and white, a political coloring: Switzerland, small enough for no one to fear, center of the Federal European government. The flags of the member nations curled idly above the entrance gates. On either side were wide strips of lawn with a token fence of white posts and nylon cord.

"That's a relief," she said. "I was afraid they'd all be security conscious, with a high wall and guard dogs."

"The wall is there, all right. Thirty feet high, they tell me. It's just that you can't see it. Improves the psychological effect."

They waited in front of the barrier while the guard checked their passes in the scanner. Abigail looked sideways at the clear sunlit air above the grass. There were birds on the ground, some of them searching for beetles, some of them dead. She saw the little notices that might have said *Keep off the grass*. They were warnings about the force-field fence. The passes tallied and the barrier in front of them rose automatically. Matthew drove through and stopped, waiting till the passes were returned to him by the guard.

"That barrier," he said. "It's armored to withstand the latest two-meter laser. There's an electronic scanner under the driveway. Also aerial radar coverage and full televisual monitoring." He turned sideways on the seat to face her. "I want you to know exactly what you're going into, Abigail. This isn't the Ministry. It's all very discreet, very pretty, very velvet gloved. But it's efficient." He turned back and started the car. "German equipment, most of it. Needless to say."

They drove along an informal, tree-lined avenue, glimpsing varied blue and white buildings through the leaves, graveled courtyards, fountains, flights of mosaic steps that made pleasing patterns against crisp grass edges. Abigail saw many small street lamps. It was a place where people were encouraged to walk slowly and talk. Matthew drew up at a corner, looking down two short roads of low residential blocks. The buildings contrived both dignity and grace.

"Well?" he said. "That out there and this in here. It's an evil contrast."

She stared around her, gnawing what was left of her fingernails. There was something about such planned serenity that made her perversely uncomfortable.

"Will I ever be allowed out of here?" she said.

"Any time you like. Remembering that the tail goes along too."

"The tail?"

"We all have tails. Yours is to be a Mrs. Foster. I haven't met her yet, but I hear she's very charming."

"You really are trying to put me off, aren't you?" She pointed at the blocks of apartments. "Will we live in one of those?"

"Good Lord, no. That's Technicians Grade I and

Junior Programmers. In this place grades are observed most carefully. Department Heads get detached houses in noble seclusion up behind the library. They're very nice, I promise you."

Abigail got out of the car. There was a comfortable scent of grass and sun-hot brickwork. Three young women hurried chattering out of a doorway, trotted to the end of the road and went over a stile into the field beyond. One of them vaulted it. They wore white shorts and were probably going to play tennis. Abigail walked around to Matthew's side of the car, testing the ground, testing the feel of the place.

"Do you yourself want to come here, Matthew?"

"That's not the point."

"It's a large part of it."

"I'm less impressionable than you. I can only say that the work interested me from the very beginning. And now there's what Gryphon asked me to do as well. . . ."

"Then we'll come."

She ran around to her side of the car and climbed in. Decisions for her were always very easy. Things happened.

"We'll find out how adaptable we are. It'll be fun."

Matthew didn't start the car. He stayed staring at the road in front.

"I wonder if everybody who comes to work here has the same doubts," he said.

"The academics won't. All they ever ask is to be left in peace to get on with their work. For them this sort of place is just about perfect."

It was all a great adventure. Force-field fences, scanners, television monitoring—the first camera she saw she'd put her tongue out at. But she wouldn't dare. She wanted him to drive on. She wanted to see their new house.

"Perhaps it's because I've always kept myself so uninvolved. Politically uninvolved, I mean." He was answering a question in his own head. "Yet I'd have expected my connection with Gryphon to rule me out from the start."

"You're good at your work. Perhaps they're just reckoning on keeping an extra sharp eye on you."

"Yes." He started the car. "That's what I'm afraid of."

They went first to the Computer Center because that was where the director was probably to be found, and Matthew said it would be civil to pay their respects before going on to look at the house. Abigail was impatient. The thought of a new house, paint to be put on, curtains to be altered, excited her. Now the rest of the afternoon would go on polite nothings with Chester Billon. She was mistaken.

They had hardly sat down to wait by the reception desk before he came out to them, festooned with computer tape. He wore a white coat over very correct suit and shirt and tie.

"Fools kept you waiting? New faces, I suppose. Won't happen again. Mrs. Oliver? Delighted. Moving in tomorrow, I hear." He talked through her protest. "Won't have to do a thing. Our men work wonders. Field where human hands and human judgment are irreplaceable."

He began to tidy his loops of tape. Abigail saw how big he was, almost as big as Matthew, with big thick-fingered hands and a big face. He was clean-shaven, had tangled eyebrows and a scar down his forehead that he had never bothered to get masked. His boxer's features and army officer's mannerism contrasted oddly with his reputed brilliance. His hair was glossy gray, consultant smooth. When he moved he moved, and when he stood still he really stood still. Abigail felt her husband getting ready to say something. Too late.

"Must get back. Thing's making sense for once." Billon started back in the direction he had come. "Twenty-two hours a day and there's still never enough computer time. You'll excuse me." The door closed behind him. Reopened. "Forgive me. No manners. Obsessive paranoia, treatable with two grains of mardil. Only then what?" He leaned on the door handle. "Start work nine thirty Monday. Know where to find your house? Good. Mrs. Oliver, forgive me. Computer time is precious." He hesitated, then quickly walked the length of the corridor back to where they were standing. He leaned forward. "And if either of you ever thinks I look at you a bit oddly, blame the plastics industry." He opened his eyes very wide, rolled them, and then tapped the left eyeball with his pen. It made a crisp, billiard-like noise. "False," he said neutrally.

The interior of the house was beautiful. The outside wall fronting on the library cloisters had worried Abigail, totally blank except for the door and a pattern of air-conditioner vents. But, once inside, she saw that the blankness made sense. The whole house looked inward to a small central garden with a deep, blue-gray pool. A tall pine tree grew out of this garden in the middle of the house, the ground beneath it soft with brown decades of needles.

As she walked quietly from room to room—Matthew had encouraged her to go on in alone, busy himself doing something to the car—Abigail felt the house fit

42

together about her. Whatever the Colindale might do outside, in here she felt safe. It wasn't like a house at all: more like a nest.

"It's not like a house, Matthew—it's more like a nest."

Matthew's reply from out in the sunlight was indistinct. She progressed further into the house, finding a study with floor-to-ceiling booksheves. So the last head of Matthew's department had also been sentimental about books. . . . Sentimental. The fir tree was sentimental. The whole house was sentimental. Which was why she liked it so much, being a sentimental person. She sat down on the kitchen window seat and slid back the glass. There was a smell of pine needles. So she was a sentimental person. Sentimental. By now the word was quite meaningless. Sentimental mental center, mental centimeter center . . . She lit a cigarette.

Matthew was a success. It always worried her how he managed it. The people who gave him commercial consultancies and departments at the Colindale, what did they see in him? If they simply saw a brilliant talent, wouldn't they be afraid of it? Wouldn't they need a willingness to compromise? So whom was Matthew fooling—her, or everybody else?

She frowned at the idea of Matthew deceiving people. He would be capable of it, of course, but would find it hard to see the necessity. . . . Except that Gryphon had shown him the necessity, and had made him accept the position almost of a secret agent. And now Gryphon was dead. And it was all sensational, and silly, and very wasteful.

She finished her cigarette and put the stub carefully down the sink waste pipe. Then she went around the house the other way, till she reached the front door.

The ground plan interconnected, and offered two ways of getting anywhere—three, if she went across the garden. She stood at the inner end of the entrance hall thinking that it was the first house she had seen that really didn't need furniture to dress it out. Its spaces were adequate, requiring only movement to complete them. She seemed to have been alone in the house for a very long time. She ran out into the wide air of the cloisters. The car was in the road beyond, but no Matthew.

His absence left a painful gap in the fabric. For a second she stood rabbit still, the tense calm of the Colindale like a weight against her face. The pillars of the arcade framed diminishing squares of sunlight on the mosaic pavement to right and left. She had lived alone, traveled alone, worked alone, made her own life for years before she met Matthew. She wasn't a child.

Then he came around the side of the house, talking to a stranger, and it was all suddenly very ordinary. She turned and he saw her, he stopped talking, the other man saw her, she walked calmly toward them, everybody smiled, everything moved on, happened all in the same moment.

"There you are, Matthew. You were a long time. I was looking for you." There was a tiny pause. Uncharacteristically, she felt obliged to go on. "I love the house, Matthew. It feels so safe . . . Just like a nest."

She had thought the words so clearly. Almost as if she had already said them many times before.

"Abigail, this is Dr. Mozart. Dr. Mozart, this is my wife, Abigail."

"How do you do." He was German, and Jewish, in his thirties, and accustomed to being found attractive by other men's wives. She judged him to have been married, but almost certainly by now divorced.

"My father christened me Wolfgang, but spared me Amadeus. He was a man of shaky convictions. . . ."

He used English as if he despised it. She shook hands silently. Dr. Mozart was looking puckish.

"In any event my father was right, of course. I grew up tone deaf. To me all loud music is Wagner, all soft music Papa Haydn."

His humility was false. In a minute he would let drop that he played the forty-nine fugues, only not very well. Still with nothing to say, she waited for Matthew to rescue her.

"Dr. Mozart has been telling me about my predecessor. Henderson." Matthew was speaking harshly. She could tell that he was going to shock her. "Henderson was burned to death in his motor car, Abigail. It wasn't an accident."

Two messengers now had brought news of violence. Violence off-stage. She wondered if the convention would continue to be observed. The tell reports of Henderson's death had implied a car crash. The director, if no one else, should have told them the truth. Dr. Mozart was looking not at her, but at Matthew. He made a small modifying gesture.

THREE

"DON'T WAIT FOR ME. It sounds as if the air-conditioner filter needs clearing. I ought to take a look. You go on in."

She left him to tinker. He stooped, unscrewed the filter unit under the dash, gave it a couple of turns, and tapped out the saturated crystals on the grass beside the car. Cement dust, burnt rubber, carbon dioxide, bacteria, urban effluent—it was a wonder anybody dared breathe undoctored air at all. From inside the house he heard Abigail calling that she liked it, that it was like a nest. He smiled. A revived housing concept, as old as sensate life. Perhaps his *People in Glass Houses* had helped after all.

"Peace shall reign within your ramparts, and prosperity within your palaces," he called. He attended Mass quite as often as she did.

When he had replaced the filter unit he closed the car door and turned to the house. He had sent her on ahead because she would prefer to make her first exploration alone. It would, if he knew her, deserve a cigarette. He stepped back a few paces to see the outline of the house separate from the cloisters along its front wall. It was one of a dozen or so, homes of departmental heads, around a large grassy quadrangle. The blankness of its outside walls could be said to make it into a nest, a fortress. It could also be called a prison, a trap.

He walked on the grass down the side of the house and around the back. Three narrow strips of clerestory window nine or ten feet up, lighting what he thought must be the back wall of the living room. Nothing else. Of course, justification was easy enough: the view from this side of the house was hideous: a high-speed train-way humping over elevated roads, some factory blocks, a big unexplained plastic dome, and as far as the horizon green fungoid rooftops, semi-detached. But windows that kept the view out also kept the people in. He frowned. One hour in the Colindale and he was already getting a persecution complex.

"Stay where you are, please. Tell me who you are, and what you are doing."

Matthew turned. A man was standing some ten yards away, his hands in the large patch pockets of his jacket.

"My name is Oliver." Matthew made the spare words sound as insolent as possible. "And I'm looking at my house."

"Dr. Oliver? May I see your identification, please?"

Casual clothes, no hat, hardly a security guard. Unless they wore plain clothes at the Colindale.

"Here you are."

The man took the card and examined it long-sightedly. "My dear Dr. Oliver . . . well met by moonlight. I am Dr. Mozart. Spectroscopy. Welcome to the Institute." His hand was cold and damp, as if from holding something metallic. Matthew wondered if everybody there was supposed to carry a gun. "We are edgy, Dr. Oliver. You were not expected until tomorrow."

Matthew understood this to be an apology, all the apology he would get.

"My wife's in the house," he said. "We're just having a look around."

"A man such as you will have a beautiful wife. I look forward to meeting her."

Very precise English, used for a very German brand of flattery. Dr. Mozart patted his back, became confidential, would have put his arm around his shoulders if he could have reached.

"I did not mean to offend you. . . . You and I, Dr. Oliver, we represent the European predicament. We must work together—for life itself we must work together. Yet I find you stuffy and you find me brash. And whatever we are, when we meet we become more so." He looked earnestly up into Matthew's face, and then burst out laughing. "If we stand here much longer we shall become pure grotesques. So take me to meet your wife."

He led Matthew back in the direction of the cloisters. Planning to spare Abigail, Matthew began to make excuses.

"We're in a bit of a rush, actually. The director has sprung tomorrow's move on us, and we really ought to get back to—"

"Did you know," said Dr. Mozart, casually, "that Professor Henderson was murdered?"

"Murdered?" Matthew kept on walking, British to the core. "No. No, I didn't."

"Oh dear. Then perhaps I should have kept the cat in the bag, out of respect to the director." Irrelevantly

48

Matthew wondered if his companion would ever learn that his English was let down by his use of cliché. "But it's too late now. . . . Yes, an incendiary bomb in the car. A few yards down the road, by the tennis courts."

Too cheerful about his indiscretion for it to have been accidental. Matthew wondered why. Why a lot of things.

"No, I hadn't heard. How very unpleasant."

"In the midst of life we are in death, Dr. Oliver."

They came up into the shadow of the cloisters. Abigail ran toward them.

"There you are, Matthew. You were a long time. I was looking for you." He detected hysteria. She was usually silent in the presence of strangers. "I love the house, Matthew. It feels so safe . . . just like a nest."

"Abigail, this is Dr. Mozart." He made the introduction to give her time. "Dr. Mozart, this is my wife, Abigail."

Abigail was shaking hands, and wilting under the halitosis blast of his charm. Matthew had to tell her. He ignored the words, simply waited for a gap in them.

"Dr. Mozart has been telling me about my predecessor. Henderson. Henderson was burned to death in his motor car, Abigail. It wasn't an accident."

She had to know while there was still time to back out. The director had lied by omission. Had he done so in case Matthew might otherwise be frightened off? What opinion must the director have of him? Dr. Mozart made a small modifying gesture.

"What you say is not completely accurate, Dr. Oliver. An element of accident did exist. The car belonged to Professor Billon and nobody could have known that Henderson would borrow it. The implication is obvious."

Dr. Mozart shrugged, his elbows bent in by his sides, his hands together, turned forward at the wrists.

"An unpleasant subject, Mrs. Oliver. But at least it suggests that your husband is himself not in any particular danger. Anyone attacking the Colindale project would go for the head, not the arms."

"Then what exactly is the Colindale project?"

As it was nearly seven o'clock they had been lucky to catch Professor Billon. He was in his private office at the computer center. A faddish room, showing the Harley Street-acquired taste of its owner. Practically nothing expressed its function. Even the windows were *jeus d'esprit*, three huge blown-up color slides of eyes which the evening sunlight projected askew onto the opposite wall. And behind the professor's desk a tall sculpture of polished aluminum and spun glass netting which revolved, catching the light.

"The Colindale project? My dear Oliver, I went over it very carefully with you. Non-political. Belonging to the European Federation. Financed by the central government. Collects scientific information, catalogs and freely disseminates it. Peaceful. Aimed solely at improving the welfare of humanity. Widest possible terms of reference."

"If it's all so peaceful"—Matthew controlled his increasing irritation—"why the hell did somebody try to kill you a few weeks ago?"

"Some people are more afraid of peacefulness than of anything else. Witness the fate of Christ. Not that I make a comparison."

"And why weren't we told about it? Right from the start?"

The director smiled with a frankness that Matthew suspected of being professional.

"You've guessed already. The only answer I can give will be unsatisfactory." He got up from his mesh chair and walked to the center window. He stared out through the eye's iris at the blue strip of grass and a blue generating station. "Buddha's eye," he said. "The eye of the soul. Of truth. Salutary reminder." He turned back into the room. "Information detrimental to national security. Official Secrets Régulations cast a wide net. Perhaps too wide. However."

"Is that all you can tell us?" said Abigail.

"Until you are sworn in. Pedantic, but there you are. I'm glad you came to me instead of going to some newspaper friend in the outside world. It looks well."

Matthew gazed steadily at him across beams of colored light.

"Then there'll be other things you've kept from me about the Institute?"

"Thousands." Billon smiled again. "But nothing material. I believe."

The director had not asked him how he had heard about Henderson's death. Perhaps he knew. Perhaps the whole episode had been a squalid test of probity. And its result had looked well.

"Well, well. Getting late. I recommend the canteen. One thing I demanded was good food. At canteen prices. Geneva can afford it and the staff deserves it. Hardly anybody eats out or in their quarters."

"We shall," said Abigail. "Mostly eat at home, I mean."

"What a way to live," she said on their way home in

the car. "I bet the cook's a computer. They'd disembody your brains altogether if they could."

"That man Mozart did mention tennis courts."

"How nice."

"Abigail love, you know perfectly well bodies are becoming more and more of a social embarrassment."

They drove on in silence. Helicopters idled overhead on their different airways to and fro. There were trains and buses and cars, movement instead of activity. Matthew turned off the North Circular and entered the approach to the Central London checkpoint.

"We're not so holy ourselves," he said. "When did we last sweat?"

"*Mea culpa, mea culpa* . . . We see everything, we admit everything—it's obscene the way we live on ourselves, enjoying a sort of mutual stimulation." She covered her face with her hands. "No, I don't mean that. But we've lost balance. There's too much time for thinking."

He hadn't realized she was so serious. He tried to play it down.

"Thinking is to be encouraged," he said. "It takes up so little space. Uses so few amenities."

"Please, Matthew, don't just be bitter. It's too easy."

He braked at the checkpoint, waited for the scanner to register his resident's sticker and let them through. By another entrance the driver of a neat gray town car was arguing with the attendant over his visitor's pass. Matthew had thought he knew all the passes—resident's pass, even day pass, odd day pass, weekend pass, midweek pass—but this man's was of a bright yellow color he had never seen before. The light changed and Matthew drove on into Central London.

"It's ludicrous," Abigail said suddenly, "to long as I do for ordinary, old-fashioned pain. For men who are dirty, and swear, and fight in anger. For the real issue to be survival."

"Not ludicrous at all. There are still places where you could find that sort of life."

"And waiting lists a mile long of people who want to go to them."

"With our qualifications, love, we could get there easily."

And with their qualifications the whole thing was made pointless. You couldn't put on simple issues like a coat—at least he couldn't. She was so much younger, of course. . . . The thought worried him.

"At least one doesn't have to go to the think-tank extremes of the Colindale," he said.

For a long time she didn't answer. They talked of other things, of his morning spent tidying up at the Ministry, of her meeting with Paul in the coffee bar. She told him of the money she had given her brother. He approved.

"Anything that keeps him busy, gets him out of the country for a bit. He's not being taken up enough by his work. Either he's in the wrong course or it's the fault of his teachers. I'll have a word with Gryph—"

But Gryphon was dead. It was shocking how easily one forgot.

"Have you realized what Gryphon's death means?" he said suddenly. They were finishing supper.

"All sorts of things. What in particular?"

"It means I don't have a contact with the C.L.C. any more. Whatever I may find out about the Colindale, there's nobody to tell."

"Don't you know any other executive members?"

"You talk as if there were an official list. I only knew about Gryphon because he happened to be a very old friend."

The C.L.C. was supposed to be illegal. As a power in society it was thus more credible. Everybody played this game, even if with varying degrees of sophistication. The executives guarded their identities. Even the printing presses were officially secret.

"Surely the government knows who they are?"

"They'd never admit it."

"Not even to you?"

She started collecting the dirty plates. Matthew lit a cigarette and considered. He had often worked closely with the Minister for Social Planning. There was friendship of a sort between them.

"I might try Beeston. I'll need to think of a good excuse."

"Easy. A private survey you're doing. Patterns of divergence in the executive classes." She went down to the kitchen, calling over her shoulder, "Why not ring him now?"

"And have Billon know within ten minutes that I'm trying to contact the C.L.C.? Don't be naïve."

He had a sudden thought and went over to the window. A neat gray town car, familiar, was parked a few doors down on the left. And in it the man who had been arguing at the checkpoint. Abigail came up from the kitchen, saw he was smoking.

"Don't I get a cigarette?" she said.

He handed her one. There was a whole box on the table—why didn't she get one for herself? Anyway, she smoked far too much.

"Thank you." She lit it. "I smoke too much," she said contentedly.

Too much? Why? On what grounds? Moral, or financial? With the health risk beaten what else was there? People who were orally fixated liked to smoke. It helped them and did no harm whatsoever.

"Yes, you do," he said, staring resentfully out at the gray town car.

The gun in his pocket made the whole outing seem basically frivolous. He ran down the front steps of his house and crossed the pavement to his car. The street was deserted, his tail apparently reading a newspaper. Matthew aimed the laser and burned holes in both front tires of the gray car, so that the bonnet end subsided abruptly. Then he ducked into his own car and drove away. He should offer the idea to *Physical Surveillance and the Free Citizen.* Except that most free citizens weren't allowed laser guns.

Two streets away he turned into a multi-story Karstak, relic of the time before the new University, when Central London hadn't yet been made a Limited Traffic Zone. He was planning to get rid of his car; a radio call from his tail would have half the police in London looking for it. He took the lift up to the fifteenth floor and parked in close to the shaft. The upper stories were silent, lined with last year's models nobody knew what to do with. The big Italian manufacturers' lobby had forced through safety legislation in Geneva that made eighty percent of not-new cars illegal. Which was good for business and gave many urban Karstaks a temporary usefulness.

Matthew took the lift down again to the ground floor,

and slipped unobtrusively into the nearest underground station. He was enjoying himself. If he was to be treated like a criminal he might as well behave like one.

Out of University hours the trains were infrequent, and by the time he reached Whitehall it was nearly nine o'clock. If Sir William were in, at least he would be certain to have finished dinner.

The Minister's roof garden was high enough to be still warmed by the last of the evening sun. Long shadows lay across the gravel. There was a pond, with lilies and fat golden carp. Matthew stood in the doorway and looked down at the Minister, sprawled virile on a traditional cane chaise longue.

"My dear Matthew, I do hope you haven't been kept waiting. I'm afraid I've only just got back from the studios."

"Then I won't trouble you, Sir William. You'll want to eat."

"Nonsense. Sit down. . . . They fed me as if I was a visiting Chinese diplomat." Matthew smiled politely. "That's why I'm so late. I . . . I don't suppose you saw the transmission?"

Matthew sat down on the low parapet surrounding the lily pond.

"I don't think I've looked at the tell for weeks," he said.

"Wise man. I was softening 'em up for some new Movement Incentives. We've got to drive 'em up into the Highlands somehow, you know. . . . They tell me it went quite well."

Obviously Sir Williams had not yet changed his clothes. He was still wearing the informal sweater everybody loved. And his hair was tousled.

"But then, of course, they would. They stroke me and I purr. Vanity, vanity, all is . . . I don't suppose this is altogether a social visit, eh, Matthew?"

"You're quite right, Sir William. I'm afraid I want something."

"It can't be money. . . . And it can't be influence because you know I haven't any." He waved aside Matthew's protest. "You've come to me for information, Matthew Oliver. Information you can't get anywhere else."

"You're quite right, Sir William." Despicable. No man should work on another's mechanisms so crudely. Worse, there might be in it something of the connivance of stooge and principal in a bad double act. "And the information I need will be hard for even you to give me without bending the rules a little."

"Rules, Matthew, are for the obedience of fools and the guidance of wise men. Place me somewhere between the two extremes"—the Minister held up a mocking finger—"and hope."

Matthew looked away, watched the silent, indifferent fish. All through his life people in authority had liked him. He wished they hadn't. Somewhere there must be a basic dishonesty in him. If he had ever presented himself truthfully to these captains of society they would have loathed him. He agreed with scarcely a thought in their heads, and frankly considered himself superior to any of them. Which made his sycophancy particularly disgusting.

"As you know, sir, I've accepted a position at the Colindale Institute as head of the Social Studies Department. Possibly because they wouldn't get men otherwise, they allow department heads a certain amount of time for their own work. The project I'm engaged on is a study of the patterns of divergence in the executive groups."

"That sounds interesting." Thanks to Abigail. "Can I take it the Government will get a look before you publish?"

"Of course." A thoroughly safe promise.

"Can't you feel the rules beginning to flex a little, Matthew? I'm sure I can."

The Minister was coy. Matthew should have been nauseated, but made allowances. For what he could not say.

"Of course, divergence takes many forms, Sir William. Political, sexual, religious, behavioral, social-relational, interpersonal-relational, and so on . . ." The Minister loved long words. "Most of these are checkable from existing records. I still have my ministry pass card to the Paris data store. There is one field, though—perhaps the most important—that is not available to me."

"Ministerial divergences—is that what you're looking for? I could give you a letter to Security. I haven't seen the files myself, and I don't want to." Sir William was adept at saying one thing and meaning the opposite. "But, for research purposes they might be—"

"Thank you, Sir William, but I'm afraid that's too specialized a sample to be of much use." Matthew took a breath. "I was thinking of the secret societies, and the C.L.C. in particular."

The Minister went carefully blank.

"But my dear fellow, the C.L.C. is an illegal organization. Nobody knows its members."

"I realize that's the official position." Matthew dabbled his fingers in the pond. Fish darted away, hid

58

under lily pads. "All the same, it is widely believed that—"

"Widely believed? I don't like your implication, Matthew. Widely believed by whom?"

"That the Government is well aware of the exact membership of the C.L.C. but chooses to take no action. There are, after all, good sociological reasons for permitting such organizations."

Sir William hoisted himself abruptly to his feet. Behind him the cane chair creaked and settled. He paced, his soft soles making scarcely a sound on the gravel.

"You are suggesting a cynicism in the Government, Matthew, that—"

"Not cynicism, Sir William. Sophistication." But he knew he had lost out.

"Cynicism, Matthew. The cynical manipulation of motives. My God—you're in the wrong bloc, Matthew. That isn't what democratic government's about."

"Then you're saying"—give him one more chance—"you're saying that nobody in the Government knows the names of the C.L.C. executives?"

"If we did, we'd arrest them. You can't make a mockery of the law; either a thing's illegal or it isn't. Dammit, Matthew, I thought you were a man of honor."

Matthew moved his hand gently to and fro in the water, said nothing, resisted a mild impulse to make excuses for himself. More than anything else, intellectual dishonesty depressed him. The Minister was working himself up.

"Sociologists as ministers—that's what some people want. Did y'know that? I'd like to show them you. You're like those bloody psychologists who tell us about God: Oh yes, He's a good thing. We see a definite psychic need for Him. . . . I'm sorry, Matthew. I seem to have lost my temper. But you assume a sort of doublethink that just won't do. Not in democratic government."

Matthew looked up, realized that to Sir William he was not, and never had been, a person. He was the dark, shiny, two-inch lens of a television camera.

When he reached home the gray town car was still in position, but its occupant made no attempt to speak to him. Matthew found a note pushed through the letter box. It was a bill for two car tires, six hundred marks. It cheered him up, and he wrote the check immediately.

FOUR

ABIGAIL CAME UP from the kitchen. Matthew was standing by one of the high windows at the front of the house, looking down into the street. He was withdrawn, and did not seem to notice her arrival. He was smoking. His hair stuck out in tufts where he had been ruffling it. She tried to reach him.

"Don't I get a cigarette?" she said.

He held his packet out to her and continued to stare out of the window. She was hurt by this disregard for one of their love rituals: the placing of the cigarette between her lips, his two fingers against her cheek steadying the flame, the smoky kiss that so often followed. She tried to remember what they had been talking about before she went down with the dirty dishes. He had called her naïve, and her mind had retorted by skipping away into other matters, the new house, the repellant Dr. Mozart. She remembered now that they had been working out a method of contacting the C.L.C. She felt ashamed, and took a cigarette from the offered packet.

"Thank you." She lit it, and tried a second time to make contact. "I smoke too much," she said.

"Yes, you do."

A silence in the room while she grappled with that one: hurt not by its abrupt truth, but by its conflict with the hundred other times he had denied the fact, and so convincingly. Did he really need his mind to be three-quarters preoccupied before he could be honest with her in little things?

"We were followed back from the Colindale," Matthew said. "The man's sitting in a car outside."

She joined him at the window, saw a man sitting in a gray car reading a newspaper.

"Are you sure, Matthew?"

"Of course I'm sure. I remember seeing him hanging around the guard house."

"Then what are you going to do about the Minister? You can't go and see him, not with that man watching. If you can't use the telephone either, then what—"

"I'll think of something."

And only two days before life had been concerned with Matthew's work, with the church, with keeping up with the technical journals, with infrequent visits to her parents, with occasional films and plays and concerts.

The first stage of Matthew's scheme worked very well. She watched from the window as he drove away, leaving the tail car disabled. The man in it did not even get out. She saw him speaking into his radio handset, and a few minutes later another car arrived. The two flat tires were replaced by the spares from both cars and then the second car drove away again. Just because she had been inside the Colindale Institute she was apparently to be watched day and night. They were children, trying to make their little activities seem important. She went out to the gray car and leaned in through the open side window.

"Good evening," she said.

"Evening, Mrs. Oliver."

"Why are you here?"

"I'm here to keep an eye on you, Mrs. Oliver."

It was disappointing that he should remain so unabashed.

"Why are you keeping an eye on me?"

"Orders."

"And that's all you know?"

"More than that'd only be trouble to me."

"Do you often have to watch perfectly innocent people?"

"Innocent's a big word." He scratched his cheek. "But I expect so."

"And that's the way you serve society?"

"I hadn't thought about it. I don't see why not. It's a job in a growth profession—aren't many of them left."

Through the open front door behind her she could hear the telephone ringing.

"Aren't you afraid I might shoot you, attack you in some way?"

"Doesn't often happen. Besides, your husband went off with the only gun."

"We might have another. Without a license."

The man shook his head.

"Not you." He was civil, but indifferent. He would push her off a cliff in exactly the same tone of voice. "We scanned the house, room by room. While you were out. No explosives, no propellants . . . and you're not the sort to come right out and poke me. Isn't that your telephone?"

She did not answer. She was furious that their house should have been grubbed around in by men like that Kahn.

"I suppose that's under powers left over from the last emergency," she said finally.

"I could quote you the subsection, Mrs. Oliver."

He arranged himself more comfortably in his seat and again scratched his cheek. The Nevershave hormone treatment had been recent, and she could see it still itched.

"Anyway, you ought to be glad to have me here." The telephone stopped ringing. "After all, you say you're innocent, and as long as I'm here I say you're innocent. That's two of us saying you're innocent. Could come in useful."

She had offered him a questionnaire and he had obligingly filled it in. She now knew how he worked. The knowledge gave her little satisfaction. The telephone began to ring again and she used it as an excuse to turn back to the house.

"And Mrs. Oliver . . ." He had leaned across the car and was looking up at her. "Thanks for the company, Mrs. Oliver."

"Why not come in and put your feet up?"

"Very kind of you, ma'am. Only I mustn't leave my radio."

Had he really completely missed her sarcasm? In the doorway she stopped.

"Have they caught my husband yet?"

"His car's been found on the fifteenth floor of the Sloane Square Karstak. Perhaps that's him trying to ring you."

She closed the front door and hurried to the telephone. If it was Matthew then her not answering would have worried him badly. She switched in the receiver.

"Hullo? Abby?" It was her brother. "Got you out of the bath, have I?"

"No. I was just . . . busy."

"I'm off in the morning, Abby. Been going around the family saying goodbye."

"You mean you've rung Mum and Dad?"

"I've been to see them. And Grandpa."

"What's going on? Are you afraid you won't be coming back?"

"I'll ignore that. Tell me instead how you enjoyed your trip out to Colindale. Pick up any good bits of scandal?"

"If I had I wouldn't tell you. They're very security minded out at the Institute."

"Which means you think the phone is bugged."

It hadn't occurred to her. Her reticence, the half-truth about why she had been so long answering, it was her instinctive reaction to an unknown situation.

"I saw the house we're going to have," she said. "And met the director."

"And Matthew's job? Has he been told much about that yet?"

"He knows about his job. He's known for weeks."

"And he's taking it?"

"Why shouldn't he?"

"No reason. Not if you don't know of one."

He was behaving very oddly.

"Are you drunk, Paul?"

"I doubt it." He seemed to pull himself together. "Anyway, I really rang to tell you about Grandpa. He's very low. You might care to go and cheer him up."

"Did he ask for me?"

"Not in so many words. It's just this dreary business of being alive. It's getting him down."

"Grandpa? But he loves life."

"That's not the way I read him."

Her brother's words made her ashamed. She had not been to visit her grandfather in more than a year, had thought of him perhaps three times in all those months. The immediate world took so much of her attention. She urged Paul off the line so that she could ring the Estate.

She looked up the number in the directory, feeling guilty that she did not know it as she knew the numbers of friends. She rang the Estate warden. He said her grandfather might have gone to bed; in the circumstances it wasn't wise to call his flat. She asked how the old man was. Very fit. Very fit indeed. Not walking so much, of course, but very fit. Perhaps he was telling her what he thought she wanted to hear. She said she'd visit her grandfather in the morning, and the warden said not before ten. He seemed unenthusiastic.

When she had rung off she stood by the telephone and said two short prayers, the first for Grandpa and the second for forgiveness of her own neglect. Then she was cheerful again.

Matthew came in shortly after ten, laughing at a bill for tires stuck through the door. She was glad to have him safely back, so she laughed as well—although she didn't really see the joke. Two policemen had been waiting by his car in the Karstak, but they'd had to let him go. There was nothing they could charge him with, and the C.L.C. was very active against arbitrary arrest.

He told her about his meeting with the Minister—although he made a great show of believing the worst of everybody, Sir William's dishonesty had surprised and upset him. They tried to think of other ways of contacting the Committee, but came up with nothing. Before going up to bed they drew the curtains and looked down into the street. The gray town car had been replaced by a red one. Night shift. They could see a tweed elbow resting on the sill of the window on the driver's side.

The Colindale removal men arrived at eight thirty next morning. Abigail, still in bed, had forgotten it was the day of their move; she had other things on her mind, especially Grandpa. But the foreman wasn't worried: his men brought in a large number of plastic crates which they began filling at once with random articles. Abigail took Matthew out into the garden.

"You must stop them. That's not the way to pack thngs. They'll rattle about in the van and get chipped to pieces."

"I expect the men know what they're doing."

That was always his reaction.

"If you don't stop them, then I will."

He went up the stairs into the house with the patient air of someone humoring a lunatic.

"Wouldn't some of those things be better wrapped in newspaper?" he said mildly.

"Waste of time, sir. We seal these crates and pump 'em full of gas. The gas solidifies in five minutes and there you are. It's not really a gas, of course: it's a sort of vaporized polystyrene. Breaks off clean as a whistle at the other end."

"Very ingenious." Matthew turned away.

It was far too early in the day for her to be able to endure Matthew being right and tactfully not saying so. She banged off into the kitchen and started taking the previous night's dishes out of the machine. But she had forgotten even to start it, and they were still dirty. She went back to bed. Yet the house was her job—if she didn't do that she didn't do anything.

"Abigail, didn't you say you were going to see your grandfather at ten? You'll need some breakfast first. I'll see to it."

If only she could believe that the reproach implicit in everything he did at these times was in her own head and not in his. It was possible to be just too good, to be just too loving. . . .

The old people's Estate was just outside the restricted traffic area, close to Richmond Park. Small blocks of flats linked by covered travelators, a shopping complex, a church, a sports and social center. A surgery with tiny hospital attached lay a little to one side, among trees. At eleven thirty in the morning the Estate was busy. Power tools buzzed in the workshop, several men and women were cutting the grass and weeding the flower beds, others were repainting the doors of the church. And there was a steady flow of the chairborn to and from the shops. Abigail sat in the car at the gate for some minutes and watched. Theoretically nothing was lacking. She went to the church to find the warden.

"I told you the truth, Mrs. Oliver." Father Carter was immediately defensive. "Your grandfather is very fit indeed."

"I'd have preferred you to tell me he was happy."

"I have two duties, my child. One to the old people here and one to their relatives in the outside world. It would have been wrong of me to give you unnecessary worry."

"Unnecessary? How can I help if you don't tell me the truth?"

The priest shook his head. He motioned for her to sit down. The room they were in was a recent addition, and still smelled of new wood.

"Your grandfather is in a terminal depression. Now only God can help him."

He began explaining what was meant by *terminal depression*. If he'd done his homework he'd have known that she had a degree in Social Geriatrics. She checked her impatience. How many old people had he in his care? And how many relatives would each old person have?

". . . It's as if there were a clock inside each of us. Science ignores that clock. Science works on the principle that the purpose of life is life. You and I know that this is not so." He smiled gently, staring into her face, making sure that he was understood. "For your grandfather the clock has run down. Yet he cannot die. So . . ."

Her grandfather's flat was on the ground floor, with full-length windows overlooking a lawn and dovecote and a dark line of fir trees, the hills of Richmond Park beyond. She paused by his front door and watched the doves circling. Two landed untidily on the dovecote and went inside. A few white feathers drifted down in the still air. There was a smell of mown grass. She rang the doorbell and entered without waiting. Grandpa was watching the tell.

"Mornin', Grandpa." She flattened her accent without noticing. "Got the kettle on, have you?"

He didn't answer. The film was a documentary, a study of post-industrial France.

"Have you got the kettle on, I said."

"Didn't know when you was coming."

He remained motionless, a well-filled bundle of clothes.

"Never mind, Grandpa. I'll do it."

She went into his kitchen, filled the built-in kettle and switched it on. Behind her the tell spoke of leisure fulfillment.

"What else is on?" she called, and got no response.

There was an old-fashioned teapot, and tea in a caddy. The details were good; the kitchen looked out onto a busy concourse. Grandpa had been there for six years and had things the way he liked them. Nothing clinical.

"How many spoons, Grandpa?"

"Four."

She made the tea and found a packet of biscuits. The old man was exactly as she had left him.

"What're you doing with yourself these days, Grandpa?"

"Bloody nothing."

"I thought you'd got a job in the bakery."

"Job? Nowt but a sop for an old fool. Packed it in."

"Somebody has to do it. The Estate can't afford to pay staff."

"Let 'em find someone else then. I've had my lot."

She poured him a cup of tea, spooned in the sugar she knew he liked. She was familiar with his condition from casework. If he'd been younger his depression could have been lifted with E.C.T. or a leucotomy. In his case the only answer was total sedation till death supervened. But all these facts applied to casework patients, not to her grandfather.

"Matthew's taking a new job, Grandpa. We're moving out to Colindale."

"The rubbish these people talk." He was watching the tell. "Every day more and more rubbish."

"Why not try another channel?"

"They're all the same. If it's not this it's music. Or that's what they call it. Or else jokes that don't make sense. And folks laughing like hyenas."

He had been born before the first world war—what could he possibly make of contemporary mass media? There were plans for a special old people's channel, but it wouldn't come in Grandpa's time. She tried again.

"I hear Paul's been out to see you. Did he tell you about his trip to Africa?"

"There's another one. Either he's mad or I am."

"He's young, Grandpa. But he means well. You shouldn't—"

"Then I don't want to hear. It's time I was dead, that's what."

"You don't mean that."

He needed to be told that he didn't mean it. He needed to believe that he didn't mean it.

"Yes, I do. I mean it."

"God loves you, Grandpa. He'll take you when it's the right time."

"You've been talking to Father Carter. Just wait till you're my age. Then you'll know . . ." He came near to saying more, but the habit of faith held him back. "There's five feet of plastic tubing in my guts, Abigail. God knows what else beside. I wish they'd never . . ."

Again he stopped short. He wished what he daren't wish. Prodding him was cruel: he was far too censored, too unprepared. Father Carter had been right. She was worse than useless, she was getting in the way.

"I'll go now, Grandpa."

An ordinary room, simple, not at all modern. Furniture and pictures she recognized from Grandma's lifetime. Sitting, uncomprehending, in the middle of it all, Grandpa. Abigail closed the door quietly and leaned against the wall outside. She would arrange with Father Carter to come more often—though whether for her grandfather's peace of mind or her own was unclear.

Matthew and Abigail stood side by side for the swearing-in ceremony, their right hands raised. Matthew felt foolish, and also uneasy. He didn't share his wife's deep reverence for oaths as such: he believed in a personal morality that might have to overrule them all. But he hoped it wouldn't need to. When the ceremony was finished the director shook hands with them and motioned them back into their seats.

"Work begins Monday morning. So you'll have a little time for settling in over the weekend. Very pleased to have you both here at the Colindale." His smile stopped abruptly. "Now. Have to start with a telling-off. Last night you took a little trip, I hear."

"I went to see the Minister for Social Planning. I—"

"Destination doesn't concern me."

"It was just a friendly visit. He and I have worked together on—"

"Doesn't concern me. But you evaded surveillance. Bad impression. Irresponsible."

Matthew felt himself getting angry. It confused his thoughts and made his eyes difficult to focus. He heard Abigail shift warningly in her chair beside him.

"I make a point of evading surveillance," he said. "I thought everybody did. It's a basic human right."

"Here at the Colindale we put up with our tails," said the director. "Make life easy for them. Anything else would be ridiculous. They work for the Government, so do we. Besides, they protect us. In three ways." Fingers held up for counting. "One, from attack. Two, from suspicion. Three, from subversion. So we give them all the help we can."

It made a crooked sort of sense. Always assuming that nobody could ever be trusted. And who was he, Matthew, to become self-righteous?

"I'm sorry, sir. It's a new idea—takes getting used to." But he couldn't resist a dig. "You see, in all my other jobs the boss has trusted me."

The director appeared not to notice.

"Good. Good. No surveillance at all within Institute

boundaries, of course. Must arrange for you to meet your tails. Decent people, as far as the job lets them . . ."

"Now that we've been sworn in," said Abigail, astonishing Matthew, who hardly ever got a word out of her in company, "now that we've been sworn in, Professor, can you tell us more about the Colindale project?"

"Of course. Start with a conducted tour. Just had a memo from Geneva. About a thing called spouse participation. Treat us all like children, you know."

The director got up from his desk.

"Start in here. Not much, only a printoff console. If I'm kept waiting late for a result I may slip in here for a kip. Let the machine wake me. No keyboard. I leave programming to the programmers. Even the new Astran would take more time to master than I can spare."

He led the way out of his office. Matthew followed, an arm protectively around Abigail. The door at the end of the corridor was a single transparent sheet that slid up at their approach. Billon walked toward it, still talking.

"It's a science of its own, programming the new associative complexes. Almost like working with live matter."

Beyond the door was the main computer room. Matthew had worked in computer centers before. The blank, gray-white cabinets, the glare of the anti-glare lighting, the coolness, the outward calm that masked an inner hysteria of machine and intellect—he was familiar with it all. But the computer center at the Colindale was different, for it was almost completely silent. Apart from the occasional high scream of tape over reading heads and the distant rustle of the six Bohn teleprinters, there was nothing but a huge pressure of silence. It stopped

Matthew in the doorway, his arm closer around his wife. Nobody spoke. Service engineers trod carefully between the bland metal surfaces, rubber shoes on rubber floor, their white coats tight about them. It was a place he did not wish to enter, bitter smelling, anti-human.

"The data processors work ninety minute shifts," murmured Chester Billon. "It's all they can stand."

He walked away down a side aisle, ran his hand jauntily along the sides of the cabinets, patted the flank of the one at the end. His manner denied any threat in the appetite of the machine he commanded. Matthew followed reluctantly, Abigail close behind him.

"Chat isn't encouraged. We'll go through to Data Reception."

The door at the far end opened, letting in a gust of activity. The area beyond was large, crowded with desks and argumentation. Sheets of blue teletype were scattered on every surface, people in groups passing them to and fro, arguing over them, smoking, drinking coffee or chocolate from the automat in one corner.

"The human touch, and not nearly as chaotic as it looks." The director's sentences were expanding with his enthusiasm. "Here we're divided up into sections according to subject. Which accounts for most of the noise. Subject barriers vaguer with every day that passes. Could get all this done by computer as well, but I don't. I believe the interplay of human minds at this level is useful, produces more surprises. Which are what we're after."

Matthew caught his wife's inquiring glance and unobtrusively shrugged his shoulders. Not unobtrusively enough.

"What's going on, Mrs. Oliver, is really very simple.

74

Data comes in from all over Europe on thirty teleprinters, each offering stacking facilities up to a hundred. So the line's practically never engaged. The data is streamed roughly by those people over there. Classified according to subject, I mean. Then it goes around to the groups who hash out the final streaming. Anything particularly awkward or interesting goes to the department heads. That's the part of your job I described last week, Oliver. Every item that finally gets into the data store is the department head's responsibility. So that's Data Reception."

He surged across to the automat and handed out coffee.

"I said we were after surprises. I meant it. Computers capable of learned responses are nothing new. But this one surprises us every day. Bohn can't have known what they were cooking. We've tried off-beat streaming, even downright perversity. Stretching the machine simply forces it to dig deeper. You see, you might say we've programmed it to trust us. So it rejects practically nothing. Spots the association even if it takes three minutes to do so. Which at ten million scanning operations per second is quite something."

He picked up a sheet of teletype and read the first few lines.

"Seismographic analysis." He shrugged his shoulders and put the sheet down again. "Myself, I know nothing about everything. Except perhaps brain physiology. And then only what sort of hammer to hit it with."

Matthew recognized his defensiveness, resulting no doubt from public distrust of "pill psychology." He distrusted it himself, for reasons part ethical and part woolly theological. But Billon himself he was beginning to like. It was interesting that in his sixties, at the height of a successful career in medicine, he had chosen to leave it for the Colindale. Matthew didn't doubt that there was some very good reason.

. "So that's Data Reception." They gulped their coffee, obviously off again. "Astran programmers are in the room over there. They put the streamed data onto ten-track magnetic tape. You have to believe in them, because what they do works."

He glanced at his watch.

"These people will be working till three. Two shifts, eight till three and three till ten. That way we just about keep up. By the way"—he turned to Matthew—"did you notice the lack of printout clatter? The Bohn 507 does it photographically. Television-type scanning on sensitized paper. Thousand lines per second. Without it we'd be output-bound. Mechanical printing had gone as far as it could."

He started herding them across the room toward the far door.

"Data output is fully automatic, emergency panels in the basement. Random access, of course—no more of the waiting around you get with tapes or disk storage. It's available twenty-two hours out of the twenty-four. The Bohn needs two hours daily for servicing. The engineers run check programs, watching for weaknesses. Perhaps I'd better explain data output, Mrs. Oliver." He didn't wait for her to answer. "We offer five services. A, you can ask for a specific data unit. B, you can ask for a transcript of a specific paper. That's where the quick printout comes in. C, you can mention a specific paper and ask for everything in that field. You then get a list of primary associations, authors, dates, comprehensive titles. If that is not enough you can ask the Bohn, D, to cast its net wider, bringing in the secondary associations, possibly three hundred or more. Lastly, you can ask for data simply by subject, in which case you may end up with a list several hundred yards long. In this case the computer will enter into a dialogue with you, and try to establish what it is you really need to know. And all by phoning in, using basic Astran from the handbook, two hundred symbols, no problem."

Abigail had known all this months ago. Advertising material from the Colindale Data Rental Service had come to Matthew through the post. They were out of Data Reception now, going down a passage lined with doors.

"What are all these?" asked Matthew, hoping to distract.

"Offices, staff amenities, door to the classified wing . . ." Billon gestured vaguely.

"Classified wing?"

"For department heads to get on with their own projects. When they've time. Computer facilities. Nothing very interesting." He turned back to Abigail, relentlessly continued his exposition. "Bohn facilities are available on a rental basis to any individual or organization in the European Federation. We install a small teleprinter plus printout, and you use it as you would a telephone. The Bohn will even correct your Astran for you as you go along. The secret is huge storage capacity —on the molecular level, in fact. Four years' use and still not at ten percent of capacity. Data Reception feeds in maybe a thousand new data items a day. And the Bohn thinks up increasingly subtle methods of interrelating them. We never really know what we're sitting on."

He broke off, as if feeling he had—incredibly—said enough. He stopped Matthew and Abigail outside a door marked PROGRAM STORE.

"Program Store," he said unnecessarily. Matthew wondered who wanted to be shown racks of magnetic tapes. Billon opened the door and obliged them to look inside. "Upward of ten thousand different programs." He glanced at his watch again. "Life wasn't always as easy as it is now. Scientists, programmers, systems analysts, took us months to make the thing work. Months of trial and error, checking miles of tape to find perhaps one tiny mistake. Now we've got diagnostic programs, do the job for us."

He ushered them out. Matthew was feeling impatient. He'd been shown nothing new so far, certainly nothing to warrant all the secrecy, all the security precautions. If Abigail could be pressing, so could he.

"And this is really all there is to the Colindale project?"

"Not precisely. . . ." The director looked at his watch, this time as a performance. "It's nearly two. Promised my wife I'd be home for lunch. What say we meet again this evening? Around six?"

It might be a genuine excuse. Matthew couldn't see that anything was gained by it—then or at six, he'd have to be told sooner or later. So he contained his irritation.

"So you see," said Dr. Mozart, leaning against the sitting room doorjamb, "there's someone in the Colindale who wants to kill the director. What interests me is what he's waiting for. One attempt, and then a three-week gap. War of nerves, do you think?"

Abigail wasn't interested. She was busy turning up curtains for the living room and she found Dr. Mozart a bore. If he was going to make a habit of popping in then she'd have to get Matthew to ask him not to. She wondered if—horrors—there was a Mrs. Dr. Mozart.

"Or simply lack of opportunity." Matthew's voice showed that he too wasn't very interested. In Dr. Mozart.

"But the director is not a careful man. There are opportunities every minute of the day."

"Is that why you carry a gun around, Dr. Mozart? Is everyone supposed to?"

"My name is Wolfgang. Please call me Wolf. And I shall call you Matthew."

"I was asking you about your gun."

"And I was evading you." He stretched his arms and yawned. Abigail bent lower over her curtain, bonding the hem with neat dabs of adhesive. Matthew hadn't told her anything about a gun.

"I might play a game with you," the German went on, "and ask you what gun. And then you would be embarrassed, because you are the sort of man whom deceit embarrasses. So I shall trust you instead."

"You're a security man?"

Dr. Mozart spread his hands in friendly admission. "I trust you because you come after the bomb incident. For a second ill-wisher to get past screening is beyond belief."

"Perhaps it's not as difficult as you think." Matthew was having a perverse sort of fun, and Abigail wished he wouldn't. She felt her ears prickling, hoped the blush didn't show. "I dislike spies," Matthew said. "I dislike security, and everything to do with it. I'm a scientist. So if trusting me means asking me to help, please don't."

He sounded so righteous, he would have fooled Saint Michael. But silence would have been far more dignified. She finished her curtain and looked up. He was sorting books onto the bookshelf, placing them according to subject and author. So tidy.

"I wouldn't dream of asking you to help. As an amateur you'd be far too inept."

"Then what are you really here for?"

"I go everywhere, laugh and talk with everybody. People don't like me too much, but I have no wife and might be lonely, so they open their homes to me. I see and hear a lot. . . . I'm here to offer you help, Matthew. Just in case you might ever need it."

"You, help me? What with?"

"Help you to stay alive."

Abigail began measuring another curtain. Boys' talk, men's talk, security, guns, staying alive . . . She told herself they needed danger, manufactured it out of nothing at all.

"You see, Matthew, it is just possible that Henderson's death was not after all an accident."

"But you told me it was. You described the circumstances."

"Circumstances that could be interpreted in one other way. I'm surprised you haven't thought of it yourself. But you're not a suspicious person. You see, there *was* somebody who knew Henderson was going to borrow the director's car."

"The director himself?"

"The director himself."

Abigail reached for the tube of adhesive. From what she had seen of Chester Billon he was certainly capable of . . . But it was getting more like a spy story with every minute.

"Why should the director have wanted to kill John Henderson?" she said.

The two men looked at her with surprise, as if they had forgotten she was there.

"Honestly, Mrs. Oliver, I don't know."

At least he hadn't got around to calling her Abigail.

"And even if he had, why should he want to kill Matthew as well?" She wanted to make the whole thing seem ridiculous. It was ridiculous. . . . "Unless, of course, you think he's planning to kill off all the leading sociologists who come here."

"I think Matthew should be careful, Mrs. Oliver. That's all."

The German took himself so seriously. Unless, to be fair, it was the situation he took seriously. A man had died. And somebody, probably still in the Colindale at that moment had killed him. . . . All her denials broke down and she was frightened. Matthew picked up another pile of books.

"Does the director know you're an agent?" he said.

"I hope not."

"What can you tell me about the Colindale project?"

"It's dangerous."

"Nothing else?"

"That's the director's job."

"I see."

Matthew was alone in the garden, prodding the pool to see how deep it was. As she hung the sitting room curtains she watched him move the stick vaguely about in the shallow water.

"The Minister has water lilies and carp. I wonder if we'll be here long enough to bother."

She saw him as a man for acres, not lily ponds. For storms and tempests, not petty intrigue, who killed whom. A cottage on an island, a field of potatoes, windblown hens pecking in the mud, Matthew coming up from his boat swinging a string of fish.

"If you went fishing in the sea off an island," she called, "what sort would you come back with?"

"Mackerel . . . if I had a motor or didn't mind rowing like hell." He put down his stick, came to the window, and leaned in. "But the islands are getting terribly crowded," he said.

"There must be one somewhere."

"You read that survey of the Orkneys."

What was the use of him catching up with her so quickly, if he then crushed her? She lowered her arms from the curtain rail.

"You were very good at lying to the German," she said.

"Only by inference. Besides, I'm keeping an open mind. I've got to find out just what the Colindale project is before I decide what to do about it."

"Perhaps"—she couldn't keep up her bitterness—"perhaps that's what Henderson said to *his* wife."

"I love you, Abigail." He hugged her through the window. "I'm not going to get myself killed."

His hands were on her shoulder blades, shaping them. He wanted to make love. It would be their first love-making in the new house. Dimly she heard the clock in the room behind her begin to strike. His hands paused, and then continued, She laughed into his ear.

"I've lost you," she said. "Tell me what you think you ought to be doing."

"Wasn't that six?"

"I expect so."

"That's when the director's expecting us."

She'd had enough of the director, of the computer center, of the Colindale. It was all so grubby somehow.

"You go. I've had enough of the computer center for one day. You can tell me all about it when you get back."

She smoothed his hair, but he still looked like a tufted guinea pig. She did not tell him to be careful—if he needed to be told then telling was a waste of time. He knew what life for her would be without him. He must simply get on with what had to be done.

After they had argued and he had finally gone alone, she drifted about the house for half an hour or so, doing nothing, waiting for him to come back. The rooms were without associations—except as dead man's shoes—and the sameness of their views of the central garden began to oppress her. They needed a past and a future that were identifiably hers and Matthew's. Then the broken bits of polystyrene from the packing cases caught her eye and she spent nearly an hour clearing them up. Finishing in the bedroom, she lay down on the piled blankets on the bed and felt that she deserved a cigarette. After that she leaped up and purged the bedroom, stuffed everything into cupboards and drawers, and made the bed. Then she cooked some porridge because she felt hungry.

It wasn't until daylight began to fail that she realized

it was late, and that Matthew had been gone a very long time. The guns and incendiary bombs she had ridiculed suddenly became real, and she rang the director's office. Getting no reply, she rang Reception. Professor Billon was busy and in no circumstances could be disturbed. The receptionist had no idea where Dr. Oliver might be—except that she was sure he had not left the building. She offered to ring around all the offices, but there were a large number and it would take time. She mentioned that she went off duty at ten. Abigail told her not to bother.

Her panic increased when she called Dr. Mozart's apartment and got no answer. There were hundreds of reasons why Matthew should have been delayed—his having come to harm in some way being the least probable. Obviously the least probable. But the emptiness in the house was becoming hard to bear. She went out, disjointed by anxiety, into the dusk to look for him.

She walked down past shadowy doorways and groups of trees and dim courtyards; already she felt better, a little foolish so that she almost turned back. But—fear apart—there was no reason why she shouldn't visit her husband where he worked. . . . Rounding a corner, she saw the low bulk of the computer center, lights spilling from it across the gray-blue evening. Its normality comforted her further, and she entered the foyer feeling totally in command. The place already had a night look about it, each feature unnaturally clear and still. The burred glass floor was now lighted from beneath, and she crossed it briskly to the reception desk, feeling as if people were looking up her skirt. She showed her pass.

"I want to see my husband."

The receptionist was now the night porter. It was a

few minutes past ten, and he'd only just come on duty. He was sorting out his keys and checking his two-way radio. He looked briefly on a chart to see if Dr. Oliver was still in the building.

"You know where his office is, Mrs. Oliver?" He let her pass without waiting for an answer. "I've booked you in for ten five, Mrs. Oliver. If you're hoping for computer time, there ain't none. Reserved solid by Professor Furneau."

Abigail liked his assumption that she was working there. She found herself wishing that she *had* been wanting computer time. Not to spoil the illusion, she thanked him and walked quickly away. Her University days had been fun, and the period afterward with the L.C.C. . . . Once out of sight she returned to reality and paused, considering what she should do next. Of course she had no idea at all where Matthew's office might be— if indeed he had yet been allocated one. She suspected not, otherwise the girl on the phone would have suggested ringing it. She decided to follow the route—the only one she knew—that the director had shown them that morning. If the director was busy, he was probably either in his office or the computer room itself. And she'd probably find Matthew with him.

Professor Billon's office was deserted and in darkness, except for the beginnings of moonlight through the three eye-shaped windows. She crossed it, and went out into the corridor that led to the computer room. The corridor itself was also unlighted. But, film-like, as if projected onto the full-width glass door at the corridor's end, Abigail saw the computer room, unbelievably chaotic, in minute and brilliant detail. The room was crowded with people. Several of the console cabinets were open, their circuit blocks pulled out in units on the floor. Folded printout sheets lay around in concertina piles, and ribbons of magnetic tape were being trodden underfoot. An assistant was going around trying to rescue them and put them up for rewind. There were also quantities of books and microfilm, and a film projector.

As Abigail approached the glass door it began to rise automatically, letting out an unpleasant murmur of controlled human hysteria. Then an awareness of her presence in the doorway spread slowly around the huge room, and the murmur dwindled down to silence. People became still, interrupted in what they were doing, fixed staring at her. Desperately she sought a familiar face, found the director and, rather in the background, Dr. Mozart. There was no sign of Matthew.

"Who are you?" From a man in a white coat she didn't know. "What are you doing here?"

She felt trapped in the surrounding silence, unable to reply. Professor Billon came toward her, stepping over curls of brownish tape.

"It's all right, Furneau. This is Mrs. Oliver. I expect she's looking for her husband."

There was a gigantic smoothness about him, filling the whole doorway so that she could see nothing around it.

"That's right, isn't it, Mrs. Oliver?" She nodded, still dumb. He smiled. "I was busy. Sent him to have a chat with his assistant." He pointed back in the direction she had come. "Along to the other end of the passage. Turn right. Third door on the left."

She turned and walked away. The glass door closed behind her, shutting off the huge uncomfortable silence.

Behind the door people would be getting on with what they had been doing. She realized that somehow she had created a crisis, and that the director had averted it. As if she had stumbled on some obscene ritual and should be grateful to him for sparing everybody's embarrassment.

At the end of the passage she hesitated, always uncertain in matters of left and right. Finally she turned the wrong way, and went through a pair of blank double doors into another passage, thickly carpeted. She counted doors. The third had the name Z. MALLALIEU on it. The initial seemed absurdly sinister. She knocked firmly and went in.

An old man was working in a brilliant cone of light, his head bent over piles of books on the desk. He was alone.

"I'm so sorry. I must have got the wrong . . ." She began to withdraw.

"Don't go." The man looked up and she saw that, although white-haired, he was young, scarcely thirty. He scuffled some books out of sight and came quickly around the side of his desk. "Don't go, I said."

She would have turned and run, but he had the flat of his hand on the door and was closing it behind her.

"Come into the light so that I may see you."

She wasn't imagining it: his voice, his physical presence, everything about him was threatening. The Colindale was peopled with madmen. His white hair moved in the darkness, nodding her forward. She walked to the desk, uncomfortably aware of her body, the mechanics of ankles and knees and hip joints as she moved. She didn't know what to do with her arms.

"I'm sorry I interrupted you. I was looking for somebody. My husband. I—"

"Your husband? In the classified wing? Forgive me if I don't believe you."

Her fear turned to weary irritation. A classified wing, a cone of light, a white-haired young man with Z for an initial and a too-carefully modulated voice . . . It was cops and robbers again. She leaned on the desk.

"I don't really care if you believe me or not. My name is Oliver. My husband is the new head of sociology. I've just come from the director. He'll identify me, if you really think it necessary."

She looked down at her hands, almost colorless in the painful light. Then across the surface of the desk, waiting for the young man to reply. She saw the books he had been trying to push out of sight. One of them was a well-used copy of the Holy Bible. And beside it, in Latin, *Apologia pro Vita Sua.*

FIVE

MATTHEW NEEDN'T have worried about being late for his six o'clock appointment with Professor Billon. The director was too busy even to notice his arrival. There were a dozen or so other people in the office, all grouped tensely around the printoff console opposite the windows. It was delivering a list of references, the sheet of sensitized paper streaming from it in a steady blue torrent. In front of the console a metal trough caught the paper so that it folded neatly to and fro. From a slot in the bottom of the trough Professor Billon was drawing out the paper in his own time, and reading the list loudly and clearly. Matthew waited in the background, unwilling to interrupt.

"Heissenger, wave theory, MW 7012x. Hill S., sub-a polarity, NP 5576. Hindl, transformer design, MF 10012k. Holt, low temperature flux, KV 99dll. Hummelmann, sub-a density variants, NP 4070 . . ."

The scientists around the console were making notes. Occasionally one of them would ask the director to repeat a title or a reference number.

". . . Lowther, beam cutoff characteristics, MW 0019. Loxton, cathode retention, CR 237Q. Mansen G., aging theory, three parts, G 6672, 3 and 4. Mansen J., petroleum catalysts, CO 79009. Mansen L., refraction indices, LW 9292x . . ." The director paused. "Any surprises yet? Buhler? Johnson?"

"The Hill S., NP 5576." An old man, bearded. "I must reread it, of course. An interesting paper, from what I remember, but I cannot see the connection. Not with the Naples discovery."

"Good, Buhler. Good." Billon returned to his list. "Maque, reentry speeds, BM 60079. Markheim K., critical masses . . ."

Matthew thought he understood what was happening. Each scientist spotted anything that was in his or her field and made a note of the reference. Presumably the list was being delivered in response to a particular stimulus. But what stimulus, and with what purpose?

"Morgenstern, Moebius extensions, QP 17d. Mort, graduated responses, SS 42—"

"Professor Billon, sir. Excuse me, sir." A young man who might have been a rugger coach. "Don't you think Boney's flipping his lid, sir?"

"Unlikely." The list continued to flow from the print-out slot by Billon's head. "What makes you think so, Furneau?"

"That's the fifth SS classification he's come up with. It's not my field, sir, but what can Strategic Studies possibly have to do with the Naples discovery?"

"You should have more faith in the Bohn." Billon turned to a man with spectacles and untidy red hair. "Coombe-Watkins, you're our strategist."

"The five papers in question all have to do with nuclear attack from satellite. I don't remember the details, but—"

"Then the connection is clear." Buhler again, excited. "I have at least a dozen papers relating to nuclear warheads."

"Which accounts," said Professor Billon, "for the sequence's high priority rating. And justifies my calling you all out at this time on a Saturday." He looked around the group. "It seems as if some of us are in for a working weekend." His one seeing eye passed Matthew, and then returned to him. "My dear Oliver, I didn't hear you come in."

"I knocked, Professor. When nobody answered, I . . ." Everybody turned to stare at him. "You were obviously busy, so I decided to wait until . . ."

"Of course. Of course. Should have sent word for

you not to come. The Bohn put out a high priority rating, so I . . . But you don't know what I'm talking about." He covered his eyes for a moment, exasperated. "No time now. See you Monday morning, nine thirty."

Apparently Matthew was dismissed. He turned to go, angry at being treated like an office boy.

"Sorry to do this, Oliver. Bit of a panic." Matthew looked back in time to catch the director's most professional smile. "Your assistant's in her office. Why not go and get acquainted? Save time on Monday."

Matthew went out, closing the door behind him. The Colindale project was as far from being explained as it had ever been. He controlled his irritation—at least the latest delay was genuine enough. He was tempted to go straight home to Abigail. But the director had suggested he should get acquainted with Miss Pelham, and he supposed he had no alternative.

He knew his assistant only by the work she had published. Steady and dutiful, it left him unprepared for the spectacularness of its originator. Margaret Pelham concealed both her intellect and her humanity behind an enormous tangle of bleached yellow hair and an amount of makeup that Matthew had previously associated only with ballet dancers. Her eyebrows were plucked bare, and she had sequins at the outer corners of her eyes. With stick arms and legs she looked—put at its most charitable—like a worn-out fashion model. If she'd got past Chester Billon with her appearance so against her, then her work must be really outstanding. Unless the director had a weakness for worn-out fashion models.

"You're Dr. Oliver? How super. I'm Maggie. And am I glad to see you—the last few weeks have been bloody hell, since poor John was killed." She kicked a large filing cabinet. "Full of problems," she said. "I've done my best, but I bet I've let through dozens of things that ought to be coded under something utterly different. Medical, topographical, God knows . . . Luckily old Boney does his best to sort it all out, poor thing."

"I see."

Matthew felt very old. But at least he didn't have to ask who "old Boney" was.

"You know, I saw you about the Institute yesterday, and I thought to myself, I bet that's him. The craggy, distinguished look. And sexy, to boot."

Matthew cleared his throat. Discipline, the establishment of authority, never came easily to him, even at the best of times.

"The thing is," she continued, "you don't have to worry. Not about me. It's my anti-social-worker's act. I learned it around the Buildings, and I'm afraid it's stuck."

"The buildings?"

"The Hampstead dropouts, you know. The community they've got there—it's smart to call it the Buildings. I did a study for my thesis."

"I've read it."

"Have you? How super . . . I've read all yours, of course. Mutual admiration soc. Shall we get on with some work?"

They got on with some work. As she explained Institute procedures her extravagant mannerism faded. Codings, classifications, internal distribution routines—she had the ability to make everything clear the first time through. She was friendly, and humorous, and easy to get on with. But the only possible relationship with her would have to be to do with work. Outside that the smoke screen went down, the distancing act. For himself Matthew was relieved. He enjoyed the company of women, but he was married to Abigail: in the Ministry it hadn't always been easy to explain the unfashionable difference. But he couldn't help wondering what had happened to Maggie to make her so defensive.

When he thought he properly understood the basic system, she fetched a file of doubtful codings and they went through it together. The work was fascinating: new data from all over Europe, much of it controversial. At this stage he didn't have to worry about statistical accuracy. The Bohn would check all figures against material already stored and send him back a list of discrepancies. Dealing with this list would be one of his first jobs each morning. And the Bohn was giving this service to all the other seventeen department heads at the same time. Besides dealing with incoming queries from more than three million subscribers.

Impressive as this was, there was obviously more to the Colindale project than just this. Otherwise, why the strict, almost pathological secrecy? And why the scene he had witnessed so recently in the director's office?

"What does the director mean," he asked suddenly, "when he says that the Bohn puts out a high priority rating?"

"It's a way the computer has of judging the importance of supplied data."

"Judging the importance? Surely that's not a job for a computer?"

Maggie looked at him sideways.

"Boney isn't an ordinary computer. I thought you knew that."

"I know it's associative. I know its capacity for observing relationships is unusually subtle. All the same—"

"You must ask C.B. He'll fill you in."

Her sudden reserve was uncharacteristic. He sat back, puzzled. She held up a warning hand, five gold-painted fingernails.

"All right. So there're things I can't tell you. The director likes to do things in his own way."

"You might tell me just one thing. Has any of this any connection with Henderson's death?"

She shook her head.

"There's too much I don't know. For one thing, I'm only an assistant. I don't get in to the conferences. John's death upset me—we'd worked together for three years. Nothing very sexual, you know, just that he was fun, and a wonderful man to work with. But questions weren't encouraged, never are at the Colindale. As for *why* he died—once again, I can only tell you to ask the director."

She paused, needing to say more but uncertain of the right words.

"The Colindale's a strange place. Frightened of itself. Not quite sane . . . I think you need to be not quite sane yourself in order to bear it." She laughed, reverted to the act. "Sane? I mean, pet, who *is* sane these days? Who'd want to be? I ask you."

He left it there. She had referred to more than just the place and the people. There was a third element she had grasped at, and then drawn back. He didn't press her because in a way he understood what she meant. Sitting beside Abigail the previous day he had shuddered as he entered the gates.

"I must get back to my wife," he said. "She's been expecting me for hours."

"Boney may be big and fast." She couldn't leave it. "But he's still only a computer. He doesn't create, you see; he only shuffles the possibilities. He spots relationships and serves them up. That's not being creative."

Matthew wondered whom she was trying to convince. There had to be some human capability that computers could not duplicate or exceed. A frontier must exist. She looked across at him, possibly sharing his thoughts, and smiled ruefully.

"You'll see what I mean. When you start working with the Bohn yourself, you'll see what I mean." She watched him get up and go to the door. "It runs away with you," she said. "It's important to keep a sense of proportion. Remember that there are limitations."

She was going to say something more, but the telephone rang. Matthew began to edge out through the door. The conversation had taken on a disturbing quality of controlled panic. He reminded himself that Maggie must have been grossly overworked since the death of Henderson. And her fears played too easily on his own. . . .

As he was going she called him back.

"It's your wife. She's along in the classified wing, with Mallalieu. Go and rescue her at once. She shouldn't be there, and certainly not with him. Of all the department heads, he's the maddest. He's so mad it's not funny."

They walked back to their house together. Abigail fitted under his shoulder, and he shortened his stride so that they walked in step. The sky was pale with the lights from the surrounding motorways, brighter than the moonlight; the courtyards and colored pavements lit at neat intervals by street lamps. The distant rush of traffic emphasized their isolation. They passed two men in white coats arguing over calculations on the back of an envelope. Matthew sighed. So much about the Colindale was right.

Abigail described what she had seen in the computer room.

"What was happening, Matthew? I've never seen a computer in such a mess."

"I have. I remember a day once at the Ministry . . . Something goes wrong. Your program doesn't give the sort of answer you expect, and you blame the computer. Just occasionally it *is* the computer that's wrong, but more often it's your program, or your expectation. It can take all night to get things sorted."

"So they've run into some kind of trouble?"

"It happens. Nothing to worry about, of course. It's only the pressure on computer time that makes people get so desperate. And at least they don't have to pay for time here as they would in any commercial computer center."

They walked on. Abigail began talking about Zacharie Mallalieu.

"Anyway, Matthew, why have a classified wing? I think they just enjoy making things mysterious."

"The director told us. It's where department heads get on with their own private projects. That's why it's out of bounds to staff."

"But Mallalieu's an economist. Even if he was reading this Bible, why should he want so much to hide it?"

"Perhaps he makes a great thing of being a rationalist."

He knew this was no explanation. Rationalists read Bibles, if only for the purpose of explaining them away.

"But he was so odd, Matthew. Terribly suspicious. For a long time he didn't even believe I was who I said I was."

"I wouldn't worry about it. My Miss Pelham says he's quite mad. Outside economics, of course."

He distracted her, told her about Maggie—omitting what she had said about the Colindale. Its closeness to his own feeling worried him. He tried Abigail's trick of dropping the whole thing out of his mind. He ran with her, sat her on a low wall, kissed her, ignored her protests. They hurried home and made cocoa in bowls, the mugs still hidden somewhere under one of the various piles in the kitchen. They went to bed. He thrust the cold hand of the Institute back till he no longer felt it.

Sunday morning they idled about the house till it was time for eleven o'clock Mass. They sorted out the kitchen and hung the bedroom curtains. Matthew spent a long time moving the harpsichord around the sitting room till he found the right place for it. The move had disturbed the tune of the upper octaves, and a further half-hour was taken up with the electronic soundwave matcher. They finally left for church with little time to spare. At the gate they were delayed while their tails were fetched and introduced.

As promised, Mrs. Foster was charming. Somebody's aunt, but with muscles, and a laser gun in her handbag. Matthew's tail was called Wilkinson. Not the man who had followed them home the previous Friday; of a better class altogether. He was shabby and thoughtful, and might easily have been an intellectual alienee, one of the thousands of middle-aged dropouts who chose to live on the social services. His car was suitable to such a man, an old model, only barely brought up to the new safety requirements. His front was perfect, giving him a reason to be anywhere at any time, idle and contented.

Since Matthew and Abigail were going out together, and were not going to separate, only one tail was needed. Mr. Wilkinson and Mrs. Foster tossed, and Mr. Wilkinson won. Mrs. Foster accompanied the Olivers to church.

The Catholic church in Colindale was new, a white, circular building with darkly colored windows. Matthew and Abigail were among the last in, and the service had already begun. Matthew walked behind his wife, not genuflecting when she did, fearing ritualized gesture, not crossing himself before the Gospel. He went to church always hoping to be gusted into complete participation. But he gave the responses for their beauty of language and joined in the prayers for the history of human aspiration that they represented. He kept himself warily separate, preferring to draw his comfort parasitically from that of Abigail. If he prayed on his own—to a God he hardly believed in—it was for understanding. He knew this was the wrong way around: faith should come first, and then understanding. He also knew that for as long as he approached the Church because it was observably a good thing, he would get nowhere. But—

He stood up so that Abigail could pass him and go to receive the wafer. Afterwards he found his joy in hers.

After the slanting purple light of the church, the road in Colindale was like a tawdry amusement arcade, with flashing signs and slot machine people. He stood beside her and let the crowd jostle past, shading his eyes. He wanted to protect her from the contrast. A young man came up to them. He was small and thick-chested—would probably have been a hunchback but for prenatal corrective treatment. He had the hunchback's sharpness of eye and manner.

"Excuse me. Aren't you Dr. Oliver? My name is Andrew Scarfe." He was the sort of young man who expected to shake hands. "I work at the Colindale, Dr. Oliver. Systems analysis."

Matthew introduced him to Abigail. They stood on the pavement thinking of things to say.

"It's our first time at this church," said Abigail. "We enjoyed the service very much."

"I come every Sunday. The priest's very good, I think. I like his delivery, and the way he doesn't hustle the responses."

"And the organist's not bad. And the layout's good—everybody gets such a good view of the altar."

This sort of in-group familiarity made Matthew uneasy. Mechanical, irreverent somehow. He wondered what young Scarfe had really come to talk about. Unless he simply wanted to strike up a friendship with fellow-Catholics.

"Can we give you a lift back?" he said.

"No thanks. I've got my own wagon. Besides, the tail wouldn't like it. He might think I was trying to dodge him."

Matthew frowned. He had been forgetting the ways of the Colindale.

"Perhaps we could give you some lunch," said Abigail, evidently not realizing that Andrew Scarfe was one to like regularity in his life. No cooking had been done so far, and they would expect to eat lunch around three.

"No thank you, Mrs. Oliver. My flat-mate always does the Sunday lunch. It's one of her few domesticities. Though it often needs half the afternoon to tidy up after her. I believe she's your assistant, sir. Margaret Pelham. Strange woman—I'm afraid we don't get on all that well. Don't misunderstand me, sir. I'm sure she's a wonderful person to work with. Good at her job and all that."

Matthew distrusted such eagerness to say the right thing. If he had to choose between Scarfe and Maggie, he'd choose Maggie every time. The young man's openness was too wide-eyed. Nobody could be as simple, as genuine, as Scarfe appeared to be.

The crowd outside the church was thinning. Along the street a procession with placards could be seen approaching, middle-aged alienees demanding the vote back. ALIENATION NO CRIME, said the placards. And PENSIONERS NOT OUTCASTS. The suburban Sunday strollers paused to stare. It was an orderly, pathetically orderly demonstration, heralded by neither drums nor loudspeakers.

"By the way, Dr. Oliver"—Scarfe cocked his head and looked up at Matthew, eyes keen and bird black—"if you ever want any help with Astran I'll be only too glad to oblige."

"That's very kind." Matthew was watching the procession. "All the same, I don't think—"

"I'll lend you a book. Bring it around one evening."

"Thank you, Mr. Scarfe. Actually, I doubt if I shall be doing much programming myself."

"Still, it'll be a help at least to know how it works. Short for Associative Transliteration, of course."

Of course. Who did the lad think he was talking to? Matthew pulled himself up, wondered why he was being so intolerant. He settled, ashamed, on Scarfe's slight deformity. In young people physical perfection was so universal, and deviation so ringed about with psychological implications, that it made him distinctly uneasy.

"Very kind of you, Mr. Scarfe. Come around any time you like."

At that moment Scarfe's tail arrived, asking if he could get back to the Colindale fairly soon as his wife was expecting him for an early lunch. A charmingly domestic touch.

"He must be very lonely," said Matthew, watching the two of them walk away in friendly conversation.

"From what you told me about Miss Pelham she doesn't sound the easiest person to share with. Though he struck me as not being very keen on women at the best of times."

"Perhaps they're not very keen on him. Anyway, he's stuck with it—Billon mixes the sexes as a matter of policy. He says it makes relationships less dependent on love or sex. They work together, so they should live together. As laid down in his quartering register."

Abigail took his hand. "The man's a fool," she said.

The procession had nearly reached them. As they watched it was overtaken by three police cars, which turned across in front of it and stopped. The marchers stopped also, and waited meekly. Policemen from the three cars went through the ranks taking names and addresses, checking identity cards. Nobody ran, or struggled, or even protested: there were two more cars and a large closed van waiting at the rear of the procession. People in general had little sympathy with alienees and their conditional pensions—being alienated was no more than an excuse for being bone idle. The idea that work was a good thing in itself lingered tenaciously, no matter how much the experts told people it was out of date.

After its members had been counted and listed, the procession was allowed to go on its way. This it did, though more from pride than from conviction or continuing hope of success. Pensions were conditional, conditional on too many things. The machinery of government was orderly and discreet.

Matthew and Abigail watched the people march by, men and women in their thirties and forties, some of them extravagantly dressed, some of them merely seedy. The purpose of their demonstration was oddly out of character; usually alienees took no interest at all in the democractic process. This untypical political interest suggested outside influence, either from the East or from the Americas. Which explained the police intervention. Usually alienees demonstrated against compulsory education for their children or in favor of better housing.

Matthew waited, saddened, for Mrs. Foster to ease her car out of the crush. The scene he and Abigail had witnessed was part of the real world; their lives at both the Colindale and in their Kensington house were totally disconnected, out of touch. Viewed like that, there was no doubt little to choose between the two. They drove home in front of Mrs. Foster, the car's air conditioner cooling the sweat on their hands and faces.

On their return they found an assortment of Sunday newspapers waiting on the doorstep, further signs of Colindale efficiency. The afternoon was hot and still, and they lunched by the pool in their central garden. The fir tree smelled rich and dark. They half expected Dr. Mozart to pop in, and were very glad when he didn't. The papers remained where Matthew had put them, on the floor just inside the front door. That afternoon he and Abigail were happier to talk about what came into their heads. If anything did.

Around six o'clock Matthew went in to try out the newly-tuned harpsichord. He felt very hot, and chose to play Couperin. After a few minutes Abigail spoke to him from the garden, not raising her voice, so that he hardly heard.

"Grandpa's lived too long," she said.

She might have been talking to herself. He went on playing. She had been to see the old man on Saturday morning. He blamed himself for not having asked her about her visit—it had been crowded out by the move, by the Colindale. No doubt she had been waiting for him to ask.

"Did you hear me, Matthew?"

He stopped playing. With even cancer controlled, what was there left to die of?

"I wasn't sure if you meant me to," he said.

"I've been thinking, Matthew. I've decided he belongs with us."

She came into the sitting room. He got up and went to her, put his hands on her shoulders.

"He'd only feel he was being a bother."

"We wouldn't let him."

"We couldn't help it. The three generation family just doesn't work any more."

"We could make it work."

Matthew would have liked things to be different. He would have liked the old man to be able to feel he had a place with them, a place where he was respected for his age and wisdom. But the two, age and wisdom, no longer went together. The tradition of respect, even of usefulness, had died.

"It can't be done, love. It's thirty years too late. He'd feel he was out of touch, nothing but an old fool, an object for our pity. You see, we don't *need* him. Anything else is so artificial."

"But everyone's worked so hard to keep him alive, Matthew."

To which there was no answer.

Monday morning was overcast, and it looked as if there might be rain. Matthew decided it would stay dry until lunch time and went to the computer center without his coat. He frequently made such decisions and they were frequently wrong. In the last two hundred yards of his walk rain began to fall heavily. He ran, and then stood under the awning shaking water off his jacket. The wet paving stones smelled of his childhood, of the first hot summer he remembered, and of the rain he had stood in, soaking his hair and face, the day that the heat had lifted.

"Dr. Oliver, the director wants to see you at once."

"I'm not late, am I?"

He hated to be late.

"Not at all. He just left word that he'd like some time with you before the conference."

"Conference?"

The girl behind the desk stared at him without expression, as if his question had been in bad taste.

"Please go through at once, Dr. Oliver."

The director's office was dim, except for a lamp over his desk. Professor Billon was talking on two telephones at once. Matthew sat down and waited. He saw for the first time that the pupils of the three eye windows were sensitized so that they dilated and contracted in response to the light outside. At that moment they were very wide. Expensive toys, and quite pointless, they irritated Matthew's puritanical soul. He tried not to listen to the director's two conversations. In any case, they made little sense. Finally they ended.

"You wanted to see me, sir."

Something to say after a long pause during which the director stared at him, his mind apprently far elsewhere.

"Seems I've got to throw you in at the deep end, Oliver." He frowned, his tangled eyebrows concealing his eyes. "Unless you've already worked everything out from the little charade you walked in on day before yesterday."

"I'm afraid not."

"At least you know there's more in the Colindale project than meets the eye. Has to be. You'll see why in a minute." Professor Billon sighed and shifted in his seat, grumbling to himself inaudibly. Then his voice surfaced. "The Bohn is a remarkable device, Oliver. More remarkable than its designers imagine. It extrapolates. Is in fact a product of its own extrapolations. Extrapolates on a sufficiently wide base to appear creative. Human creativity works by selection, sorting through the individual's memory store and selecting items that interrelate unexpectedly, amusingly, interestingly, profitably. It is the subtlety of this selection process, the criteria it employs, that determines the creative ability of each individual person." He leaned forward across his desk to point his next sentence. "And the criteria we have given the Bohn are the subtlest we here at the Colindale Institute could devise."

"You're saying that the Bohn invents."

"I'm saying that the Bohn perceives relationships and extrapolates logically from them."

Which was the same thing. This was what Maggie had been trying to tell him on Saturday evening. He hadn't wanted to know then, and he didn't want to know now. Knowledge would force decisions on him, force him to think of Gryphon and what the man had or had not died for. . . . The director sat back and smoothed his already smooth hair.

"So we have a machine that—if you like—invents. Plots future trends. Tells us what will happen *if* . . . And does all this better than any other person or organization in the world, simply because of the unique supply of data at its disposal. So what do we have, Oliver?"

Matthew waited to be told.

"We have a unique way of carrying every new discovery, every complex of discoveries, to its most imaginative conclusion. And doing so in a matter of minutes. Months, perhaps years before anyone else will arrive at the same point. . . . Saturday evening you walked in on the Bohn at work, Oliver. It was responding to a discovery received that afternoon from a team of scientists in Naples working in the field of electromagnetics. In itself a small item. But to the Bohn it was like the last piece in a gigantic jigsaw puzzle only the machine itself knew about." He frowned and tapped the desk with the fingers of one hand. One-two-three-four. One-two-three-four. "No. I choose words badly. I don't want to suggest that the Bohn had known about this puzzle for some time and had been waiting for just the right last piece. What I mean is that its scanning techniques are so rapid and so complex that all the relationships made possible by the Naples discovery were perceived in virtually the same instant. To choose the more meaningful of these was, for the Bohn, a simple matter. You watched the result of this process being delivered. A list of ninety-six different papers, the contents of which—taken together—made up the whole picture. My team has been checking this list for the last thirty-six hours. Soon we go into conference to hear their conclusions and to decide what is to be done."

"Done?" Here was the crunch, the million dollar question. "If an invention exists, it exists. What can possibly be 'done' about it?"

"I'll tell you a story, Oliver." the director paused. They were coming to a part of the script that was familiar to him, complete with stage directions. "In 1933, Oliver, a laboratory was built for the physicist Pyotr Kapitza. For its facade he ordered the head of a crocodile in stone. 'The crocodile of science,' he said. 'The crocodile cannot turn its head. Like science it must always go forward with all-devouring jaws. . . . ' " Again Billon paused. He turned his chair one complete revolution. "A generally accepted fact, Oliver. But one that we here at the Colindale deny."

"You mean you try to suppress discoveries of which you do not approve?"

"Suppression is seldom necessary. You can't suppress what hasn't yet been discovered, what only exists in the circuits of the Bohn. Prevention is another matter. Once you know what a particular invention is to be, there are many ways of preventing it. Research is so specialized. The right hand of science so seldom knows what the left hand is up to . . . and then, of course, there's money. The administration of research funds. And so on. And so on."

"You take a lot on yourselves."

"We have to. Scientists have refused responsibility for their discoveries for far too long. We've left that to the politicians and the philosophers." He gestured widely, indicating the resultant state of the world. "We now have machinery for intelligent, imaginative extrapolation. With this as our basis we can, we *must*, accept responsibility. Accept it and exercise it." He sighed. "And exercise it secretly. People in a democracy dislike being told what is good for them."

It had stopped raining. For a moment Matthew's attention was distracted when a ray of sunlight caused the centers of the windows to scrape softly as they contracted. He feared what the director was telling him.

"No delusions of grandeur, Oliver. Every decision is a committee job. Imperfect system. Better than nothing. Better than the free-for-all that has landed us where we are today. I'll give you an example from your own field. Sociology. To do with organ transplants. . . . You know why they're no longer carried out on people over fifty?"

"The risk's too great. The drugs controlling rejection leave older people too vulnerable."

"Right. But last summer a thesis on compatability came in from a Bristol student. Extrapolation showed its line to be new. Probable result: trouble-free organ replacement in all age groups. We needed to know what this would imply. The Bohn gave us the percentage increase in average life expectation. Relating this figure to housing and pension schemes produced a crippling increase in national expenditure. This was set against an index of life fulfillment patterns devised by your predecessor. Even allowing an optimistic increase in productive working life, the deficit was still far more than the European economy could stand. A study of terminal depression rates, together with an estimate of possible drug control in this field, confirmed the conclusion on purely humanitarian grounds."

"So?"

"So the girl from Bristol didn't get her post-graduate grant and was forced to go into industry."

So Gryphon had been right. Decision making on this basis would produce no detectable pattern: the criteria were far too wide-ranging and variable. Individual academic freedom sacrificed for the ultimate good of the whole. A dangerous but attractive possibility. If it worked.

"What if the work doesn't come from a helpless undergraduate?" Matthew asked. "What if it comes from a famous scientist?"

"Who pays, Oliver? Pays for his equipment, his laboratory, his staff, his food even? Where would any scientist, no matter how great, be without Government money? The important thing is not to do it crudely, to shape the direction of research by giving a little money here and taking a little there. And never giving reasons. Existing legislation offers plenty of loopholes."

Matthew saw that it could be done. Even the private

sector of industry was dependent on the Government for subsidies, grants, tax concessions—besides needing the data facilities of the Colindale. It could be done, but would it?

"What does the Government have to say? How did you persuade them to give you such enormous power?"

"But we have no power at all. No real power. Purely an advisory capacity. Politicians, you see, are seldom scientists—they have to believe what we tell them. Apart from anything else, we save them money. The system can be seen to work. And politicians are pragmatists."

Science in control of itself. The quality of life at last as the deciding factor. And who was better trained to make judgments on the quality of human life than the sociologist, the ethnologist? He would have to come out from behind the protection of his impotence, his power to do more than theorize. He was being taken onto a high mountaintop and being shown the kingdoms of the world.

"Humbleness, Oliver. Above all, humbleness. We need to listen to each other, we need to listen to ourselves, we need to pray." This was unexpected. Matthew had made his spiritual uncertainty quite clear during the first interview. He shifted awkwardly under the director's steady gaze. "Pray to anything you like, Oliver. To the good in yourself, if that's all you believe in."

Professor Billon sat back, his elbows on the arms of his chair, his fingers interlocked under his nose, staring out over them, missing nothing. Behind him the tall sculpture revolved endlessly. The scar on his forehead was unpleasantly clear in the brilliant overhead light. He was considerable. He could talk of humbleness so that Matthew believed him and did not mentally turn away to vomit. He was considerable.

"You needn't stay here at the Colindale, Oliver. After my exposition to senior staff I always give them the chance to leave."

"Do many take it?"

"None. So far. But there's always a first time."

The Colindale project. He could refuse. He could betray it to the C.L.C. He could do what Gryphon had asked him to. He could rouse righteous democrats all over Europe . . . the kingdoms of the world. With Abigail to help him.

"I'd like to stay, sir."

The director nodded briefly, and blew through his nose onto his knuckles. A sign perhaps, or an expression of satisfaction. He got up and walked to his place beside the central window. The sky behind him had closed over again, hot and heavy.

"Now," he said. "Business. Today's crisis. Conference starts in five minutes. You'll pick up most of the form as you go along."

Summer lightning flickered, momentarily bleaching the room's thick shadows. Both men waited for the thunder. When it didn't come they felt cheated.

"We'll be discussing an electromagnetic shield. A technique for deactivating nuclear warheads. Total immunity. We're shaken out of our mere recommendations, Oliver, out of our memoranda to the Appropriations Board. We've got to *do* something."

Matthew shook his head, not fully understanding. It sounded thrillerish and improbable, quite outside his field.

"The bloc that first sets up this shield, Oliver, can

initiate atomic war and win. You realize what that means?"

There was a second flash of lightning, brighter than the first. Neither man noticed it.

"Don't worry," said the director. "Get it sorted out by lunchtime. There are precedents. Thank God." He walked to the door. "Conference time, Oliver. After you."

SIX

THE SOUND OF RAIN on the pool outside their bedroom window was soothing. Abigail curled up in the big bed and was comforted. She felt very alone now that Matthew had gone. The house was not yet his, not yet theirs, not yet solidly inhabited by the two of them. His warmth was still beside her, her shoulder still smelled of sweat from its place close under his arm. Yet he was completely absent: somebody she distantly hoped would reach the computer center without getting wet.

The Colindale should have reminded her of the University. The University buildings had been taller, but similarly thoughtful, expressing the movement of people with a conscious logic of material and mass. The colors had been similarly mannered. The purpose had been similarly to provide an intellectually stimulating environment. Yet for her the two places held nothing in common. The Colindale, adroit, pretty, costly, of noble aspiration, was totally alien. She rolled over in bed and stared at the ceiling. The University had been open, and the Colindale was closed. And in its parts it was closed, one part against the next. In the Colindale even Matthew, when he was away from her, was closed to her.

The first flash of lightning came when her eyes were half shut, and she thought she might have imagined it. The second, brighter, caught her with her face turned toward the window. She sat up in bed, waiting for the thunder. When none came she got out of bed and went to the window. Storms excited her, prickled her skin. The rain had stopped, leaving the air heavily moist and hard to breathe. The garden outside the window seemed tiny, and its four glass walls reflected each other's black surfaces opaquely. It was like looking into a dead aquarium.

She went to the back of the room and stood on a chest to look out of the high strip of window there, seeing an empty expanse of wet grass, the side of the cloisters, and the blank wall of another building. Over to the right were rooftops and motorways, city to the far horizon. She climbed down from the chest and looked for some clothes to put on. She would be sensible, would go out and do some sensible shopping.

It was while she was hunting for a shopping bag in the kitchen cupboards that she found the first of the microphones. It was no thicker than a piece of paper, with hair-thin leads at one corner—just like the illustrations in Matthew's C.L.C. leaflet. Searching carefully, she found four more, two in the sitting room, one in the bathroom, and one in their bedroom. They had not been in position two days earlier, when the house had been unfurnished: somebody must have broken in to fit them, presumably while she and Matthew were at church. She supposed that bugs for the spare rooms and the lavatory would come later.

It was pointless to be angry or disgusted. The hiding places were hardly more than a matter of form. The breach of etiquette was hers for having uncovered them. She sat down and lit a cigarette. People would often break into her home: to approve it, to bug it, to search it, to protect her from herself and Matthew from Matthew. All this would happen, and more, because she was living at the Colindale Institute.

She thought of Gryphon, and his suspicions about the Colindale. She could believe now that his death had been arranged, that there was indeed something needing to be hidden. She would help Matthew to uncover it. She felt closer to Edmund than she had ever been. . . . Suddenly Matthew was unpredictable, his reactions. He claimed to approach every decision from first principles, but he possessed none—nothing but an expedient, humanistic, woolly sort of love. He would understand her hatred of the Colindale, and he might say he shared it.

The telephone rang.

"Mrs. Oliver? Main gate here. We have a man who wants to see you. He's dressed like a priest. Says you know him. Name of Hilliard."

"Father Hilliard? Of course I know him."

"Regulations say you should come down and identify all visitors personally. Then we issue a day pass."

Father Hilliard had been one of the priests attached to the new University of St. Paul. Abigail had known him well: a very old man even then, vague in his movements, but his mind still clear, with a Jesuitical clarity that she found herself temperamentally unable to appreciate. Years of dealing with undergraduates had given him a professional elusiveness, so that—although he basically never gave an inch—he seemed always to be in a state of agreeable retreat, always willing complacently to admit doubts that to her were inadmissible. She had never been able to discover the exact boundaries of his faith. He would smile, and shift his ground, and tie his questioners in knots that for all their obviousness were irritatingly difficult to unravel. He relied on experience alone to evade the inept sincerity of his young opponents. To her his words were thin things, inadequate, irrelevant to matters that could only be dealt with by faith.

Father Hilliard was the only priest she had known whom she could not respect. She had not seen him now for more than five years. She wondered why he had come to see her, and almost wished he hadn't. Paul never mentioned him; it surprised her that he should still be alive.

She saw him while she was still a long way from the gate, sitting with his feet close together, his hands folded in the lap of his old-fashioned soutane, on a chair the guard had placed for him under the awning outside the guard house. He was tiny and frail, far older than the five years since she had last seen him. Such a helpless old man—it angered her that the machinery of distrust should have kept him waiting there like a supplicant. She thought of asking the guards why they hadn't stripped him and probed in his anus for bombs. Except that the scanner would do the job better, and with at least a show of dignity.

She vouched for him. The guard reluctantly called him *Reverend* and let him through.

"It's refreshing, my child, not to be trusted. I've worn this uniform for too long. I'd quite forgotten what non-acceptance felt like."

She caught herself suspecting this of being mannered-ly innocent, and offered him a silent apology. Not that he wouldn't contentedly have agreed with her.

He had arrived on foot from the bus stop, carrying a large black umbrella. She took it from him, it looked so thick and heavy. They walked up slowly under a lowering sky, lit by infrequent flashes of lightning. Father Hilliard said little, saving his breath for the gentle ascent and the occasional short flight of steps. Beside him Abigail felt indecently robust. She identified a few of the buildings for him, and then fell silent. His ascent was single-minded, leaving room for nothing else. She shared his effort.

By the time they reached the house they were both exhausted. She offered him a chair in the unfinished sitting room, and he chose an upright one from which it would be easy to rise. She made him tea as she remembered he liked it, trying not to despise him for all the infantile milk and sugar. If his mind had been infantile too she would never have objected.

"I worry you, my child. I always did. Yet there is more than one way of skinning a cat."

"Of course, Father."

"But you are far calmer than I remember you. I like that. You do not pester me with questions. You let an old man take his time. I like that."

He had that ability of the very old to pay compliments that neither embarrassed nor needed answering. To disclaim his praise would be impolite, an unsuitable criticism. She stood by the window and waited, keeping herself apart. She had hated his cliché about cats.

"You are well, Abigail, and your husband? Your marriage is well, you are happy and strong in your faith?"

These statements, not questions, seemed a necessary grounding, as if he wanted them out of the way as quickly as possible. She allowed him their truth.

"I'm here to speak to you about your brother, my child. You may be able to help me."

"Paul? He's been to see you?"

"We have talked." He drank his tea, holding the cup in both hands, looking up at her over the rim. "Not within the Confessional, you understand. It is possible that he has done this as a way of leaving my hands free—more than that, as a way of demanding that I take some action."

"I saw him a few days ago." She still gave nothing. "He seemed all right then. A little overexcited, but he's like that."

"Seven years younger than you . . . You know him well?"

"Not very. He has his own very close circle."

"I need background, you see. . . . What can you tell me about your parents?"

Her inclination, which she knew was wrong, was to tell him nothing. But Paul had gone to him for advice.

"Father, what did he talk about? If I know that, perhaps I'll be more able to help you."

"About militancy." An upward inflection. "About the Church's definition of a righteous war."

This shocked her. She thought Paul had moved on from that. Instead his thoughts had simply become secret. She went nearer to the priest and sat down.

"I thought Paul had moved on from that."

"Moved on?"

"Nobody wins wars. In societies as closely ordered as ours militancy does no more than provide excuse for further repression."

"That's what you've told him?"

"It's obvious. The only alternative is social disintegration, which we can no longer afford."

Father Hilliard shifted on his chair and stared into the half-empty teacup. If he didn't continue with the argument it would not be because he agreed with her but rather because he had other things to do than differ. Perhaps he thought her reasoning over-sophisticated, even slick. She felt obliged to press the point.

"There are other methods of resistance," she said. "Surely you see that?"

"For you certainly there are."

The sort of open-ended remark that had always annoyed her. She said nothing, fearing in her bone marrow to be rude.

"I fear this isn't going very well," said Father Hilliard. "We'll be safer on the neutral ground of your parents."

She offered him a second cup of tea and brought in some biscuits. The circumstances were like those of her visit to Grandpa, and with as little communication. Yet

Father Hilliard was perfectly capable of understanding, if he would.

"Dad retired a few months ago." She leaned toward him, forearms on her knees. She saw her thin wrists. "I don't really know what he thinks about anything. He was very hard on me as a child, and on Mum. Then, when Paul was born, the usual thing—he spoiled him completely. Mum went along, only too glad of the new atmosphere. It's a long time ago now, Father. I promise you I'm being objective."

The priest nodded tolerantly.

"A resentful man, would you say?"

"He couldn't adjust to the new patterns of work. He'd never learned a trade, so the only virtue work could have was in its length and its arduousness. He found post-industrial attitudes very worrying." She broke off, aware of sounding too much the sociologist. "I don't want you to think he didn't care for me. Only that he could never manage to show it."

"And your mother?"

"A good Catholic wife. Afraid of Dad, very working class, very old-fashioned, very simple."

"Which your father is not, I take it. Or there wouldn't have been two such intelligent children." He mumbled a biscuit, dropping crumbs down his black front. "So your brother's image of a man is of one frustrated, powerful, but never able to realize his potential. Something of a demagogue in the home where it was easy, but impotent elsewhere."

Abigail disliked this sort of slot machine psychiatry. But she had to admit that this particular analysis was good. If she'd ever made it herself she might have understood Paul more readily. She changed the subject.

119

"I've been very worried about his retirement," she said. "But his counselor has got him really fired up. He's busier than he's ever been before."

"And Paul knows this?"

"I suppose he does. He'd be blind not to."

She realized for the first time how much they both resented this, and Paul even more than she. Father Hilliard finished his tea and put the cup down very carefully, as if he were in the habit of breaking things.

"He did well at school, your brother? Pushed on perhaps? Not allowed to choose his own friends?"

"Of course he chose his own friends." She couldn't allow that. "I was the one with the unsuitable friends— or so Dad said. Paul always chose the goodies—he had a sort of instinct as to what would please."

"Meek boys, probably his intellectual inferiors?"

She wanted him to stop. It was unworthy, like fortune-telling after you'd seen the family album and examined the souvenirs in the china cupboard. She filled in by fetching a cigarette for herself and lighting it. Belatedly she offered the priest one, which he took.

"I suppose they might be described like that. Though it doesn't make him seem a very nice person."

"Nice person?" Father Hilliard concentrated on making his cigarette burn. He seemed to be lacking in suction. "Come now, my child, morality is overloaded as it is, without making it a basis for choosing our friends."

She nearly answered as Matthew would have. Matthew made everything a question of morality. The number of times he brushed his teeth in the morning, even that was a success or a failure to meet a self-imposed target. Remembering quirks of Matthew's mind comforted her. The conversation with Father Hilliard had taken her further from him than she had been in years.

"I can imagine circumstances, Father, in which one might choose one's friends immorally. Simply as flatterers, for example."

"Is it really immoral to need flattery? It's all a question of levels, my child. I tend to reserve morality for questions of the eternal soul."

She saw he was almost mocking her, matching her own pomposity. To her relief he began raising himself attentively to his feet. "Thank you so much for our little talk, my child. It has been very helpful. I must go now. The bus journey is long, but most comfortable, I'm glad to say. Such a change from the buses of my youth. And if I could just use your lavatory before I go?"

She showed him where it was, and blanked down on a sudden mental picture of him using it. Not from disgust, but from sadness, wondering if celibacy finally withered a man's body. Afterward she felt tender toward him, and motherly. In a way that he would least suspect he had reminded her of God's glory. She fetched his umbrella for him and walked with him down to the gate, holding his hand.

"You've been very helpful, my child. The more I can understand your brother the more likely I am to say the right things to him next time he comes."

"I'm afraid that won't be for some months, Father. He's just gone to Africa on a project."

"Are you sure, Abigail? He made no mention of it when he saw me yesterday."

"Yesterday? But he was leaving on Saturday, catching the morning plane."

"I don't think I'm that muddled. . . ." He wasn't muddled at all. "Yesterday *was* Sunday? Yes, he came to the Presbytery yesterday afternoon. Perhaps it was to-day he was going. Or next Saturday, even."

"Yes, Father. Perhaps it was."

But she knew it wasn't. She felt afraid for Paul, afraid of his reasons for setting up such an elaborate deception. Going around the family to say careful goodbyes while all the time he intended to stay in London. She could think of no satisfactory reason, and she was afraid for him. . . . Beside her the old priest stumbled a little. She supported him, and they continued down to the gate. She handed him his umbrella.

"Goodbye, my child. God bless you." She tried to listen to him. "And don't worry about your brother. That he came to me is a good sign. With God's help I shall be able to advise him."

She stood for a moment, watching Father Hilliard drift uncertainly away, the wind blowing his robe tight against the backs of his thin legs. He paused, perhaps for breath, and waved his umbrella. She waved in return.

As soon as she got back home she rang the University and asked if they could contact her brother. After a delay, the secretary returned to say he was not available. He had gone to Africa on a merchandising project. She expressed surprise that Abigail, his sister, should not have been told. The secretary thought everybody had been.

The conference room at the computer center was cir-cular, like a tiny Roman amphitheater, with five white, deeply-cushioned steps leading down to a low area in the middle which contained a small Bohn keyboard and printoff console. Dark blue telephones lay around on the cushions, and computer-linked doodle pads. The ceiling was a shallow cone of cedarwood, its point a long way off center. Panels of complex prisms were set in the cedarwood, and the patterns of light from them changed continually. It was a room that, although circular, had no obvious focal center.

Matthew and the director were the first in. Billon walked casually down over the cushions and started explaining the facilities available at the computer desk. Matthew followed him, worried to be walking on what looked like white velvet. But their feet left no trace. Another of Billon's expensive toys, showing a delight in technical ingenuity for its own sake. Curiously eighteenth century.

". . . Knowledge is power, Oliver. For too long we've regretted that fact. We've said that knowledge is unfortunately power. Reflection of our inadequacy. Our lack of control. In this room we control the head of the crocodile. Close its mouth. Science guiding science. Real power."

Matthew remembered the director's protestations of humbleness.

"We know it's dangerous, Oliver. Men of good will. That's the answer. You're one. I've got seventeen others. You'll see. Of course it's dangerous. Isn't the alternative more dangerous?"

A phrase occurred to Matthew, coined back in the sixties, increasingly apt in each successive year. *The runaway world.*

"What about the other powerblocs? This may work for Europe, but what about the—"

"A start. Besides, we must be grateful for the curtains. Behind their curtains the East and the Americas may still be hell-bent. But precious little gets through. With care we'll survive the both of them. Quality of life, Oliver. We don't define it, but we know what it means." Voices were heard approaching. "All right, Oliver? I'll introduce you."

The members of the committee began to arrive. Matthew was bombarded with faces and famous names. It intrigued him that he might be considered as distinguished in his field as they were in theirs. A new thought, but not unpleasant. In the end he could only confidently identify the men he had seen before: Dr. Mozart, Zacharie Mallalieu, and Professor Buhler. And the rugger man, Furneau. They settled themselves, informally, the director among them, Matthew at his side. If there was a floor, it was held by the austere gray cabinet of the Bohn 507.

"Begin by confirming the findings," said the director. "You've had time to check, Buhler?"

"The calculations were simple enough, once I was sure of the direction." Professor Buhler looked tired and worried. "The Bohn checked them for me last night. It's the Littgen paper on molecular polarity, of course. Plus the work being done in Sweden on high-gain generators. Taking into account Parden's revised theory on wave frequency and some of the findings of that man in Switzerland whose name I forget."

"Morgenstern," someone said unnecessarily. Buhler smiled.

"Thank you," he said. "The paper came in a month ago. For myself I would have said it was mostly nonsense. But Furneau let it through, and the Bohn made no fuss, so here we are." He smoothed his beard. "Fission would definitely not take place. Theoretically the shield is feasible."

"Gardner?" said the director.

Gardner turned out to be a woman. Sexual equality at last. Matthew wondered if Gardner thought this a triumph. From her scraped-back hair she might.

"As far as practical considerations are concerned there should be no difficulty at all." She drew a quick diagram on her doodle pad. It appeared as it was made on all the other pads. Matthew was fascinated. "Horizontal beaming in the two kilowatt range would blanket an area of ten square miles. Refractive beaming from ground level would need a bit more." She laid out calculations and Matthew watched the answers come up. "Three point seven-five kilowatts. Roughly." She looked around. "With today's cheap power, what's that to the Defense Department? You could cover all major population centers for around a thousand kilowatts."

"Side effects?" said the director.

"None at all. Unless Evans has any radio problems."

"Not that I can think of." Evans was as Welsh as his name, small and bushy. "It's the frequency, you see. Far too long. And laid too close. Today's transmitters would go straight through it without even noticing."

Dr. Mozart cleared his throat, straightened his spectacles, made sure that everybody was listening.

"As I see it," he said, "there might possibly be some risk of X-ray interference. Clouding of negatives that would result from spillage. This of course would depend on the limits of the beaming. How narrowly could they be defined, Miss Gardner?"

"You underestimate current band limitation techniques." Gardner appeared to have taken this as a personal insult. "Spillage is almost unheard of. Down to point o-o-one, at the most."

"Thank you, Miss Gardner."

Dr. Mozart removed his spectacles and cleaned them unnecessarily, seeming to have made some private point of his own. From the speed with which the director cut in Matthew guessed that the team was not without its internal stresses.

"Then we're agreed. The shield is practicable." He glanced at Furneau. "Counter measures?"

"No trouble there, sir. A suitable mask for the warhead could easily be devised. An anti-shield shield. It would mean modifying all existing missiles, of course. Which would inevitably take a bit of time."

"So," said the director, "the bloc first discovering the shield would immediately make war." He was unself-consciously playing ticktacktoe with himself as he spoke. "All-out war. Us in the middle. Probably attacked from both sides."

"Unless we ourselves perfected it first," said Mallalieu. "We could then be the aggressors. Both ways, simultaneously."

"What the hell would we gain by that?" said a man who hadn't spoken before, his name lost to Matthew in the flood of introductions. Mallalieu shrugged his shoulders. "The possibility exists. Therefore it needs considering."

The director had stopped doodling. Matthew felt him stiffen.

"Advantages?" he said.

Several people began to speak at once. Matthew wondered if it was a game they played, or if it was for real. Billon nodded to the strategist among them, a man called Felsen, recognizable from the dustcovers of his books.

"Europe possesses over-kill," Felsen said, "even against the two opposing blocs at once. Destruction of industrial potential in the East and in the Americas would simplify her position. Less of the G.N.P. would need to be spent on defense. As we have no territorial interests there would be no problem over policing. A massive relief program would need to be mounted, but this would be aimed solely at alleviating immediate distress, and would be of short duration. Our position then established, we could command a permanent lead—especially in the field of scientific control being pioneered here. The outcome could be the greatest happiness of the greatest number." He paused. "As for the economic results of a drastic reduction in world population, I leave that to my friend Mallalieu."

"The results would be excellent." Mallalieu drew a square on his pad, then another inside it and another inside that. "Europe is at the moment largely self-sufficient, but with an inevitably low growth rate. Markets are retracting, and our post-industrial society competes badly with the totalitarian regimes marketing in Africa and India. Although we have largely adjusted to our lack of oil by the provision of cheap electric power, the possibility of favorable import rates for oil would provide room for expansion. There would in general be no difficulty regarding payment for goods supplied to the newly-devastated countries since they have ample resources for settlement in kind. This combination of new markets for consumer goods and new sources of raw material could increase our growth rate tenfold over the first few years. The loss of several hundred million consumers would make little difference."

The squares inside each other had continued, down to a tiny square dot. Such a mind would be comforted by the tidying of people into consumers. Matthew could keep quiet no longer.

"And the moral issue? The effect on conscience? Professor Billon—each one of us has a view of himself, and of the society in which he lives. We survive by believing ourselves to be right. You may not be able to compute a thing like national conscience, but that doesn't mean it doesn't exist."

"Of course it exists."

The director stood up, walked down to the Bohn, and began sorting through a file of storage disks.

"First of all, if the others will forgive me, proof for Dr. Oliver that intangibles like national conscience can be usefully computed. Your predecessor, Henderson, did a lot of work in the field."

He passed up to Matthew a disk with the classification *Indices of Pride, National and Personal. Jan. 87.* Matthew believed it because it was there.

"You see, Oliver, once you have an associative capability you can use it in non-quantitative fields. Anything may be expressed in terms of anything."

He took the disk back and looked around the rest of the group.

"We were talking about national conscience. I think I can say the national conscience at large need not worry us. Malleable. Easily subject to shaping. Drugs, abreaction, the cruder propagandas. I could deal with it in a matter of weeks."

He paused. Matthew stared at him, appalled. Suddenly he was every scientist that Matthew had ever feared: passionless, an offerer of facts, not even boastful. It was in him a cause neither for pride nor for shame that he could deal with the national conscience in a matter of weeks—the fact existed. It was, like Everest, like the storage disk, there.

"But, Professor—"

"I referred to the national conscience at large, Oliver. This is, as I said, shapable, worthless. But there is another national conscience. We in this conference room. Self-appointed. All the more aware. Whether we like it or not, we are the conscience of the European Federation."

It was disturbing. But at least it followed. Everything that the director said did that.

"So?"

"So we have developed a method of discussion here. First the practicalities, then the intangibles: pride, love, hate, work incentives, conscience, aesthetics and so on . . . No point in taxing our higher centers before it's absolutely necessary."

He turned to the other members of the group.

"So here we have it. Matter of conscience. Conscience personal to each one of us. Ends that might be beneficial to humanity. Means that could not possibly be. Anybody in favor?"

His tone made it clear that he considered the question to be no more than a formality. Nobody said a word—not even Zacharie Mallalieu. It was not that before they had knowingly been playing an intellectual game, and now they had stopped playing. It was more that they found it necessary to keep morality as a separate issue. And it was only morality that could turn the head of the crocodile.

"Nobody in favor. Possibility ruled out."

Obviously the meeting was being recorded. Professor Billon glanced across at a man who had not yet contributed.

"Political solution, Blake?"

"Either we all have the dratted shield or none of us does. May we take it that the thing couldn't be kept quiet forever, Furneau?"

"Independent discovery is inevitable, sir. I happen to know that Littgen's work is already duplicated in the Argentine."

"Then we all have it, and the sooner the better." Blake was tall and lean and brisk, the image of a successful negotiator. "International control treaties would be piffle. So the answer is simple. We all have it, we all use it, and we all develop anti-shield shields for our missiles." He shrugged his shoulders. "Political solutions tend to be crude. I'm sorry."

A disapproving fidget ran around the group, like a wind ruffling the feathers of roosting birds.

"A lamentable drain on the Defense Appropriation," said Mallalieu. "But I suppose it can't be helped."

"Come along now, Zack"—this was Dr. Mozart, the first time he had spoken in far too long—"we all know Defense is the great adjuster. Haven't you been worried by the imbalance in the Danish economy caused by that improved bacon yield we got a couple of months ago? Surely all these shields are just what's need to mop that up?"

Mallalieu shook his head angrily, the white hair flopping like a sparse mop.

"It's easy to see you're no economist, Mozart. I should have thought it was perfectly clear that—"

"Then we're all agreed." The director cut in firmly. "Blake's solution must be adopted. I'll get the machinery in operation at once. Same procedure as before?" Nobody argued. "Right. Then we'll have a ten minute break."

He sat back and closed his eyes. The committee members broke up into groups and began talking about other things, the rest of the morning's work ahead of them. The problem of the nuclear shield, now settled, had no further interest to them. Phone calls were made, and Professor Furneau went for some coffee.

"Is it really as easy as that?" said Matthew, under the general conversation.

Billon shifted, but didn't open his eyes. "I told you not to worry, Oliver. There's an established procedure. We've done it before. New nerve gas and its counter, for example. Two years ago. We organize a handout in Geneva. Fullest possible details to everybody. Then we develop it neck and neck and nobody either wins or loses. Childish, but there you are. Excuse me." He reached for a telephone. "Need a systems analyst. The Bohn will even do the handout, given the right program."

Matthew stared at the people around him. Gryphon's question was answered—with an answer so big that it made the question unimportant. All the secrecy, all the unpleasant superstructure of the Colindale now made sense. With Gryphon dead and Sir William uncooperative, Matthew now had no immediate way of contacting the C.L.C. He would do nothing to find one.

A technician in a gray overall came in down the white velvet steps. He was the systems analyst Professor Billon had rung for, Andrew Scarfe with a neat folder under one arm. Billon got wearily to his feet and went to join him at the computer console. Scarfe recognized Matthew and waved. Matthew waved back. He was thinking of Abigail, and he was—in a sudden moment of clear-sightedness—fearful.

SEVEN

ABIGAIL FACED HIM across the kitchen. Behind her the machine was beating eggs for omelets.

"I think it's insane. And you accused Gryphon of paranoia."

"I know all that, love. But isn't the alternative worse?"

"The alternative is education. We're all being taught a new awareness. We can all choose, we can all accept or reject. Science can only do what people let it do. We've rejected nuclear war, haven't we?"

"Of course we haven't. It looks over our shoulders day and night."

"But it doesn't happen because we don't let it. We've been given free will—we are responsible for ourselves. It may not be comfortable, but it's how we are. The future is between God and each one of us: not something to be shunted off onto a bunch of faceless, soulless experts of whose existence we haven't even been told."

She saw his incomprehension, and it frightened her. They had been arguing now for ten minutes; the eggs would be like plastic foam.

"But that's how it has to be, Abigail. People's vision is limited. They go for the short-term gain, the immediate benefit. That's the big thing wrong with democracy. And they can't be told about the Colindale for the simple reason that they're so bloody stupid they'd immediately blow it up. Or something."

"We are responsible for ourselves, Matthew. All we can do is trust in God."

She watched his bitter reply remain unsaid, and for the wrong reasons: out of respect for her, out of an intellectual understanding of her position, out of a wish not to hurt. She couldn't reach him. She couldn't make him see the sin in relieving people of the basic human agony of self-determination. Before his return her mind had been full of Paul, wanting Matthew's advice. What should she do, knowing that he had lied? What had he really wanted the money for? What was he doing? The questions had gone around and around. Now they were unimportant.

"Abigail, it seems to me that you see God like a father handing his child a box of matches. He tells the child that the matches are dangerous, but he goes on handing them, box after box. . . . I have a feeling that God might be very pleased if some of the matches were taken away."

She wouldn't listen to him. She wouldn't hear him betraying his intellect, damaging her respect for him, ultimately—through hurt—her love. She turned away and switched off the egg beater. She had never felt less hungry in her life.

"We've always had leaders, Abigail. People who make decisions for us. What's the Pope if he isn't the ultimate responsibility shift?"

She heated a pan, didn't answer.

"You'll say the Pope is guided by God. Why can't we in that conference room be guided by God? On earth peace to men who are God's friends?"

God's friends—who inhabited a devil's trap of secrecy and intrigue. Who murdered each other. Who lied, and carried guns, and sought through all this for an earthly salvation. . . . But the argument wasn't only in her mind. She was thinking now with her whole body, with her whole life. For her it wasn't a matter of reason, it was a matter of knowledge. Everybody must make their own world, the world they lived in. Everybody.

"Listen to me, Abigail . . ."

"I won't listen. You only argue so hard because you know you're wrong."

"Of all the—" She turned and stared at him, seeing a man she had known and ignored. "Of all the easy ways out, that is the bloody easiest."

She cooked omelets and he ate them. Nothing ever put him off looking after his body. She watched him snouting for several minutes.

"I ought to have told you," she said. "They've bugged the house."

"That's nice. That's lovely." Shoveling food. "Now the whole place knows how you feel about the project."

"Don't you mind being spied on? Doesn't the whole outfit make you want to be sick?"

"Of course I mind. It's just that I can see their point

of view. With a project as important as this they obviously can't afford to take any—"

"Eat your food, Matthew. Just eat your food."

He was a stranger. She stood by the sink and waited till it was time for him to go back to the computer center.

"Well?" he said. "What are you going to do about it?"

He spoke loudly and clearly for the benefit of the microphones. She could have stuck kitchen knives in him. She could have taken his hands and ground them in the waste disposal unit.

"I don't know what I'm going to do about it."

"That's a change. I thought you always knew."

"Please, Matthew . . ." Suddenly all her hatred had ebbed away.

"I'm sorry. That was cheap. . . . It's just that I see here the most hopeful thing that has happened in six hundred years of science, and you—you see it as the devil going forth like a raging lion. Yet we both start from the same point."

"I wonder if we do."

"Abigail, think of the men who worked on antibiotics. They looked no further than the immediate problem. You might say they were directly responsible for the misery and starvation that followed. If the Colindale had been in charge then, work on population control could have been started at the same time."

"If the Colindale had been in charge," she said bleakly, "wouldn't it have seemed easier simply to suppress the antibiotics? Avoid creating a problem for which at the time there was no solution? Don't you think so?"

Matthew's eyes flickered. She watched him trying to evade. She knew she was wasting her time.

"That's where basic good will comes in," he said. "Obviously Billon has chosen his men carefully."

Abigail fetched his briefcase from the chair by the door.

"You'll have to hurry or you'll be late."

"You haven't told me what you're going to do." Thinking of the microphones?

"Nothing for the moment. I promise."

He went away down the cloisters, paused at the corner to look back. At that distance he was familiar, all of him precious. She ran after him and hugged him, held on to the size of him. What he had told her was so monstrous, so insane that it shifted life off onto a completely different level, a level where neither of them belonged. They were too close to each other; she couldn't have lost him to such a system of ideas. She wanted instead to talk to him about Paul, but that would have made him late for the afternoon's conference, spoiled the punctuality that meant so much. He was edging away even as she hugged him.

When he was finally out of sight she walked back a few paces toward the house, then leaned on a pillar and tried to think what she should do. Do about Paul. The other thing she had put away as unreal, nothing to do with her and Matthew, basically irrelevant. She trusted that the truth of what she believed would come to him in its own good time. But Paul's trouble was immediate.

She was afraid. Father Hilliard interpreted her brother's avoidance of the Confessional as an appeal for practical help. Abigail saw another possibility: actions that Paul was not yet ready to confess. He had lied, he had obtained a large sum of money from her, and he had gone into hiding. And he had asked the priest for a justification of violence. . . . She stared out across the grass at a distant line of trees, pylons and point blocks behind them. The conclusion was obvious. Paul had joined some subversive organization and had contributed her fifteen thousand marks to its funds.

She turned back to the house. If Paul was in hiding she was sure she knew where. There was a vast underground carpark near the University, left over from the time when the buildings had been offices and unlimited cars had been let into Central London. He had often explored there during his first year, fascinated by the total emptiness and silence and lightless desolation. He had described to her corners where for seven years the dust had lain undisturbed by so much as a breath, where there were fungi like trees and shallow lakes of reeking water that stretched beyond the beam of his strongest lamp. The place delighted him almost to the point of perversity. And it was an ideal hiding place. For him, or for a small army.

She found Matthew's flashlight in one of the still unpacked crates. She would go and see her brother at once, and talk to him. At once, before the idea lost urgency or was even thought better of. She must first think of a way of ditching Mrs. Foster. She smoked two cigarettes while working out a plan. In the end the simplest seemed the best.

She changed into her most uncharacteristic dress, a pink affair given to her by her mother, and covered it with her rain coat. She chose a hat into which she would be able to stuff her hair. Mrs. Foster's number was on the pad by the telephone.

"Mrs. Foster? I'm just going in to the University library. St. Paul's University. I'll be ready in about half an hour. Meet you at the gate."

She then drove quickly down to the guard house and parked close outside. She waited with every sign of impatience for ten minutes. After that she went in.

"I really can't wait any longer," she said, in a charming state of agitation. "I phoned up my tail simply ages ago, told her exactly where I was going, and when. Look, be a dear and tell her I've gone on."

The guard looked doubtful.

"It's Mrs. Foster. She can't possibly be much longer. She knows where I'm going, to the University library. She'll find me there easily enough. I think it closes at four, so I'm sure she'll understand."

The library stayed open until at least five thirty. Abigail had hoped she would find the deception a challenge, fun even. She didn't. It was dreary, squalid, and too easy. The guard let her through; he really had no alternative. It wasn't his job to hold up department chiefs or their wives. If the surveillance staff was slack, that was their affair. But he made a note of Mrs. Oliver's white raincoat, to show he was aware of his responsibilities.

Abigail wasn't a good fast driver, but she made it somehow to the University. Parking in a prominent position, she ran in to the library and chose a book at random from the shelves. She checked it out and left the University buildings. There was still no sign of Mrs. Foster. Paul had told her about the sealed entrances to the carpark—there was one in a side street that had a loose section of shuttering, perhaps used by students needing privacy, and small boys.

The entrance was at the bottom of a ramp between Victorian terraced houses off Cannon Street. Once their ground floors had been rented by importers of jute and by wholesale button agents. Now they were shops, serving the University with microfilm and magnetic tape, anti-bug devices, clothes, TV repairs, gimmicky sports equipment like power-boosted roller skates. Abigail was able to mingle with the shoppers and slip unnoticed down the ramp to the carpark entrance. The shuttering could easily be prised away to make a three-foot gap. It sprang back into place behind her.

At first she thought the place was totally dark. Then she began to see dim patterns of slatted light from ventilators overhead, and cracks around the shuttering at other entrances. When she switched on her flashlight they vanished, adjusted out by her eyes in the new brilliance. A square repetition of beams and pillars, gray undressed concrete, continued as far as she could see. She had expected movement from rats, but there was none: the place was too dead, too inorganic for them to bother to come. There were black rubber tire marks on the plastic floor. She looked for footprints, needing a direction, but the area around the entrance was too scuffed.

Once she had left the entrance it would be difficult to find it again. So she wedged the shuttering open a few inches with a piece of wood, making a broad crack of light, easily identifiable. Then she walked away down a corridor of pillars, quietly, shining her light onto the ground a few feet in front. She wanted to know as little of the place as possible. She found that the corridor of pillars was not straight, but curved away to the left so that one side of it made a wall to conceal the entrance from her. She called her brother's name, but softly, afraid to rouse echoes from surfaces she could not see. It was useless for her to look for Paul. If she moved, and showed a light, and occasionally called his name, he would find her. Providing he wanted to.

She began to hear water dripping. The morning's rain had stopped long ago, but here it would seep on down for hours. She came on a black skin of water and paused, watching it spread, its tiny lip bulging infinitesimally, held back on grains of dust and burnt rubber. She skirted the water, shone her torch on its surface to convince herself it really was the centimeter deep she knew it was. The reflection told her nothing. She walked on.

The sound of the water faded. Darkness pressed against her face and her clothes. The carpark was more than a mile square—it was idiocy to offer herself to be found in such a place. Besides, if Paul knew of it, who else did? If others, would they stand motionless behind pillars and let her pass? Instantly the dark became peopled. She reasoned that they would not want to be discovered, that they would not harm her if she did not see them. She kept the beam of light close, and her head low.

The air was stale and heavy, and sour with smells of cement dust, of dead damp, of long-departed motor cars. She had left the ventilator shafts behind her, and the darkness around was infinite. She didn't know how long she had been underground. She never wore a watch: usually the exact time was of no interest to her. But she realized that the longer she was away the harder it would be to fool Mrs. Foster on her return. Suddenly at the very edge of the light from the torch she saw a movement away to the left, the definite movement of a pale hand and a face above it. She had planned what she should do when this happened. She switched off her light and ran to the last pillar she had seen ahead.

"Who's there?" Her back to the pillar, darkness bearing in on her. "Paul? Is it you?"

"You're a brave woman, Abby." After a torturing pause. "It might just as well not have been."

"I'm here, Paul."

She switched on her torch and shone it in his direction. He was dressed in black, clothes she had never seen before, with some sort of gun by his right hip.

"Paul—are you on your own?"

"There's a group of which I'm a member. You wouldn't approve."

"I meant, are you on your own down here?"

She couldn't bear to think of it, being alone for even an hour in that dark place.

"Point the light down, Abby. I can't see a thing." She did so, and he came nearer. "I like it here," he said. "It appeals to me."

"I asked if you were on your own."

"And I didn't answer you."

She listened for the movement of others, would have been glad to hear it, to have had people to fear rather than emptiness. Nothing moved. She fastened instead on the reality of Paul's shoes in the trembling disk of light. They were dusty, the laces knotted. She didn't want to know about his plans, about the other people in his group, about what her money was to be used for. She simply wanted to get him out.

"We mustn't quarrel, Paul. I came here to help you."

"I thought Hilliard would have the sense to keep his mouth shut."

"You should have known he wouldn't. You're lucky he came to me. He might have gone to someone much more awkward. Your tutor, for instance."

"But he didn't. He came to you, and you remembered this place, and put two and two together, and here you are, saying you want to help. If you really want to help—"

"Please, Paul. Don't stay here. Not in this terrible place. Come with me, and—"

"If you really want to help, Abby, just go away and forget you ever saw me. Would you? For your own sake as well as mine? Please?"

She turned her torch up onto his face. He closed his eyes but didn't try to move away. The light told her nothing, produced a disembodied mask hardly recognizable.

"You were going to Africa, Paul. It's still not too late—"

"For your own sake, sis, just shut up and go away. I mean that."

She switched off her torch, disliking the melodrama it made of his face. Their voices came back at them at odd angles from the flat sides of the pillars. The place was cold. She closed her eyes, and in the darkness it made no difference. To like being here Paul must be a little mad, she thought.

"I suppose you think all this is exciting and romantic. An exciting plan to set the world to rights."

"One has to begin somewhere."

"You're behaving like a ridiculous little fanatic. I thought you'd grown up."

"Grown up?" He moved away from her, raising his

voice. She had the distasteful impression that he was talking to others than just herself. "Grown up? Perhaps I have. Perhaps it's you who's stuck. It's not enough simply to be well-meaning. There's something beyond the dot— you can go through and come out on the other side."

"Paul, listen to me—"

"Everything, sis—art, politics, religion, philosophy, everything reduced to a tiny, self-regarding dot. Push a little harder and you come out on the other side."

"Into anarchy?"

"You have a labeling mind. Tidies everything up. You call it being grown up."

"Into what, then?"

She heard him come close, felt him in front of her, the pressure of the air he displaced. She thought he might be going to strike her.

"Into anarchy, if that's the only word you have. Into people. Into death and hatred and disease and suffering and injustice and a thousand things we thought we wanted to be without." She tried to concentrate on the hysteria rather than the words. "Sweat, Abigail. That old fool's blood and sweat and tears. If he'd added joy to the list he'd have had the whole of life. Except that he wasn't a fool—he knew the respectable Christian mind. Blood and sweat and tears are respectable— joy isn't."

She would have preferred him to strike her. The words he used were closer, more painful. She shifted her ground.

"You asked Father Hilliard for the definition of a righteous war," she said quietly. "I don't believe there is one."

"It's your way of life, Abby. I can't talk to you. With

your reasonable husband and your half-starved soul, I can't tell you anything."

She let his theatricality pass.

"Please, Paul. Come with me."

"No."

She recognized finality. There was nothing more to be said.

"I'll come again. Tomorrow, perhaps."

"For God's sake don't. It only makes things difficult. You know where I am now, and you know I'm all right. So there's no point." He lowered his voice. "And I'm sorry I cheated you over the money."

She reached for his hand in the darkness, touched it, and felt it drawn away.

"And you can trust me to go away and not say anything?"

"You're my sister."

"But—"

"And you're more than half with me."

She denied it.

"I want things to be changed, Paul. But I—"

"You won't betray me, Abby. Come on, now. I'll show you the way back to the entrance."

He switched on his own flashlight and took her arm. He led her firmly, counting pillars half-aloud as he went. She kept quiet so as not to interrupt him. At the thirty-third pillar he turned right, and from then on he didn't need to count, merely followed the curved line of pillars till they reached the entrance. Still she didn't speak. He paused close to the shuttering, with his hand still tight on her arm.

"Now, sis, there's no need to worry. Nothing's going

to happen for some days yet. And anyway, you'll be safe enough when it does."

"You're telling me this plot you're involved in has something to do with the Colindale?"

"I'm telling you nothing."

"Stop playing at cops and robbers, Paul. If your group's planning to sabotage the Colindale I can tell you it's quite hopeless. You'll never get through the—"

"Be quiet, Abby. Just be quiet." He gripped her arm till it hurt. She could see him listening. All that she could hear behind the silence were the distant sounds of the street. "It's all right. I think they trust me. Just as I trust you. All I can tell you is that you mustn't worry—you'll have plenty of warning. Now you must go." He began easing back the shuttering for her and peered out. "It's clear. Go along now. And be careful . . ." He helped her through. "And Abby . . . lie for me. If you have to. As you find out about the Colindale you'll see that ours is a good cause."

He closed the shuttering behind her. The gray daylight hurt her eyes. Her hands were still patterned from the pillar she had leaned against. She walked up the deserted ramp, finding it hard to believe in the crowded darkness behind her, hard to believe that she had spoken to Paul, hard to believe in what he had told her. The opposing pressures of him and Matthew were more than she could bear. They demanded decisions from someone who had happily given up decision-making in favor of her husband, and who even before marriage had been content to let things happen. Prayer and right thinking had always been enough—the rest had been seen to by God.

She took refuge in the immediate, in coping with

Mrs. Foster. To this end she removed her white coat and hung it over her arm, disclosing the surprising pink dress. She made sure that the library book was still in the coat pocket, just in case Mrs. Foster asked.

The foyer outside the University library was as crowded as always. Abigail had to stand around for some minutes before Mrs. Foster found her.

"Where have you been?" Abigail got it in first. "I chose my book ages ago. When there wasn't any sign of you I went up to the canteen for coffee."

"I looked in the canteen," said Mrs. Foster coldly.

"Well, I was there . . . such a crowd. Perhaps you missed me on account of this awful dress. And the hat. I *knew* they were a mistake the moment I put them on."

Certainly Abigail bore no resemblance to the slightly mouse-like person, always hatless, with long dark hair, that Mrs. Foster must have been familiar with. Abigail chatted on cheerfully. Even if the woman was unconvinced, there was still nothing she could do about it. Finally they returned to their cars and drove back to the Colindale in very close convoy.

When she got home, Abigail was pleased to find Matthew still not back. She needed time to think. Suddenly hungry, she hydrated a small beef casserole for herself. Necessary decisions crowded in on her. She wanted the Colindale project put an end to quite as much as Paul did, but she could not see that violence was the way. Publicity would in the end be far more effective. If she could get details of the project to some member of the C.L.C. committee, she could make the plans of Paul's organization quite unnecessary. Public opinion, as Matthew had admitted, would close the

Colindale in a matter of days. The snag was that she didn't know how long she had before the sabotage plan was put into operation.

Then there was Matthew to think of. She poked in the casserole, looking for fat. If Matthew still supported the Colindale project—and she had to admit that this was very probable—then she couldn't tell him anything about Paul: once he knew he would feel obliged to pass the information on to the authorities. For the first time in their marriage she would be forced to tell him less than the truth. It was necessary to contact the C.L.C. without his knowledge, and as soon as possible.

How she was to do this she had no idea. She ate her stew at the kitchen table, staring unhappily out into the garden. She chose not to consider the implications of going against Matthew in a matter as central as this. The sooner the lid blew off the project and he was out of a job, the better.

For Matthew the afternoon was spent in the conference room, going over Bohn extrapolations. Most of these were unexciting, a cheaper substitute for neon, a growth accelerator for conifers, two new applications for laser analysis techniques. But Matthew did have occasion to join with the philosophy group head, Schatten, in opposing a chromosome shift likely to make fetal sex a matter of paternal choice. Its implications were considered too far-reaching for an immediate decision and the paper was put on one side pending a Bohn study of the relevant distribution statistics.

Matthew walked home from the computer center very slowly, dreading any more discussion with Abigail. Around him people were hurrying, turning off into courtyards, running up the short flights of steps between lawns that led to the different residential areas. Zacharie Mallalieu passed him going in the same direction, grunted something supposed to be friendly. Most of the department heads lived around the same large quad-rangle; Matthew supposed a social life must exist among them, a coming and going for bridge or cocktails or talking endless shop. He and Abigail would have to decide whether or not they wanted to compete.

Abigail . . . he couldn't see how the present situation between them was to be ended. For once their basic differences in matters of faith seemed insurmountable. There was no middle ground on which they could meet. Perhaps it was true after all that any structured re-ligion—no matter what—acted as a strong reactionary force, holding back moral and physical progress. This was something he would very much rather not be-lieve.

Therefore he was relieved, when he arrived home, to find a pot of tea waiting for him, and Abigail cheerfully upacking the last two crates of belongings from the old house. If there was constraint between them, it was far less than he had expected. She told him she had been visited that morning by Father Hilliard from the Uni-versity. The priest was worried about Paul.

"He would be." Matthew stirred his tea. "Nobody seems to take the demands of our society into considera-tion. His tutor, the principal, you, and now this Father Hilliard—none of you seems to have heard of normal adolescent rebellion." He was glad of something external to talk about.

"But he's twenty-three, Matthew. Hardly adolescent."

"So he's a bit late getting things sorted out. You must

admit society hardly encourages people to grow up nowadays. Anyway, this trip to Africa's just what he needs. Work him hard and keep him out of mischief."

Her face went blank on him, and she didn't reply. Not that he blamed her; his comment had been off the peg, not even dusted down. He drank his tea meekly, aware of the danger of being forty.

"Matthew, I've got to talk to you about these microphones. Is there really nothing we can do about them?"

"I don't see what." She would want him to be more indignant. "Friend Billon will say they're just something more for our protection. We'll get used to them."

"But there's one in the bedroom. They can even listen to us making love."

She seemed to be whipping something up, keeping it going. In a way he was grateful to her.

"I doubt if they'll be bothered."

"I wouldn't be too sure. Who knows what secrets we mightn't whisper to each other in our post-coital stupor."

"It's no use being bitter, Abigail. If I work at the Colindale I have to accept the limitations it places on me."

"Exactly."

He'd walked straight into that one.

"I have to do what I believe is right, Abigail."

"I don't."

He didn't care that the microphone listened. There were many other things more important. Besides, each one couldn't be monitored every hour of the day.

"That's true, Abigail. Both of us, we can only do what we believe is right."

"You'll work here then, whatever I do?"

"Abigail . . ." The situation was unbearable. He reached

across the table to take her hands, and she let him. Because they were inert, hardly hers. He squeezed them, trying in vain for some response. "I have to do what I believe is right," he said again.

There was a long silence. The kitchen, the rough bark of the fir tree outside the window, the chair he was sitting on, everything seemed unreal. Even her face. Was there really anything in the world more important to him than her?

"I have to, Abigail." Even as his heart rebelled. "I have to."

"Yes."

Utter helplessness in her one word. This was the confrontation he had dreaded, the confrontation that in honesty could not be avoided. She moved around the table to him, and he felt her go through the motions of putting her arm around his shoulders, her cheek against the side of his head. He was faintly nauseated, but it would have been cruel to draw away.

"We'll sort something out," he said.

"No." She ruffled his hair. "But nothing goes on forever."

He wanted to ask her again what she intended to do, but he had not the courage. So he hid behind trust that he did not altogether feel.

Without the matters largest in their minds to talk about, they talked trivia with false ease. She told him she had been in to the University library, and then seemed disinclined to show him the books she had brought back. He guessed they would be theological works relevant to her side of the present situation. He countered with the news that Professor Billon had asked them both to dinner some time, to meet his wife. The mouse wife would break his heart, Matthew said. Nonsense, said Abigail, she might be a positive virago. A lot of dominating men became doormats when they entered their own homes. Time was passed imagining the home life of Chester Billon.

A brief spark was struck when they started talking about Abigail's grandfather, but it quickly failed.

"There's a case in point," Matthew said. "Wouldn't it be better if the operation that's kept him alive had never been invented?"

"Why not kill off everybody over eighty and be done with it?" said Abigail.

So it was pleasant to have the doorbell ring shortly after dinner. Matthew answered it, and showed in the young systems analyst, Andrew Scarfe. He brought the promised, unwanted Astran Primer. They welcomed him, and gave him coffee.

"It's very good of you," he said. "You may not realize it yet, but free evenings in the Colindale are few and far between."

"Shift work?" said Abigail. "I thought that was only for Data Reception."

"Not shift work, Mrs. Oliver. I wish it were. No, it's the chief's special project, unpaid overtime. When he gets Dr. Oliver going on that you'll hardly see him from one week's end to—"

"Special project?" said Matthew.

"Well, obviously you'll be taking over where Henderson left off. Since his death we've been marking time, more or less. So the sooner you can pick up the threads . . ."

He tailed off, seeing Matthew's puzzled expression and misinterpreting it.

"Bugged?" he said, in an efficient whisper.

Matthew nodded, still not understanding.

"I'm sorry. I should have thought." And he started talking loudly about the tennis club.

The director's special project, so special that not even the camp guards should know about it. Boxes within boxes within boxes. Matthew's first reaction was to be pleasantly intrigued. Then he looked uneasily across at his wife. Whatever the project was, on present form she would be unlikely to approve. Scarfe was still babbling, trying to cover his indiscretion. The principles underlying everything at the Colindale were so rational, so alien to Abigail's nature. He would prefer to avoid anything that might damage their relationship still further.

"By the way, Mrs. Oliver, did you know I was up at University with your brother?" Scarfe shifted his thick shoulders to get more comfortable. "I got to know him quite well. I was in my third year when he was in his first, of course, but we met at the Union. He's an interesting debater."

"I'm glad to hear it. We've gone our separate ways. He's seven years younger than me, you see."

Her coldness surprised Matthew. Normally she would have been delighted to talk about Paul with somebody who knew him. There had been a similar freeze earlier in the evening. Yet a subject as uncontroversial as her brother would tide them excellently over the rest of Scarfe's visit. He decided to try to help the young man along.

"Paul's in Africa now," he said. "Did you know that?"

"I had heard something. There's a team gone out to study merchandising. Isn't that it?"

And they were off. Social anthropology, one of Matthew's favorite subjects. And Scarfe was agreeably willing to learn. But even as he talked Matthew was aware of Abigail's reserve, and of the occasional efforts she herself made to break through it. Twice he lost the thread of his argument, watching her and wondering what was wrong. At the second blank he gave up.

"I'm sorry, Scarfe. I must be getting tired. It's been a long day."

"And your first in this sweat shop. I should have thought. I'll be on my way." The young man stood up. Seated, you forgot how short he was. "Very good of you to put up with me as long as this, Mrs. Oliver. It's been very interesting."

Abigail smiled and shook hands. She was charming, and invited Scarfe to call again. Matthew recognized the effort it was costing, the set to her jaw that made her almost ugly. At the front door Scarfe drew him out into the quadrangle and lowered his voice. The long summer evening was over, and—incredibly—from somewhere on the Colindale Matthew could hear a nightingale. He could have done without Scarfe's muttering.

"I really am sorry I didn't think before blabbing about the special project. I've been here long enough to know better."

He was protesting over-much. Matthew felt annoyed.

"As a matter of fact, I haven't been told anything about it. Not yet. So perhaps you were a bit premature."

"You haven't? That makes it worse than ever. I suppose the chief just hasn't had time to get around to it yet."

Probably true: the day had been very full. But Matthew, with a jangled evening behind him, was pettish. Besides, he didn't like Scarfe, and he was obviously going to be working with him on the special project, whatever it was.

"It doesn't matter," he said. "I've got used to people dropping me hints about my work and then shying away. Perhaps it's intended to make the whole thing more mysterious and interesting."

"I say, I do hope you don't think I did it on purpose." Still not able to leave it. "I mean, why should I?"

"Don't worry. As you said, I'm sure to be told just as soon as the director has time to get around to it."

Cowardly, taking out on Scarfe his general anger against Life . . . Matthew watched him walk away, merging quickly into the gray dusk. The nightingale had stopped singing, and might have been imagined. It had been a gray day, and mist was rising. There was something about the young man that was false. His public school vocabulary, perhaps. That sort of aspiration irritated Matthew very much. He turned and went back into the house.

"What was all that about?" he said to Abigail. "Why the sudden freeze-up?"

"Do you like that young man?" She was clearing away the coffee cups.

"Why not?" He attacked to avoid being attacked. "He's friendly, intelligent, not in the least conceited. I expect he hoped his knowing Paul might give him a link with us."

She shrugged her shoulders, and carried the tray away into the kitchen. It was unfair of him to argue with her rather than with himself. He helped her stack the day's dirty crockery in the machine.

In bed that night they made love because not to do

so would have been worse, would have been an admission. They made it quietly, neither having the need to do otherwise. And they pretended to each other that it made things right between them. She lay in her place at his side, his arm around her, her head in the hollow of his neck, and quickly slept. Matthew was wakeful. He regretted the cold dampness against his thigh. He couldn't retreat into sleep as she could. He asked himself again if anything was more important to him than she was. This mess couldn't last. They were dramatizing. In a day or a week or a month they'd come to their senses. He prayed vaguely, knowing neither for what exactly nor to whom. In the Colindale dark a sense of proportion was difficult.

EIGHT

TUESDAY MORNING the sky had cleared, and with it all Abigail's worries. About Matthew, about Paul, about the ominous special project. Nothing stayed complicated in her mind for long: she had the sort of faith that accepted right solutions as inevitable. Thus she saw in Matthew's quietness over tea and bed and then at breakfast proof that her prayers were being answered. He was being helped to do what was right. It might not be easy for him, his niggardly reason might fight all the way, but the outcome was a foregone conclusion. There was no need at all for her to contact the C.L.C.—Matthew would do so himself, if not that same evening then at least within the next day or so. Then none of it, least of all the special project, would matter.

The oath she and Matthew had taken did not worry her; she could dismiss it as merely a civil affair. Ultimately one was responsible only to one's own conscience.

Not even the discovery that her absence at the University the previous afternoon had been used to place microphones in the spare bedrooms and the lavatory— even the lavatory—could depress her. Soon they'd be out of the place for good. Even if they left under escort, on their way to jail—a possibility she didn't really credit, public opinion would be so strongly on their side—even that would be preferable to staying. There would be nobility in suffering jail for such a cause. She thought.

She collected Mrs. Foster and went shopping in the complex nearest to the Colindale. The manager was used to Institute executives, and arranged card facilities at once, without reference to the central finance information bureau. Abigail wandered around the shops, buying food and a few clothes. Nothing for the new house —they wouldn't be staying there long enough. She asked Mrs. Foster's advice over a new shirt for Matthew. If they had to go about everywhere together there was no point in being polite enemies. The shops were cool and gently lit, and smelled carefully enticing. She realized that she didn't mind the many tell cameras set up between the counters: surveillance was part of the normal shopping background. It only took time, and one could get used to anything.

When she had chosen everything she could possibly think of—the rich had a social duty to spend their money—she went up to the manager's office again to arrange delivery. The complex ran special packing facilities for easy inspection at the Colindale gate. Mrs. Foster stayed downstairs choosing herself some stockings.

"Some time this afternoon, Mrs. Oliver?" The man was a new generation manager, an individualist liking a rigid framework, running the complex on extended franchise. "No sooner, I'm afraid. One of the vans is in for a battery overhaul, and I—"

"There's really no hurry. Any time before six or so. I don't start thinking about the evening meal till then."

"Dr. Oliver works late, I expect."

"Not very. Only by leisure society standards."

She realized that the man had given Matthew his doctorate. An intelligent guess.

"You know my husband?"

"I've been told about him."

The reply was carefully significant. She waited while the manager stamped her dockets and returned them to her. She was still bemused from the adroit techniques of the shops below. And now the bright, restless colors of his office.

"I've been instructed, Mrs. Oliver, to say that when your husband is ready to make contact I am in a position to help him."

"Contact?" She was genuinely slow to catch up. Once a difficulty was solved she no longer thought about it.

"With the Committee, Mrs. Oliver." He mistook the

slowness of her reaction. "No need to worry—I've a jammer going just in case. We retail them here, so there's no problem."

He knew of Matthew's attempt to get in touch with the C.L.C. She wondered how.

"I see. . . . I didn't think the C.L.C. knew anything about it. Or were you in touch with Dr. Gryphon personally?"

"Gryphon?" The man's face was expressive, showed genuine incomprehension. "Wasn't he the University lecturer murdered a few days ago? No, I didn't know him."

"I'm just surprised that anybody knew we might want to . . . to get in touch."

"News travels, Mrs. Oliver." He stood up and smiled, selling her his own integrity. "Now you'd better get back to your Mrs. Foster before she starts getting edgy." He accompanied her to the door. "Just remember, I can put your husband in touch within a matter of hours. . . . And thank you for your custom, Mrs. Oliver. If there's ever anything you want, please don't hesitate to ask."

Abigail went downstairs slowly, gathering her thoughts. She wondered who, except Edmund, had known that Matthew might want to contact the C.L.C. From what Matthew had said, Edmund had been playing a personal hunch, working very much on his own. So who else could know? Nobody. Unless of course one considered—assuming that he had been astute enough to see the real reason for Matthew's visit—Sir William Beeston. Not that considering him made any sense. But whatever else Sir William was, he was certainly astute enough for three . . .

". . . I rather fancy these gray ones with the copper

thread, Mrs. Oliver. But maybe a bit too young. . . . What do you think, Mrs. Oliver?"

Abigail focused on the concerned, motherly face of Mrs. Foster. It was hard to believe that she carried a gun, and had been trained in unarmed combat.

"I'm sorry. What did you say? I'm afraid my mind was wandering."

Maggie Pelham repeated what she had just said, a little peevishly. She gave her full attention to whatever she was doing, and naturally she expected Dr. Oliver to do the same.

"The last up from Data Reception, Dr. Oliver. I've checked all except these three. I'd like you to have a look at them."

Matthew took the three blue sheets of teletype from her. Tuesday was a day for catching up with data queries, confirming classifications before the material was transliterated and fed into the Bohn. The morning's work had been hard, and made harder by the way his thoughts strayed continually back to Abigail or wandered curiously around the special project mentioned by Scarfe. He stared at the teletype, seeing instead Scarfe's sharp young face and in the background Abigail watching. It came to him suddenly that she had been frightened. The Colindale frightened her, and Scarfe represented the Colindale in its most essential form.

"Maggie, tell me something. Did John Henderson ever talk about a special project, something he was working on with the director?"

"I knew of its existence. He kept stacks of paper locked away in that drawer."

She indicated one of the filing cabinets, a drawer with a blank label.

"Are they still there?"

"How should I know? I've been far too busy. Anyway, the drawer's locked, honey. I told you."

Matthew tried the drawer and it opened easily. It was completely empty, folders swinging loosely on the side runners.

"That's funny." Maggie began to take interest. "There were masses of stuff in it—sometimes it would hardly close. John used to work on it till all hours. Either here or tucked away in the classified wing. And he always kept the drawer locked—used to make little jokes so I wouldn't feel hurt."

"This lock—who else has a key?"

"No idea. Come to that, who has John's key?" She paused, and sat down again very slowly. "Not that there'd be much left of it. Not if he had it on him when he . . . died."

Matthew slid the drawer shut. There were too many things still being kept from him. He found the continued secrecy insulting.

"I'm breaking for lunch." He clipped the three teletype sheets together. "These can wait till this afternoon. Then we can start on the backlog."

He rang the director's office and spoke with his secretary. Professor Billon would be away from the Institute for the whole day. Matthew struggled to keep a sense of proportion, to believe that the director had other things to do than simply to evade and insult Dr. Matthew Oliver. He got up and went to the door.

"Walking home, Maggie?"

"Lunching in the canteen." He saw that she was still

upset from talking about Henderson's death. There were other concerns in life than his own. She pulled herself together. "The young turd I flat with—I daren't use the kitchen except on Sundays when he's out at church. He's the house-proud type, has a dinky little apron."

"Scarfe? I wouldn't have said he was one of those."

"Perhaps he isn't. Then again, perhaps he is. He's never tried anything with me, but that don't prove much. Me and him wouldn't mix, love. I mean, would we?"

She flounced away, stridently cheerful, trying a little too hard, even for her.

In the foyer Matthew caught sight of Dr. Mozart. He hurried to catch him up; if Professor Billon wasn't available then perhaps the security man could help him. They walked away from the computer center together, along paths thronged with other staff members, some in white coats and some in bright hot weather clothes. Again Matthew was reminded of University scenes, and again there was something wrong. In this case the distant band of rich green turf set with warning notices about the force-field fence.

"It's a lovely day," said Dr. Mozart. "I trust you are settling in after yesterday's trauma. Usually new boys are brought to the water more gently. I'm glad that you intend to drink."

Matthew had no time for idiomatic fireworks.

"I want to talk to you," he said. "My house is bugged —why didn't you warn me?"

"My dear fellow, a man as intelligent as you should need no such warnings. Also you must remember that I work with the system, not against it. But you should have noticed how I came to pay my respects while you were still moving in. They leave empty houses clean. It makes a better impression on the incoming tenants."

"You're very cynical." And untrustworthy? Matthew walked a few paces in silence. "Tell me, if you're not connected with the security organization within the Institute, to whom are you responsible?"

"Faceless men, Matthew. Faceless men in Geneva. . . ."

"Are you here to find out about Henderson's murder?"

"Not particularly. It interests me, of course. But the indigenous guard force has excellent machinery to deal with that sort of inquiry. I've been here nearly two years now, Matthew. My brief is much more general. . . ." They were walking past a row of glass-fronted laboratories. Dr. Mozart covertly watched his reflection. "You had something you wanted to say to me?"

"I wanted to ask you if you knew anything about a special project. Something the director was hatching with my predecessor."

"Henderson was one of the group? I suppose I should have guessed."

"You know about it, then?"

"No details. Even its existence is only a matter of deduction. I got interested in it six or seven weeks ago." They were walking slowly, and most of the crowd had left them behind. "As you know, we department heads are supposed to be allowed time for our own work. I wanted to seem willing, so I cooked up a bit of a theory and then tried to book some evening computer time for its development. This proved to be very difficult. One of four people was always ahead of me—Mallalieu, Schatten, Dingle or Blake. And very occasionally, Henderson. Anyway, I finally went to the director to complain. He was most charming. Too charming. Of course I had a right to complain, he said. Of course I had a grievance. He'd see to it that I was fitted in at once. And so he did." Mozart shrugged his shoulders. "Such consideration made me suspicious. It wasn't typical. He had something to hide."

"But you still don't know what sort of work they're doing."

"An economist, a philosopher-theologian, a politician, a historian and a sociologist . . . what unites these three with our psychologist director?"

"Many things might."

"Quite so. So I still have no idea what they are doing. And it's probably none of my business. What makes you so interested?"

Matthew told him about the empty drawer in Henderson's filing cabinet. Mozart was silent as they walked up the path toward the Institute library. They were almost alone, now that they were approaching the higher, more exclusive residential areas. Mozart turned off the path and sat down on the grass under a small group of lime trees. Matthew leaned on a treetrunk beside him, hands in pockets. The sun flickered down through the leaves. They might have been discussing Nietzsche or the Test Match.

"This interests me very much, Matthew. . . . Just let us suppose that this special project had in some way got out of hand, started moving in a direction Henderson did not like. He only has to try to stop it, and there at last we have a motive for his murder."

"Billon again?"

"It has to be."

"But you're making far too many assumptions."

"I find it useful. Theories exist to be refuted. It's their only purpose."

Matthew withdrew from the discussion. He had been interested in what Mozart knew about the special project, not in refuting his murder theories. He did not have a murder mystery mind.

"The director isn't available," he said, cutting through whatever his companion was saying, "but the moment he is I intend to go and see him. He can't refuse to tell me about the project, not if Henderson was so deeply involved in it."

"I shall be interested to hear what you find out, Matthew." There was an element here almost of threat. "But he's away for the day, explaining yesterday's discovery to the Prime Minister and the Chiefs of Staff."

"Then I'll go to his house this evening, after he's got back."

Mrs. Alice Billon turned out to be no virago, but more of a mouse even than Matthew had feared. He'd walked up to the director's house after his evening meal. He was rather glad to get away: Abigail treated him with curious care, as if he were nine months pregnant with something only she knew about. And she asked him odd questions, mainly about Sir William Beeston, shying away when he tried to find out why she should want to know. They were no longer able to be honest with each other; he was forced to be evasive when she asked him why he was going to see the director.

At the front door of his house he paused, looked back at her, as beautiful to him as ever, dark hair loose on her shoulders, doing simple things about the sitting room; as beautiful and as desirable. But he observed her from the outside, as a stranger. Between them nothing touched. She was as far off, in the low golden light, moving between the balanced shapes of the furniture, as if she had been a projection, a three-dimensional hologram. And he had to do what he believed was right.

He was glad to get away, up the path beyond the quadrangle, through a round white archway with a Spanish wrought-iron gate, to Professor Billon's low white house. Unsurprisingly the director liked beautiful things: there was a jade fountain by the entrance, spilling pale green water into a tiny pool of white and gold mosaic. And sculpture, steel strip and rod, exact upon the paving stones. And when Mrs. Billon opened the door, she showed a hall with a huge photo-sensitive mural, shifting from blue to silver in the evening sunlight.

Viewing Mrs. Billon against this background, Matthew liked her husband less. It was as if the setting had been chosen to make her cease to exist. Billon himself, Matthew had no doubt, would dominate it with ease.

"You wanted to see the professor? I'm afraid he's not in."

"I'm sorry I troubled you, Mrs. Billon. I thought he'd be back from London by now."

"Oh, he got back from the meeting two hours ago." She said the pronoun as if with an upper-case H. "But he's gone down to the computer center now. I'm alone in the evenings a lot, you see. He often doesn't get back till two or three in the morning."

It might have been self-pity, but it sounded more like a simple statement of facts. At that moment Matthew had no wish to be caught up in her troubles. He spoke briskly.

"The computer center, you said? Perhaps I can find him there."

"You may try, of course . . . but he's always very busy."

"My name is Oliver, Mrs. Billon. I'm the new sociology man."

"Replacing poor Mr. Henderson. . . . Well, I expect it's all right, you going down to the center, I mean. But I wonder if you would be good enough not to suggest that I sent you." Head on one side, hair retained by old-fashioned pins at all angles. "Because I didn't, you know."

"Of course you didn't. There's no need for me to say I came here at all." He smiled as warmly, as comfortingly, as he knew how. "I'll be going, then. And I'm sorry I disturbed you."

She pattered after him to the gate.

"And please, Mr. Oliver, do not say definitely that you were *not* here. Chester has a way of getting things out of me—out of one. And lying is so seldom a good thing. Don't you agree?"

Matthew reassured her. What strength she had ever had must have been given away years ago. Chester Billon in his mid-sixties was boundless, undauntable. His wife was an old, old woman. She stayed by the gate, watching him, till he went down the last short flight of steps into the cloisters.

The girl on reception in the computer center said that if Professor Billon wasn't in his office he was probably at the Bohn desk in the classified wing. She looked at Matthew doubtfully. He glanced up at the computer register and saw Schatten's name against the evening period.

"I'm working with Dr. Schatten," he said. "I believe computer time has been arranged."

He smiled down at her and she let him through. He never thought about it, but in general he didn't have any trouble with receptionists. Unless they were elderly, ex-service, male.

The director's office was empty. Matthew went through it and along the corridor to the classified wing. He found the Bohn desk there without much difficulty. It was up a short flight of steps, under a transparent dome that overlooked most of the Institute. Only Schatten and Professor Billon were there.

"Dr. Oliver, you make a habit of walking in on me unexpectedly." Matthew drew breath to explain. "You can be of use, however. Now that you are here. Pre-Christian Palestine, twenty or thirty A.D. Effect sociologically on the Jews of being a subject people? Hmm?"

It sounded a serious question, expecting a serious answer. Matthew was reminded of his schooldays, a waiting silence stretching ahead of him like a long, too brightly lit tunnel. He found words.

"A general hardening of attitudes . . . a tightening of the internal structure. Also a group shame, I should think. Causing a sort of fierce dignity."

"Rather as we have in society today?"

"A dangerous analogy. I wouldn't think so. We have this total lack of a unifying element. All we share is a generalized anti-them feeling." He sat down opposite the two men, now more or less in control. "I could do you a study, of course, but I've never found that sort of comparison very valuable."

Billon laughed, short as a cough. "Very good recovery. Resourceful. Very good indeed."

Matthew flushed, placed his hands on the arms of his chair, got slowly to his feet.

"Professor Billon, I'm the head of your sociology department, not a little dog doing tricks. Perhaps your purpose is to test my spirit. In that case your object has been achieved: you are now the man I most love to hate. Which I know is a perfectly good and workable relationship."

He would have gone on longer, but for his awareness of how foolish most people looked when angry. The director waited, tapping his pencil on the plastic surface of the desk. Schatten collected his papers.

"I'll get off to the canteen, then. I could do with a break." He stopped by Matthew. "The last few days have been unusually hectic. That's not an excuse, Dr. Oliver, merely a statement of fact."

He smiled, and came near to taking Matthew's arm, near to making some gesture of understanding. Then he went away down the steps. Matthew waited for the director to speak. The glass dome came down to floor level, exposing them on every side to the sky. Behind the director's head, and to one side, Matthew could see the asymmetrical roof of the conference chamber. And above it fine weather clouds in a high, pale sky.

"Sit down, Oliver. We could exchange psychological jargon all night. Contrary to what you may believe, I don't 'handle' my staff members. Mutually degrading. I simply react. I can't work with people who are too eager to please."

Eager to please. The words dropped coldly into Matthew's head and stayed there. Eager to please. They were a crushing indictment: of his life, even of his marriage. He remembered all the ways in which he had shaped himself to Abigail's image. Eager to please. And now that he wasn't, now that he was opposing her, she withdrew from him completely. Was this the real basis of their relationship, his eagerness to please?

"You see, Oliver, to be director here is to be a blind man led by the partially-sighted. They can only proceed at my pace. I need to be convinced that each step is safe and is in the right direction. It may be that I lead. But from behind. Like a wise general."

Matthew thought of the previous night, his question to himself: Was anything more important to him than Abigail? Than pleasing Abigail, should he have said? If so, then the question answered itself.

"People have been dropping me hints, Professor, about a special project you were working on with Henderson and some others. These hints are embarrassing. If I am not to work on the project I should like to be told. And if I am to work on it, then I should like to have it explained to me."

"Reasonable." Billon felt the need for a change in the relationship and stood up, going to lean his head against the glass of the dome to the right of the desk. "I had intended to introduce the project to you gradually. It is not easy. But other people talk, of course, so here we are." His breath laid a mist on the glass and he moved his head. "My starting point for the project was the accepted theory that any new development, practical or philosophical, needs to wait for its moment in history. For the right mental climate. Examples abound. Da Vinci's discovery of the principles of steam power went unnoticed. The time wasn't right. Philosophical theories change from decade to decade. . . . Look at the arrival of Jesus, followed by Paul, at exactly the right historical, emotional moment. A hundred years earlier, and they'd never have made themselves heard. But the Middle East was ready for them, and even Rome."

"Which was the point of that extraordinary question you greeted me with?"

"Except that we already know the answer. Or hope we do."

Matthew was unsurprised. His arrival had annoyed Billon, and Billon had accordingly—to use his own word —reacted. The director turned back to the computer desk.

"Scarfe will be here in a few minutes to do some transliterations for me. Not much time." He picked up a roll of magnetic tape and tightened it smaller and smaller in his fingers, "We did a study of the entire Romano-Jewish ethos, Oliver. Plenty of literature, Roman, Greek, Arabic, Egyptian, as well as non-Biblical Jewish texts. We've analyzed the factors governing the phenomenal spread of Christianity, and we think we understand them. We've attempted a similar study of the Buddhist inception, but the sources are less good." He petered out, frowning perhaps at the inefficiency of the Oriental chroniclers.

"And your reason for all this work?" said Matthew.

"The important thing to remember, Oliver, is that a need for Pauline Christianity had to exist before such teaching could get itself heard. Observably this need exists no longer. Different needs have arisen, to which Pauline Christianity is almost an irritant."

"You admit then that we do still have spiritual needs?"

The director didn't bother to answer.

"By extrapolating from what we know of the relationship between the Romano-Jewish ethos and Pauline Christianity we can determine the precise quality of spiritual teaching that would satisfy our present-day ethos. Extrapolation, Oliver. Extrapolation by association. The special province of the Bohn 507."

If this was going where Matthew thought it was, he didn't like it.

"And when you have determined this precise quality?"

Professor Billon looked down at his hands, arranged them to touch lightly the keys of the teleprinter. He pattered on them, making no mark.

"Our social balance is precarious, Oliver. Sustained by oblique oppression. Democracy is eroded almost beyond recognition. The established churches have become little more than social clubs. The—"

"All right. We're in a bad way. But how—"

"We're leaderless, Oliver. And needing leadership. Crying out for a relevant messiah."

"Which the Bohn is going to supply?"

"Determine the exact nature of the need, and then satisfy it."

Matthew stared at him, finally incredulous. Either the man was mad, or this was some elaborate joke. Some new test of his character.

"You talk a lot about humbleness, Professor. Yet here you are, proposing to supply a messiah, tailor-made, just like any other consumer durable. Humbleness? Is that what you call humbleness?"

He remembered Mrs. Billon's use of the capital H. Billon sat down, leaned his face forward on his two clenched fists, looked out under raised eyebrows. It was a characteristic attitude.

"God works through the minds and the consciences of men," he said. "You agree? Up to now the provision of great spiritual leaders has been the divine prerogative. Why? Because the minds and the consciences of men have not been sufficiently developed. But if we believe that the present explosion of technology is part of God's plan for the world, then what follows? We have new tools. They can bring about our destruction, or they can help us to our spiritual salvation."

"And giving people precisely what they want will bring about their spiritual salvation?"

He was indeed talking to a madman.

"Not what they want, Oliver. What they need. And not from a position of superiority—from a position of humble involvement. From understanding. From the ability to correlate many variables. From knowledge that has been given to us by God."

"So the Bohn is an instrument of God's will?"

"We can make it one. On its own it's nothing. It would be equally a sin either to misuse this potential or to ignore it. We have been given the means of our own salvation." He paused, then spoke softly, hardly more than a whisper. "We must use them."

The sky was stippled with long feathers of pale orange cirrus. The sun had dropped to the top of the generating station, and cast a long shadow on the roofs around them. They seemed alone, supported in its radiance. The only sound was a faint electric hum from the computer desk between them. Matthew stared at his companion, trying to fix his thoughts. Instead he found himself irrelevantly wondering which of the two piercing blue eyes fixed on him was human tissue. One of them was a triumph for the plastics industy. But he had forgotten which.

"It's an interesting argument." Shying from commitment. He sought a way out, shifted his position, broke the tension. "Even so, your custom-built messiah still has to be accepted. If he's to offer people what they need instead of what they want, he's going to have to say some very unpopular things. And the enemy is better armed than he was in Christ's day. Won't the battle go to the big battalions?"

"Two points, Oliver. First, faith. In an ultimate good. Second, the harnessing of science to the propagation of that faith. Where I come in. Why I'm in the group at all. Conversion is no new science. Greek writers describe methods of mystical initiation. You should read Plutarch or Pausanius. Remember the conversion of Paul. And that the authorship of the Acts is attributed to Luke—the physician. Conversion techniques are respectable, Oliver. In case you thought otherwise. But the ancients used them pragmatically, not understanding. . . . Under the more emotive name of brain-washing, techniques of conversion are now a well developed science. The brain is a mechanism, Oliver. Pavlov found out how to interfere with its function over seventy years ago. Modern pulse generators do the job even better." He closed his eyes, perhaps to dissociate himself partially from what he was about to say. "Given a cause I believed was right, Oliver, I could spread it through Europe within a matter of weeks. I could bring converts to their knees in millions. In itself this is no great achievement. Even Hitler, using the crudest methods, inspired thousands. Genuinely inspired them. But the cause needs to be right; it needs to be a seed that will grow."

Matthew had done some work himself on drug abreaction and cerebral wave interruptors. He could believe that the director was not making a vain boast. The success of revivalist meetings proved this. What the revivalists lacked—mercifully—was large enough backing, especially in the reinforcement stages. Professor Billon's resources, with the weight of the Colindale behind him, were probably unlimited.

"For the last three months," the professor went on, "we have been storing data in the Bohn. Sociological surveys, educational analyses, hospital reports, historical comparisons, political influences, reports from economists, philosphers, theologians, psychiatrists . . . I won't bore you. Any day now the program for relating all these will be complete. In response to it the Bohn will deliver a precise definition . . . the canon of a new faith. A spiritual framework to satisfy contemporary needs. The program is uniquely complex. We can only work at it humbly, as men of good will."

His words ended, but his reasoning continued in Matthew's head. God existed. It was only man's way of reaching Him that changed from century to century. Today human needs were increasingly understood and catered for: sex, companionship, ritual, challenge. If God was anything, He was all of these. . . .

But Matthew still refused to accept what his reason told him. His objections were emotional, irrational, amounting to an almost physical revulsion. They could be related to no objective truth, and he distrusted them. Racists felt just as violently about what they called miscegenation. But his objections, no matter how untrustworthy, were loud in his head, shouting down reason so that he could only cope with them by deferring them, by screening them off, by diverting his thoughts onto more practical, more encompassable matters. He took refuge in the peripheral, in a question sparked off by a sudden recollection of Dr. Mozart's face under the flickering green light of the lime trees.

"John Henderson," he said, "did he approve of what you are doing?"

"Henderson? He was the mainstay. A great loss."

"With the project nearly completed? Hadn't he in fact served his purpose?"

"My dear Oliver, the project only really starts when we receive the Bohn's specification. A representative has to be found, for example. There are months of work ahead—interpretation, selection, presentation, so much still to be done."

Matthew's question had amounted to a near accusation. That Billon should simply not have noticed it seemed a sign of innocence: a murderer would have been more sensitive. Yet the project was of total importance to him. Was it not conceivable that he would have been willing to kill in order to preserve it? Had the director killed John Henderson or had he not? To Matthew this relatively superficial question assumed great significance. He was faced with a decision for which he was morally ill-equipped. So he fixed on the director's guilt or innocence as a safe, easy, externalized deciding factor. Almost like flipping a coin. He would judge the project by the conduct of its chief. He would help no man who could kill coldly, for the sake of an idea.

"Miss Pelham tells me Henderson had papers relating to the project. I can't find them."

"Naturally. I could hardly leave them there for anybody to read. I got Blake to pick them up for me the day after Henderson died."

"May I see them?"

"I was going to suggest that myself. You'll find them in the drawer in my office. Bottom right." He handed over a bunch of keys, a gesture of trust. "I'd come myself, but I'm expecting Scarfe."

He stopped Matthew halfway down the steps.

"One thing more. Your wife."

"My wife?" He felt himself flush. Had their differences been noted down, discussed, passed about the place from hand to hand? "What about my wife?"

"Only that she's a Catholic. Bound to disapprove. You know your own business, of course. Handle with care, I'd say. Any reason she should be told?"

Matthew went on down the stairs without replying. If it was necessary for him to deceive Abigail, that was a matter between him and her. He was entering into no compact with the director about it.

Abigail had spent the evening in a state of pleasurable anticipation. In her mind there was only one reason why Matthew, after a day of obvious mental indecision, should go to see the director: he was offering his resignation. Which would be accepted. She thanked God devoutly. Matthew would leave the Colindale, they would contact the C.L.C., and the whole evil business would be brought to an end. Without violence. Paul would see how much more effective it was to use public opinion than bombs.

She sat and watched the tell. The house no longer interested her, for they would soon be leaving. Their house in London waited for them, the strands of their old life there to be picked up. Not even the possibility of jail—reformative custody—worried her. God never tested anybody beyond their strength. So she sat and watched the tell, and waited for Matthew's return.

"Well, love—what did he say?"

"Say? What about?"

"When you told him."

Matthew was carrying a pile of thick plastic folders. He looked at her with genuine incomprehension. Suddenly she felt very sick.

"You didn't tell him."

"Tell him what?"

"It doesn't matter. Tell him you weren't staying. It doesn't matter."

It did matter. She got up wearily, and turned off the tell. She would make one last appeal, and after that another, and another last appeal.

"Matthew, what have you been thinking about all day? And last night, when you couldn't sleep?"

"Work. I've been thinking about my work."

He was striding about the room, trying to hide from her in aimless movement.

"You have a conscience, Matthew. You know the project is wrong. You know it is. Please, love, don't—"

"Project?" He rounded on her, unexpectedly savage. "What project?"

"Don't be foolish, Matthew. There's only one project. You know quite well what I'm talking about."

She watched him relax, had no idea why. Most of the previous night's conversation with Andrew Scarfe had passed her by: mention of Paul had sent her off on tracks of her own, recollections of the place where he was hiding, a script of words she would use to tell him what she and Matthew had done. This at a time when she had believed in Matthew, in the essential rightness of his mind. Now she watched him, inexplicably relieved, circle her as if she were a wild animal and place the plastic folders in a drawer which he then locked. He took the key and put it carefully in his pocket. Once there had been trust between them.

"Abigail, please remember that we may be overheard."

"I don't care. I want to be overheard. I want them to know that everybody isn't as corrupt as they."

"Darling, be reasonable." But he came no nearer to her. "What good will it do to get yourself put away where nobody can hear you?"

"Put away?"

"You know they have the power."

"And you'd let them?"

"What else could I do?"

He spoke to her patiently, in sadness. Only then did she realize how alone she was.

"You'd stay here working, Matthew, while I was taken away?" It still had to be spelled out. "You'd do that?"

"Abby . . ." He never called her that. Now he came toward her and she backed away. "Abby, there's no need for you to be taken away. No need at all. If you'd only—"

"But you'd stay here working?"

He turned from her and went to the mantlepiece for a cigarette. He offered her one, which she refused. He lit his own carefully, delaying beyond everything that was possible the moment when he would have to reply.

"Abigail, we all have to do what we believe is right." His words disgusted her. "Would you respect me if I betrayed my principles, went against my conscience, just in order to keep you out of jail?"

How could she tell him that conscience was so often the prompting of the devil? That only God's help, which he had never humbled himself enough to ask for, could truly show him right from wrong? She sat down, leaned her face in her hands.

"We're married, Matthew. We don't need to—"

"And what does that mean?" He spoke so fiercely that she recoiled into the corner of her chair. "Does it mean that I should do only what pleases you? Or that you should sometimes do what pleases me? Where are your marriage vows now, Abigail?"

There was nothing she could say. In three days their relationship had come to this: childish talk of vows and who pleased whom. A weak, degrading, irrelevant word, and applied to the thing she had thought strongest in the whole world. She closed her eyes and prayed for it all to end. But he could not let it rest.

"Abigail, you must promise me. Promise me you will do nothing to endanger the Colindale. For your own sake you must promise me." For her sake, or for the Colindale? "Do you hear me?"

She heard him. If she did not promise, the microphones would come and take her away. Or Matthew himself would arrange for her to be removed. She would be silenced either way. She did not blame Matthew; she did not even blame the Colindale.

"I promise."

She lied. She lied loudly, for the microphones, with every sound of sincerity. Her framework of habitual truth was such that she expected to be believed. She said her lie again, more quietly, for Matthew.

After she had gone to bed, Matthew sat on in the sitting room, trying to read Henderson's notes on the special project. His mind kept returning to Abigail. He'd been pushed far further than he had intended. Perhaps her Catholic faith was the root cause of their present situation: the belief, when pressed, that she had divine authority for what she thought, while he had none. This made for an imbalance of intensity between them. From where she stood the things he did wrong were often sins; from where he stood the things she did wrong were never more than understandable mistakes. So it had always been harder for him to hold out against her, easier simply to give in and please. Billon's word ate in. Each time he had agreed to ideas of hers that basically he thought mistaken, he could at least comfort himself with the certainty that she had arrived at them intelligently, and from the highest motives. Besides, quite often she turned out to have been right after all. In those circumstances no mere idea had been worth endangering their relationship. It had been so much easier to give in and please.

She would keep her promise to do nothing. Knowing her, he was sure of it. Not that there was much she could do, with things the way they were at the Colindale. . . . Not much either of them could do. Still tortured by indecision, he turned back to Henderson's notes. There was a chance they would in some way prove him to have been killed by the director. In that case the coin would have come down tails: both projects would have been shown up for what, perhaps, they were, the children of madness. He sorted through the plastic folders.

The room was gentle, green curtains from floor to ceiling along the inner wall, his harpsichord glowing burnished amber, the chairs metallic gray and white, the whole area dimly blue under the background lighting he had chosen. And the variable tick of the clock slow and calm, defining the aural limits of the space.

Above the corner of the sofa where he sat was a single untapered column of light, clear white for reading. He saw that the folders were dated, and found the one with the latest date, the last one Henderson had been writing in, many of its pages still unused. The notes were mostly in diary form, often quite personal, detailing experiments and developments in chronological order. He turned to the final page. Handwriting neat, steady and unhurried.

Wed. 4th June.

Boney up with some good stuff, but impenetrable. Answering Schatten's query about contemporary attitudes to ideal age of prophet. Offered this a.m. expressions of p.'s optimum age in terms of a 6-language etymology! Makes you think.

Basic concept still bugs me. E.g. sunset = grid = of integers = graph = equation. Equally well, sunset = grid of integers = electrical impulses = sound/music. As CB says, anything can be expressed in terms of anything. Don't altogether get it, but not to worry. It seems to work, so who cares.

NOTE Regional nature of p. worries me. CB says 300 mill Euros are enough for a beginning. I expect he's right.

NOTE Refer to Boney re. Danish marriage survey—Hinks MG 70791 (I think). Must do before evening session.

Wednesday, the fourth of June. The day Henderson had died. Died, involved up to the last minute in the director's special project. Supporting it. Enthusiastically. Perhaps it had only been a few minutes after writing his notes that he had borrowed the director's car, and driven down past the tennis courts, and died. . . . Matthew let his eyes slip out of focus. The coin had come down heads. He was tired. Also he was committed. He knew, had always known, that Professor Billon was no murderer. The Colindale staff was huge; any one of hundreds could have placed the bomb in the professor's car. Perhaps Mozart himself. Mozart who would be on to him in the morning, wanting to know about the special project. He'd be told nothing, and he wouldn't like it. Matthew was tired. The coin had come down heads, and his prejudices were stirring. He turned back to the beginning of Henderson's notes. He was tired, but he didn't want to go to bed. He didn't want to go to Abigail. In spite of everything, he felt guilty.

NINE

SHE WENT through the morning business of getting Matthew off to work. In the middle of the night she had woken, found herself alone, and got up. He had been asleep in the corner of the sofa, surrounded by papers. She had helped him into bed, leaving the papers to be tidied in the morning. Moved by his sleeping, blind-kitten helplessness, she had treated him tenderly, and he had responded, not waking, drawing close to her, curled up in the big bed. She had watched him against the early dawn. Then they had woken together, as on any other morning, staring at the day beyond the curtains. Till, suddenly rigid, he had torn away and hurried into the sitting room, modest in quickly grabbed trousers. There had been no tea in bed. And when she had gone there later, the papers were all tidied and locked away. She went through the morning business of getting him off to the computer center.

When he had finally gone she sat down in the kitchen and lit a cigarette, let reality flood in on her. She knew what must be done, and she knew that she must do it alone, unaided. Everything depended on her being right about Sir William Beeston. She must explain the situation to him in person—sending a message would be far too complicated. She decided to check first with the shop manager to make sure that her guess about Sir William had been right.

If Mrs. Foster was surprised to be called out on a second shopping expedition so soon after the first, she made no comment. It was no concern of hers how vocationalists spent their money. They found the manager down on the shop floor, checking stock with one of his assistants. Abigail encouraged him to explain to her the relative merits of different ultrasonic washers, asking him questions till Mrs. Foster drifted idly away to a mixer demonstration.

"Yesterday you offered me a certain kind of help."

"Indeed I did."

They squatted down to look closely at a turbulence control unit.

"I want you to tell me the name of the person who would receive my message."

"Nobody has names."

"But you have met him?"

"On one occasion."

So it was a man.

"Is it Sir William Beeston?"

"Nobody has names, Mrs. Oliver. I told you."

But the sudden lack of expression on his very mobile face told her what his words denied. He was likable, she thought, but not a very good intermediary. They moved around to the front of the machine.

"Have you a message you wish passed on?"

"No, thank you."

Caution prompted her to tell such a transparent young

man as little as possible. He shrugged, and began explaining to her the control panel of the Mark VII Bendix.

The Minister's secretary said that Sir William was very busy. Abigail replied that she would not be bothering him if the matter was not very urgent, and that her name was Oliver—her husband had worked with the Minister on several important schemes. The secretary checked in the Minister's diary and found that he had a cancellation between twelve thirty and one. Abigail said she'd be there.

One of the advantages of calling on a senior member of the Government was that one was unlikely to be suspected of sedition. Abigail left Mrs. Foster firmly outside in the waiting room. It was a personal visit, Matthew having worked with Sir William so many times in the past.

"Mrs. Oliver, how good to see you. Do sit down."

His office was light and airy, cantilevered out over the Thames, giving a view of the new South Bank heliport and the hovercraft landing ramp. The Minister seemed relaxed and cheerful. She looked at him, thinking how she had never liked him, yet now she was to trust him completely. His life seemed to be one long public-relations operation. Yet an act of some kind would be necessary to a man in his double position—it was the, stuff of all the best spy histories. Of course he would have put Matthew off the way he had, while he asked around, made sure.

"I expect you know why I'm here, Sir William." His face carefully showed nothing but a polite interest. "The shop manager . . . spoke to me."

"Shop manager? Forgive me for being slow, Mrs. Oliver, but I don't think I—"

She grasped the nettle. "About the C.L.C., Sir William." His gaze didn't flicker. "I think you are a member, Sir William."

"Nobody belongs to the C.L.C., Mrs. Oliver."

"That's what Edmund Gryphon always said."

"Gryphon . . ."

He pushed a cigarette box across the desk to her, killing time while he made up his mind. She took one and he lit it.

"And you say that some shop manager in Colindale gave you my name?"

"Not your name." No point getting the man into trouble. "I worked that out from . . . from internal evidence, if you like."

"So?"

They could circle around each other for the rest of her half-hour.

"I need someone I can talk to in the strictest confidence, Sir William."

He sat forward abruptly. "I am a Cabinet Minister, Mrs. Oliver. One of the privileges of my position is an office free from microphones. If you have something confidential to say to me, I can assure you it is quite safe to do so. I tell you this because I think we share a concern for the liberty of the individual in these perilous times."

She suffered a last-minute panic. She came down to telling herself that he had a kind face when his mask was down.

"You must have the courage to trust your internal evidence, Mrs. Oliver. I can give you no proofs—we hardly carry membership cards about with us. You take a risk, of course. But no doubt your husband sent you. I respect Dr. Oliver, in spite of what he might have gathered from our last meeting. Anything he has to tell us—to tell me—will receive careful attention. All human relationships come down to this, Mrs. Oliver: at some time or another the risk has to be taken, the gesture of trust made. . . ."

The shadows from the window uprights were moving across the floor. She had little time, and a lot to say in it.

When Matthew got home for lunch the house was empty. Fearing for a moment that Abigail had left him, he went into the bedroom and opened the cupboards. Her suitcases were there, and all her clothes. Her brushes were on the dressing table, and her identity card was in the top drawer. Typically, wherever she had gone, she had forgotten to take it. He wondered for how long he could live on the precipice edge. It would be better if he sent her away himself, perhaps to stay with her parents. A break might help them both. He cooked himself some food, miserable to be alone, and returned early to the computer center.

He had cleared all the queries from Data Reception by the time Maggie came in. Work was a way of not thinking. She closed the door and leaned against it, blowing down the front of her dress.

"Stone me, but it's hot. Did you know we put the stopper on climate control as too controversial? Bloody faint-hearted, if you ask me."

She walked limply across to her desk.

"Still, without the weather, what'd there be left to

complain about? Except the Government, of course." She sat down. "Maybe that's why they left us the weather."

Matthew hadn't noticed the heat. He decided he liked Maggie; the limited openness her act allowed her was easy to get on with.

"Maggie, are you happy working here at the Colindale?"

"Happy? Who's happy? What a question."

"The tails, the secrecy, the microphones, don't they worry you?"

"Haven't you heard the handout?" She closed her eyes and held up a benedictory hand. "We at the Colindale are privileged to be taking part in uniquely meaningful work. Whatever price we pay for this historic role is amply justified."

"Professor Billon?"

"None other."

"And it satisfies you?"

"The hell it satisfies. I like to work for people who trust me."

"Yet you stay."

"Just you try leaving."

They all knew too much. Matthew hadn't thought of that. Abigail was with him, whether either of them liked it or not.

"Look, Matthew, in the official mind there can be only two reasons for not wanting to stay here, for not loving every minute of it. First, political deviation. And second . . ."

"Insanity?"

"Well done. You're not as naïve as I thought."

She laughed, but he didn't join in. Gryphon had called him naïve. The director had said the same thing, in different words. Abigail too, in every aspect of their relationship. It was time he stopped being naïve.

"I surprised myself," he said.

She laughed again, this time more because it was expected of her than because she thought his reply funny.

"By the way, I've been thinking about my flat-mate. How kinky do you really reckon he is?"

"I don't know enough about him to be able to say."

"Well, either he's that or he's some dreary sort of agent. I'm sure he pokes in my drawers. And I once caught him reading one of my letters."

"What sort of letter?"

"Well, that's the point. As it happens, the letter was the purest porn. There's a boy gets a thrill out of writing them to me; they do me no harm, so I let him. Other people's quirks are sad, don't you think? Anyway, there you are. At the time I was furious, accused him of being a spy, threatened to go to C.B., had a grand *crise* . . ."

"Why didn't you?"

"Go to C.B.? Well, there's enough spying in this place already. I reckoned I'd frightened Andrew good and proper. Anyway, now I come to think of it I'm bloody glad I didn't tell on him. I bet that letter was making him bust his jockstrap. And I bet he rummages in my panties for the same reason."

Admittedly it was hard to see what Scarfe, in his central, privileged position, could hope to learn from reading Maggie's letters. But if Mozart could be a spy, then why not Scarfe? And a spy for whom? Come to that, Matthew had no real idea for whom the German was working either. . . . He was beginning to see the extent of his own naïveté.

Maggie was sorting through the litter on her desk. She uncovered the telephone.

"Look at this. Must have come in during lunch." She tore off the paper that projected from the phonoprint. "For you, by the look of it."

Scarfe says program fini. Running this P.M. *CB.*

The director's notes were as telegraphic as his speech. He must be referring to the special project program. Matthew had hoped for longer in which to get used to the idea. He felt slightly sick.

"You don't need to tell me what it's all about. Whenever John got cryptic notes from C.B. he always slipped them into the special project drawer. I take it you're now an initiate?" Matthew nodded. "Good luck to you. All it ever gave John were lines around the eyes and gray hairs from lack of sleep."

When he got in that evening he found Abigail waiting for him. He had walked up from the center warily, not wanting to meet Dr. Mozart. He trusted nobody. The house was cool, air-conditioned. Abigail had pulled down the sunblinds to keep out the glare, and she was standing by the sitting room window, watching a blackbird hunt for worms in the shadow of the fir tree. He kissed the back of her head, and talked about the weather. He didn't ask her where she had been at lunchtime—he felt he no longer had the right. But the question existed, and she answered it.

"I'm sorry I wasn't in at one, Matthew. I felt I just had to get out. Mrs. Foster and I went in to the Finchley shopping center."

"I hope you enjoyed yourself. Did you buy anything?"

"No."

He believed her. Except as a social duty she seldom made purchases unless they were greatly reduced in a sale, or the result of a long discussion. This wasn't meanness, merely a way of living with their wealth. He could have checked with Mrs. Foster about the expedition, but he preferred not to insult Abigail by doing so. It didn't matter where she'd been: he had her promise.

He told her he had to go back to the computer center immediately after dinner and she accepted this, also without question. There was so little left for them to say to each other. How long he could keep it up he didn't know.

She had his food ready, and served it at once. Some people could live lives on a level of domestic efficiency and not much else. They ate in silence, his mind on the coming night's work. He was obscurely afraid of what the Bohn might tell them.

Back at the center the receptionist directed him down to the basement. He found the other members of the special project group in a long low room beside the shielded storage banks of the Bohn. Small sounds filtered through the wall, a constant clatter of relays as the machine dealt with incoming queries and with data being fed in from the teleprinters of Data Reception. The room was intended for the use of research teams and was comfortably furnished, recognizing the long sessions that were sometimes necessary before the program ran right. At one end of the room there was a long tropical fish tank, a brilliant microcosm, salutarily uninvolved, silent.

Professor Billon was sitting at one of the three teleprinters, checking a tape against the hand-printed master. Scarfe was beside him, at a large drawing board. As Matthew entered he looked up from a sheet of flow diagrams and penciled calculations, and waved.

"Glad to have you with us."

Matthew wondered if it was hypersensitive of him to see this remark as an abrogation of the director's position. Certainly Professor Billon was too busy to notice. Scarfe had taken trouble to acquire a necessary technique, and it had won him a place with distinguished men. He wasn't a man to cope wisely with such a situation.

Zacharie Mallalieu sat on one of the couches, reading the day's *Financial Times*. All that could be seen of him was his white hair and his young pale hands. Schatten and Blake were setting out the pieces of a pocket chess set. Dingle, the historian, was filling a large meerschaum pipe. There was a feeling in the air that nobody expected anything to happen for a very long time.

Matthew sat down beside Professor Dingle, put on the cheerful friendliness he used with strangers.

"Looks as if I ought to have brought a pack of cards."

The older man finished filling his pipe, then dusted shreds of tobacco off the front of his jacket. He spoke carefully, and with great good manners.

"You will be Dr. Oliver. My name is Dingle. We were introduced in passing the other day. How do you do."

Matthew wondered if he should stand up to shake hands. Dingle employed the typical distancing mechanisms of a converger. It often surprised Matthew that people should behave so much as their profession suggested they would.

"Cards are supplied, as a matter of fact. Should any of us care for a game."

"What could we play?" The evening was fantastic—why not compound the fantasy with a game of cards? He looked around. "We seem to be the only two not fully occupied."

"I expect Mallalieu will be glad to join us. Henderson and we used to have some fine old tussles. Been quite at a loose end since the poor fellow's sudden departure." Dingle leaned slightly closer. "But I feel I should warn you that friend Mallalieu likes very much to win. It's as if the whole efficacy of a mathematical turn of mind were at stake."

"Friend Mallalieu also possesses excellent hearing." The *Financial Times* had not moved a centimeter. "Five mark ante, just to make the game more interesting?"

"I'm willing," Matthew said.

Apparently the game was to be poker. Mallalieu folded his paper carefully and put it in his pocket. He rose and, nudging a small table across the floor in front of him with his foot, came to join the other two men. The table legs made an unpleasant noise on the floor. Andrew Scarfe bent lower over his flow diagram and clicked his tongue in loud irritation.

"If we are expected to be here," Mallalieu said, to no one in particular, "we can hardly in addition be expected to preserve a monastic silence." Matthew foresaw an edgy poker game. "I'm surprised, Oliver, that you did not come better prepared. Every computer session I have attended here has turned out to be a considerable waste of everybody's time."

"I expect," said Dingle mildly, "that Dr. Oliver is used to more normal computer operations, employing a large number of technicians. The secrecy of our work here makes that impossible."

"In other words, Oliver, we're expected to blow the thing's nose for it. And wipe its arse."

Matthew disliked self-conscious man's talk. But then, he disliked Zacharie Mallalieu. It would be pleasant to take his money from him. Dingle fetched a pack of cards, and began to take out all those under seven. Then he put them on the table and Matthew cut. Mallalieu dealt. Matthew anted the five marks and picked up his hand. Two knaves and three odd cards, ace high. He kept the ace with the knaves and changed two.

"Hmm," murmured Dingle. "Drawing to a three."

"Rubbish," said Mallalieu. "Pair and an odd ace. They all do it."

Cards betrayed people more than any other single activity. Except perhaps driving. The two cards he gave Matthew were ace knave. Dingle changed three, and the dealer one. Matthew, with a good full house, tossed out a ten-mark piece. Dingle folded and Mallalieu, snorting, raised to twenty.

Matthew hesitated. He had no idea how the other two played. He reasoned that he had been placed either with a three or two good pairs. Mallalieu was either filling a straight or a flush, or drawing to two pairs. A further raise should tell him which. He kept the raise at ten. Mallalieu put it up again a full twenty— either bluffing or with five of a kind. Unless he'd matched one of his pairs. Matthew paid the twenty to see him, feeling the money well spent, if only to find out how the other man played.

Mallalieu put down five odd cards, king high. The chat was obviously an integral part of his game. Matthew showed two of his knaves and gathered in a profit of fifty marks.

They played several more hands and Matthew, never a distinguished player, continued to win. He enjoyed cards for their own sake: their precise shape and texture, the excitement of each new hand, the skills of dealing and shuffling, he enjoyed it all. So that, within limits, he had no objection to losing. Mallalieu was different—to put down a hand better than his was to offer him a personal insult. The money was of little significance to any of them. It was the sense of personal success or failure that troubled Zacharie Mallalieu.

At any other time this situation would have made Matthew play to lose. He would have felt no game to be worth anger, tension, unpleasantness, a possible row. But tonight he was a new man. Anyone as small-minded as Mallalieu deserved all he got. So he played hard and tight, and kept on winning. It was one of those nights.

Behind them Professor Billon finished checking the tape. He and Andrew Scarfe muttered together, heads bent over calculations on various bits of paper. Matthew was aware of their activity all the time, as a background to the game. He watched the director take the final tape and move toward the computer desk. Scarfe called him back. The two of them conferred over an Astran service manual.

"I've raised you twenty, Oliver."

"See you," said Matthew, not concentrating.

When it was too late he remembered that he held four queens and had intended going up with every mark he possessed. Mallalieu showed four triumphant kings. It was one of those nights.

Finally Billon and Scarfe were satisfied. They

mounted the tape on a twenty-four-inch reel—Matthew saw that it barely fitted. He was used to seven-inch reels, with a running time of two or three minutes. The present program might take up to half an hour. Professor Billon was at the computer desk, threading the tape across the heads, clumsy with excitement.

"First run, gentlemen."

There was a slight rustle of interest.

"Tenth run and I might begin to take some notice," said Mallalieu, very audibly.

"I raised you five," Dingle said. The cards were beginning to run his way.

"Five? What sort of raise is that? Either they're worth raising on, or they're not."

Dingle pursed his lips and said nothing, let his bet stand. The second filling of his pipe had just gone out. Mallalieu, his temper worsening, raised a further twenty and lost again. The chess players, who had looked up at the director's announcement, returned to their game. And the Japanese fantails circled contentedly between their pillars of pink coral.

It was Mallalieu's turn to deal. Meanwhile, the first few cleaning feet of the tape ran through quickly. Then the note changed: there would be a brief ugly scream till the heads reached a stop combination and paused. The sounds from the next room would intensify. Then the tape would rush on again, chattering and shrieking. Matthew had the feeling that if only the noise could be slowed, as on a tape recorder, it would make human sense. He was hearing thought. He was hearing an intellectual process. And to his mind intellectual processes were inseparable from words. Computer logic—anything expressed in terms of anything—frightened him.

"How many are you changing, Oliver?"

Suddenly the monitored, synthetic perfection of their environment nauseated him. The careful lights, and the jibber of the computer. And the people. Scarfe, all brain, studying his flow diagrams as he had on another occasion, all body, studied Maggie Pelham's letter. Billon, quite without movement or apparent emotion. And the other four men, manneredly absorbed in their own irrelevancies.

"Make up your mind, Oliver. How many are you changing?"

"One."

He didn't even look at his hand. The machine screamed and paused, screamed and paused. Schatten offered his opponent a quiet *Check*. The scene should have been completed with a palm court orchestra playing *The Flight of the Bumblebee*. Badly.

"I've put up ten, Oliver. Are you in?"

He fidgeted with the cards in his hands, but still didn't look at them.

"Raise you fifteen," he said.

Dingle met this, and Mallalieu upped it fifty. Scarfe got up from his drawing board by the group of teleprinters and joined Professor Billon at the computer. He checked the tape counter to see how far the program had advanced. The tape feed had been badly aligned, and used tape was beginning to spill out across the floor.

Matthew automatically raised a further fifty, and then dragged his mind to look at his cards. Mallalieu must be desperate, putting in raises of fifty. . . . At first Matthew thought he had five odd ones. Then he saw that they could be sorted into a straight—ten knave queen king ace. His blind draw had turned out incredibly well. But he hadn't been attending, and he had no idea what the others had drawn. Mallalieu with his fifty raise, and Dingle quietly meeting even the hundred now needed.

Mallalieu folded his cards into a neat stack, put them facedown on the table, and raised a hundred. Matthew had allowed his attention to wander on the hand that was apparently to be the showdown. Betting blind, not knowing what was against him. Under such circumstances he would normally have got out. But Mallalieu's gross confidence annoyed him. The room's hysteria was infectious.

He tossed out a two hundred note. "It's a shame to take your money," he said.

Dingle met the two hundred, and the four subsequent raises—never raised himself, but always kept level. He was staying in, believing he had a good chance of picking up the pieces. Mallalieu ran out of money, and had to borrow. He hadn't looked at his cards since putting them down on the table. Matthew kept his in his hand, needing constant reassurance that he really held what he thought he held. At any moment the knave might turn out to be a queen, or the ace a seven. His cards were nowhere near good enough for the level of the betting. Mallalieu *had* to be bluffing. Dingle he would lose to with pleasure.

Suddenly the note of the computer changed, and the console put out a short blue paper tongue. Scarfe tore it off.

"Error in phase seven," he translated aloud. "Loop incompatability. Holding." He referred to his flow diagram. "Phase seven . . . there's a hierarchic loop, three-level structure. Worked well in isolation."

"Copy misprint?" said the director.

"We'll have to see. Might be a simple data error. Dr. Mallalieu . . . ?" Scarfe had wound back the tape and was reading it off straight through on the printout. "Dr. Mallalieu, your stage. Stand by, please."

Mallalieu appeared not to have heard. He was entirely focused down to the act of willing Matthew's cards to be worse than his. Suddenly Matthew felt sorry for the man, that it should really be so important.

"No point in throwing any more money down the drain," he said. "I'm running."

"But you can't run. Not now."

"I just have."

"But—"

"As far as I'm concerned the kitty's all yours. Must be upward of two thousand marks."

He turned away to watch Andrew Scarfe. But out of the corner of his eye he saw Dingle pay to see Mallalieu's hand. And he saw Mallalieu's flush go down to Dingle's four nines. His own hand had been the weakest of the lot. And nobody would ever know. The relief that he felt told him that he had backed down not out of compassion but out of cowardice.

"Dr. Mallalieu. Please. I have a list of figures here for you to check."

The game was interrupted. Dingle gathered the money he had won, and scooped it unobtrusively into his pocket. He and Matthew stared, embarrassed, at the scattered cards on the table, waiting for Mallalieu to return.

"It's a strange game for men like us to choose to play," he said. "Which probably explains why none of us is very good at it."

"Men like us?" said Matthew, preferring speech to silence.

"Not gamblers by nature, I mean. At least, I don't think we are."

"So we gamble with money, which doesn't really matter."

"I wonder if you are right. I receive the distinct impression that we have been playing for something far more important than money." He began refilling his pipe. "If I were prone to generalizations I would say that with no gambler is money ever more than a tertiary motive. If that even."

"Nobody likes to lose."

"You, my dear Oliver, are being intentionally obtuse. Perhaps you are wise."

A long silence followed, in which the movement of the chess pieces and the background clatter of the relays next door became unnaturally loud. Mallalieu could be heard muttering over his data list. . . . Dingle had been partially right. Matthew *had* offered a remark that was knowingly inadequate. But certainly not out of wisdom.

"I suppose we have to go on playing," he said at last.

"Sportsmanship demands it. Zacharie is losing—whether we stop or continue must be his decision."

"And he'll want to go on. So we'll just have to hope that luck changes."

"Which is egregiously patronizing of you, my dear fellow."

The *dear fellow* and Dingle's charming smile robbed the retort of its edge, if not of its truth. Matthew collected the cards and began to shuffle. His companion's fusty appearance and turn of phrase sorted badly with the technical chic of the room they were in, with the special project, with the Colindale.

"Tell me," Matthew said, his eyes on the cards he was shuffling, "what made you agree to help with this particular project? I'd have thought it out of character."

"It's perfectly simple. The project won't work."

"Won't work?"

"Of course not. I look on it as an intellectual exercise and a harmless way of keeping our director happy. But please, never tell Zacharie that. It would mark the end of an indifferently beautiful friendship."

"Why won't it work?"

"Because it's a logical impossibility. While it might be possible to deduce grass from the needs of a horse, to work the other way is utter nonsense. The ability to deduce a horse from the properties of grass is quite beyond us."

"But you're saying one can't deduce man from the properties of God, which was never in question. Anyway, this project has nothing to do with God. It's man we're analyzing, not God."

"We start from different points, my dear Oliver. You see, I believe in God, and you don't."

The penetration of this remark shocked Matthew into silence. Since his marriage he had believed in God rather in the manner of the Red Queen's advice to Alice that she should believe six incredible things every morning before breakfast. And it had never quite worked. He didn't believe in God; instead, he believed in Abigail, and she believed in God, and that made everything all right.

Mallalieu returned to the table, and they began playing again. But the tension was broken, the hands dull.

Scarfe rethreaded the tape—the error had not been in the data but in the copying—and the Bohn continued where it had left off. Scream, pause, scream. Schatten won his game against Blake. Neither player seemed inclined to start a second. The program tape jerked through its last few yards, its end finally rustling down among the coils that moved secretly on the floor around the computer desk. The calculation phase began, the associating and cross-referencing. To fill in, Scarfe found the end of the tape, clipped it into a new spool, and began winding back. The coils were gathered up from the floor, rubbing together like snakes. The rewind rose to a high whine, then cut abruptly as the last few inches flipped, slowing, around and around. Finally the room was left to the faint considering chatter of the relays. The card players laid down their hands.

Professor Billon seated himself by the printout console, rigid, resting no more than he had done throughout the program run.

"Five minutes," he said. "Perhaps less."

Nobody moved. Matthew noticed that Dingle had put his cards face upward, two tens, an eight, a queen, and a king. He couldn't remember if his own hand was better or worse.

"Of course," offered Andrew Scarfe, his voice abnormally normal, "it'll be a miracle if it comes through right first time. Much of the flow is pure guesswork—beside straining Astran to its limits. I wouldn't be surprised if all we get is a sound of popping elastic."

It wasn't a good joke, and nobody even smiled. But the atmosphere relaxed. To try that particular brand of schoolboy risqué perhaps Scarfe was public school after all. Thought Matthew.

There was a general stir of activity as the five-minute wait became real, an absurdly long time to remain silent and motionless. Conversations were instituted. Dingle saw his turned-up cards and pushed them into the middle of the table.

"I was folding anyway," he said.

Mallalieu threw in also. No incentive remained for another deal. Slowly the five minutes passed, then six, then seven. At last, with a faint turning of wheels, paper began to flow from the printout console. Billon switched in the big monitor screen so that everybody could see.

INRELATE FAZ NOTKOM POINSTOP TENPREFIN SM 101 POINSTOP LATERAL KX THOZE FEET IN ANSIENT KAKBKK TENPREFIN SM 101 TIME WALKIN WALKIN WALK BIASS UNKOMPAT AST OBJEKON BIPA AST OBJEKON BIPA 2 SM 101 POINSTOP KAKBKKKDKEKF KAP FAZ ERROR NOBIPA POINSTOP 1 123 123456 12345678910 1234567891011 121314-15 1234567891011121314151617181920211234

The printout ran on as far as this before Scarfe could switch it off.

"Slipping into a very simple progression curve," he said. "It's the interrelations in the capstan phase. They'd leave a blank series all the way."

"And the recurrent objection?" asked Professor Billon.

"The whole aesthetics loop is hunting. Or we wouldn't get that breakthrough. But at least we've succeeded with the nationalism block."

Matthew lost interest. Their language was too private.

All that mattered was that something had gone wrong. He wondered how long he would be expected to stay. An error in the capstan phase—what was the capstan phase anyway?

"Gentlemen"—the director stood up—"gentlemen, this SM 101 reference. Mean anything to any of you?"

Matthew jumped, as if caught talking in class. "S is a sociology prefix," he said. "But I've not seen an SM. At least, I don't think so. I'll check if you like."

"Would you? We'll get a redefine first, but it seemed consistent."

The redefinition produced nothing helpful. Matthew went up to his office to look in the classification index. There was no SM listed. Outside his window the night was clear and starlit. He leaned on the windowsill, staring up. Astran demanded a basic humorlessness, yet there was no real reason why KAP FAZ should seem to him so irresistibly funny. The typically British habit of laughing at the natives, maybe.

Back in the basement room he found Scarfe handing around sheets of codified data for checking. Apparently the capstan phase provided the central motivational impulse and was returned to between each associative operation. Thus its interrelations involved all departments. At first glance Matthew could make no sense of his data list at all. He had several hours' work ahead of him.

Abigail spent the evening alone, alternately exultant and appalled. Exultant at the success of her meeting with the Minister: he had promised her a special meeting of the Committee within two days, the publication of a broadsheet within a week at the most. He had shown a reassuring, unhysterical determination; he would get things done. Now that she had started an irreversible process she experienced a pleasant dissociation from it. Already in her mind her visit to the Minister was completely innocent. Her good intentions spilled over onto actual events, transmuting them . . . until, appalled, she thought of Matthew.

She had betrayed his trust in her; to this the rightness of what she had done was irrelevant. She needed time in which, with God's help, to walk slowly with him till he understood. It was for this reason that she had lied about where she had been. It was in his power to have her taken away, committed to reformative custody, and in the immediacy of his hurt this would seem justified. She needed time. Events towered about them both, a windowless city. If she was taken away that night she would carry with her nothing of him. He would snatch back the past even. If he simply knew that night that she had lied to him, she would go alone. And this she feared far more than jail, far more than anything. She needed time.

At midnight she went to bed—to stay up would be to erect a barrier of significance against his return. Later she was woken by the familiar, four-year-long sound of him brushing his teeth. Instinctively her body opened to him, then closed, suddenly remembering.

"Matthew?"

"It was a long session. I'm sorry."

Their bathroom door was ajar, letting a narrow strip of light fall across the floor and the bottom of the bed. The strip widened, and was filled by his shadow. Then darkness. She heard him undressing: shoes, socks, the zip of his trousers.

"I hoped I wouldn't disturb you."

"It doesn't matter. I'm glad you're back."

He turned back his side of the bedclothes.

"It's a hot night."

His weight depressed the bed so that she had to prevent herself from rolling toward him.

"I love you, Matthew."

"My eyes hurt. If this goes on I shall have to see about glasses of some sort."

"Don't you believe me?"

"It's after two, Abigail."

"You must believe me."

"All right. And I love you too. But I can't. Not tonight. I honestly can't."

"That wasn't what I meant."

"No. No, I suppose not."

She listened to him breathing, felt him slowly unwind. Then he slept. A warm summer wind blew across the Colindale, causing the fir tree to scrape soft green needles against the bedroom window.

TEN

AT THE coffee break next morning Matthew received a call to the director's office. From the look of him, the director had been up all night. He was as sleek as ever, but the sockets of his eyes were gray and the skin at the base of the scar on his forehead was twitching.

"SM 101," he said. "Are you sure you've nothing in your index?"

"I've checked several times. There are no SM classifications. None at all. Either the Bohn's mad or this isn't a classification at all."

The director screwed up his face with the pain of his tiredness.

"I've sent Scarfe back to his quarters. He's done all he can. For the last six hours we've got nowhere."

"Might I suggest you went home yourself, Professor?"

"I know my resources. There's an answer here somewhere. Couple of hours ago we ran a diagnostic check. Nothing wrong, Oliver. Nothing there to diagnose. This one reference, it's all we have. All there is to show for three months' work. It must mean something."

"No change in the final printout at all?"

The director gestured in the direction of the console. "See for yourself. A miracle might have occurred."

Matthew crossed to the machine. The long hours of the previous night had taught him a lot about its controls. He dialed the repeat sequence.

FINDEF SM 101 POINSTOP REQ STA2 POINSTOP FINDEF SM 101 POINSTOP REQ STA2 POINSTOP FINDEF 101 SM REQ ST

He stopped the machine and ripped off the piece of paper.

"Request stage two? What's this stage two it's asking for?"

"Well, well . . ." The director smiled wryly. "It's getting impatient. Stage two is the campaign stage. Not even begun on yet. We have to understand the final definition first."

"What happens if you ask for a redefine?"

"Thing goes wild. All its party tricks. Kings of England, Haydn symphonies, passages from the Revelation of St. John the Divine—anything and everything. We had to stop it. Looked like keeping it up all day."

"And there's nothing wrong with the program . . ."

"Of course there's nothing wrong with the program. And yet there must be. SM 101—what sort of definition is that? How can the whole thing possibly be brought down to just one series?"

Matthew scrumpled the neat rows of symbols and tossed them down the waste chute.

"I'm afraid I can't help you, sir. I'm sure it's not a classification anywhere on my files."

He started to move toward the door. Professor Billon called him back.

"You, er . . . you think I've bitten off more than I can chew?"

"Not at all, sir." There was too much at stake. The director's entire career might have been directed toward meeting this one challenge. "There must be other S's. What about Dr. Mozart's subject: what about spectroscopy?"

"Thought of that. All SP's."

"And seismography?"

"Been through every S classification we have. Anyway, what single scientific paper could possibly . . . ?" He tailed off. But he didn't want to be left alone. "Sit down, Oliver. Time I told you about my dud eye."

Matthew had a duty to be generous. He sat down in

one of the mesh chairs. He might have lived a hundred years since he had sat there beside Abigail, making up his mind if he wanted to work at Colindale. In less than a week his life had been enlarged till he was a different person, a Colindale person. He believed in the director and he believed in the Bohn. He saw the special project as logically, beautifully inevitable. And he accepted it as being larger than himself, larger than himself and Abigail.

". . . Student days," the director was saying. "I used to go around the closed wards, asking too many questions. Closed wards they had in those days. Felt it my job to stir things up for the regular staff. Far too resigned. Complacent even. . . . Maybe they did it to warn me off and maybe they did not. Might have been quite accidental. Not that it matters." For once he paused not for effect. He was reliving the moment. "Somehow the poor woman had got hold of a knife. Interesting tradition, strength of ten men. Sound physiological explanation. Anyway, there you are." He made a quick slashing movement with his right hand. "Sorry as hell about it afterward, of course. Made me think. You see, it was all psychoanalysis in those days. And who benefitted? Not who needed it most. Couldn't get near the seriously disturbed. Never claimed to. That woman changed my life. It was she needed help, not the wets afraid of their virility. And to help her, Oliver, some other way was needed. Surgery. Drugs. Unpopular ideas even now. But they work. The brain is just as much a machine as the heart or lungs. . . . Story of my life. Case you've ever wondered how I landed here."

Matthew had reservations. His eye wandered away to

the sculpture revolving in the corner. He had been warned about trying to please.

"The brain may be a machine, sir. But isn't it something else as well? Hasn't it other qualities?"

"Careful here. Only talk about what we know. You refer to the soul: repository of higher emotions, conscience, love, hate, honor, duty, faith . . . Right?" Matthew nodded. Billon held up fingers, started counting them. "First thing, as defined, the soul exists. Second thing, we don't know where. Third thing, its nature can be changed. Drugs, applied hysteria, illness, even the simple processes of time—all these can modify the nature of the soul. And all these act on a physiological level. Fifth thing, what then is the soul?" He leaned forward. "And if you see where that takes us and don't like it, neither do I. Keep an inquiring mind, Oliver. And humbleness. Nothing else will do."

Matthew was uneasy. In spite of his admiration for the director, there was at the back of his mind a nagging distrust of people who professed humbleness. Perhaps, like children, it should be seen and not heard. The director closed his eyes and leaned back in his chair, his tiredness doubly returned now that his story was finished.

Abigail was enduring a visitor. Wanting nothing more than to be left alone, she was having to be polite to the resident Colindale doctor.

"I'm really very sorry not to have called before, Mrs. Oliver. I make this routine call to all newcomers, just so that they'll feel welcome, looked after, you know the sort of thing."

"Of course, Doctor. Sit down, won't you?"

"Thank you, thank you. Only a fleeting visit." He looked around the room, saw the harpsichord. "You are musical, Mrs. Oliver? Or is it your husband?"

"I like music. But it's my husband who plays."

"You have no children?"

"No."

"You are a practicing Catholic?"

"Yes."

All this had been in the preliminary written questionnaire. But no doubt he had to find something to talk about. Suddenly she thought how unreasonable it was that the assumption between her and Matthew had always been that she was the barren one.

"If you want any help in that direction you know I'll be only too glad to do what I can.

"Of course." She dared a bitter note. "Perhaps you'd care to talk to my husband."

The doctor would have to have been a complete fool not to see that this was a subject best left.

"You're settling in well? You've made the house quite delightful. . . . Tell me, how do you like it here at the Colindale?"

"Not very much." No harm in that much honesty.

"We do our best to make you comfortable. Why don't you like it?"

"Perhaps you do too much. I don't think being comfortable is all that important."

"A well-ordered life makes you uneasy?"

"It depends on who's ordering it."

She could spar like this all day. The doctor smiled disarmingly.

"Believe me, Mrs. Oliver, I'm not trying to get at you. I simply have a professional concern for your comfort.

Yours and your husband's. A move is more disrupting than many people think. *Autre pays autres moeurs . . .* Both of you are well?"

"You're right, doctor. The Colindale *is* another country."

"I think you'll settle down, Mrs. Oliver." He paused, looking for a comforting noise to make. Abigail lit herself a cigarette, unhelpful. Behind her she could feel the mid-morning garden, hot and still. "There's a very active social life here, Mrs. Oliver, which you probably haven't yet come much in contact with. I expect you're suffering from a sense of isolation. It's very common among newcomers. You should get out more. I'll ask the Leisure Counselor to call."

"Please don't."

She'd been a Leisure Counselor herself, immediately after leaving L.S.E. In the days when she'd been in love with Edmund. She couldn't face the patter, and the life it would remind her of.

"Not if you don't want me to." Unconcerned. "Her number's in the book, should you change your mind."

"I'm afraid you'll think me very uncooperative, Doctor."

"Of course not. Most of the people here are sufficiently intelligent and well-adjusted to run their own lives." He got up. "Another hot day. Chance for me to sweat off a bit at the tennis courts. Stir up the old circulation."

He paused on the way to the door.

"I expect you're not yet used to the microphones. Do they worry you?"

"They stand for distrust. That worries me."

"Distrust, Mrs. Oliver?" He smiled down at her, almost as tall as Matthew. "Don't we all long to know what happens in houses when the doors are shut and the curtains drawn? I'd say it shows a healthy curiosity. I think you're jealous, Mrs. Oliver."

Or guilty. Why didn't he say what he was really thinking?

"Observing a phenomenon changes it, Doctor. Nothing happens in houses when the doors can never be shut and the curtains never drawn."

The remark came out more violently than she had intended. The doctor seemed not to notice.

"You'll be surprised how quickly you forget all about them."

"I doubt it."

She wouldn't be staying that long. He went out into the cloisters, looked at the smooth grass and the other houses generously spaced around the sides of the quadrangle, the trees and the informal shrubberies, and was pleased with what he saw.

"You have my number," he said, "should you ever want me. Anxiety states are easily dealt with, you know."

"I am not suffering from an anxiety state."

"You might find it cleared up your . . . other trouble as well. Often a matter of tension, nothing more." Cheerful to the end. "Good morning."

He deserved no medal for noticing she was tense. She went quickly into the house and closed the door. All right. She was tense, she was anxious, she was barren, she was guilty. She lit another cigarette. Also she had an oral fixation. She curled her bitten nails into her palms, hiding them even from herself. If the doctor had been sent to undermine her, he had done a good job. And Matthew soon to be in for lunch.

She rang his office in the computer center. He wasn't

there, so she left a message with his assistant, asking him to lunch at the canteen. For wasn't that the purpose of the canteen, to help wives whom the Colindale had turned into screaming neurotics? She went into the kitchen and prayed, leaning against the sink, staring at the taps.

Hail, Mary, full of grace, the Lord is with thee: blessed art thou among women, and blessed is the fruit of thy womb, Jesus. Holy Mary, mother of God, pray for us sinners, now, and at the hour of our death.

Amen.

She prayed the single simple prayer for a long time, not repeating it but listening to its echoes. Then she went down to the canteen, to the public table where nothing could be expected, nothing said.

Early in the afternoon Matthew's routine work was interrupted by Andrew Scarfe. He put his head experimentally around the door.

"Afternoon, Dr. Oliver. Afternoon, Maggie. Room for a little one?"

Maggie sighed audibly, and went on checking classifications. She didn't have to be polite to Scarfe; she lived with him. Matthew had wider obligations.

"Come in, Scarfe. I thought you'd been sent home to get some sleep."

"Sleep? Could you sleep with this thing on your mind?"

"I managed a peaceful six hours."

"But you're not really involved. I'm supposed to be

the computer man. When I close my eyes all I see are compensating loops and differential feedbacks."

He sat down in stages, like an old man. He certainly looked as if he hadn't slept much. His self-importance of the night before had gone.

"I'm at a complete dead end. I could understand it if the Bohn weren't so specific. Usually when there's something wrong all you get is a load of bunk. But this—" He checked himself, glanced across at Maggie. "Well, it's something quite new. And I can't even shop around for a second opinion."

Maggie got up, glad to be able to get out and at the same time register I-know-when-I'm-not-wanted.

"I'll take these down to Data Reception. It's a good thing to show the rest of the group that we are real people in here—people with problems, people who make mistakes. Not like bloody old Boney."

She went out, taking a bundle of classifications with her. Scarfe turned in his chair to watch her go.

"She doesn't like me."

"I wouldn't say that. . . ."

"I would. She's a bitch. God, how I hate women like that."

Matthew fiddled with the papers on his desk. He had work to do. And to have a row with Scarfe in his present state would be pointless.

"If I were you I'd try to occupy myself with something else for a day or two. The subconscious grinds on —you'd probably find the thing solved itself if you gave it time."

"And the director? What's going to happen to him? He's far nearer to breaking up than I am."

Matthew had seen few signs of disintegration when

they'd talked that morning. Perhaps Scarfe needed to prove something.

"Maybe he's stronger than you think. I was with him a few hours ago, and—"

"All you've seen is the act. And he's good at it. But I tell you, the better the act's going the worse he is inside. You should have seen him the first few days after Henderson's death. As bright and busy as a light bulb. And just about as brittle." He laughed at his own word-play. He might have been talking about someone he hated. "If I don't come up with an answer soon, Dr. Oliver, he'll just fall to pieces."

Computers exacted from people a service equal to their own tireless, elusive circuitry. It was the Bohn that drove Scarfe on, not his sense of responsibility to Professor Billon. Matthew had seen computer men before, the same sharp bright talk, the same sleeplessness, the same need to personalize their servitude. And with Scarfe there was something more, some additional tension. He should think himself lucky the Colindale wasn't a commercial concern, where each misrun cost somebody thousands.

"I don't suppose there's anything I could do to help?"

"Do? Just tell me you made a mistake. Tell me there's an SM on your file, a paper about some noble guru living near West Woking with all the answers." Matthew smiled and shook his head. "Well, failing that, there's not a thing." He started to get up. "Unless . . . Well, there is just one thing you could do. Stupid thing, really."

Matthew waited. With Scarfe it could be anything. The deeply personal things men asked men to do in books. Matthew waited, looking helpful, feeling apprehensive.

"I ought to ring my mother. I wonder if you'd do it for me. Here's the number . . ." Ring his mother? It might have been a lot worse. "Just tell her I'll be working late for the next few nights, so I won't be over as I promised."

"Wouldn't it be better if you rang her yourself?"

"I suppose it would. But, hell, you know what mothers are." Matthew didn't: his own had left him with an aunt so that she could get on with her career. "You see, she'll want to know why, and I won't be able to tell her. Then she'll say it's some girl, and why can't I at least be honest with her. Then I'll deny it, and she'll say . . . and I'll say . . . and so on and so on. So I'd be very grateful if you'd do that little thing for me."

Matthew wondered if it was his imagination, or if Scarfe really had said *girl* as if it were a dirty word. If that was the sort of mother he had it was no wonder he'd turned out a little odd. Matthew took the number and dialed. It was his first outside call, and he could imagine the recorders grinding.

"May I speak to Mrs. Scarfe, please?"

"Speaking." Formidable indeed. The one flat word.

"I'm calling from the Colindale, Mrs. Scarfe. I have a message from your son. He says he's very sorry, but he'll be working late for the next few nights, so he won't be able to get over as he had promised."

"I see. Nothing else?"

Matthew raised his eyebrows at Scarfe and the young man shook his head vehemently.

"No, nothing else. Except that he's sorry. It's a very busy time here at the computer center."

"I see. Tell him I'll be writing."

She rang off. If that was motherhood, Matthew was glad to be without it.

"She'll be writing," he said.

"So I heard. You know, I wish she wouldn't. Pages and pages of nag. I feel such a fool if I ever have to go down to the censorship office." He stood up. "Anyway, you're a hero. Now I'd better get my nose back to the grindstone. . . . By the way, I'm forgetting what I really came in for. Could I possibly borrow back that Astran primer? There's a couple of points I think I ought to look up."

"I'm afraid it's at home. I could ring my wife, ask her to bring it down for you."

"Please don't bother her. There's one in the library. I was only trying to save myself a couple of minutes."

After he had gone Matthew tried to get back to his work. *Ring my wife, ask her to bring it down for you . . .* such easy, such proprietary words. Words that lied, words he must stop using. Once she had said that he was the fire, she the fuel. And the desolate present, that too would pass, giving place to a quality of life he could not imagine. He didn't know how long he could continue to burn without her. He didn't believe that everything could founder, not on a ragged lifeless ideal. That evening he would talk to her, try to reach her.

When Maggie came back from Data Reception he filled in his own silence by telling her about the phone call to Scarfe's mother. She stood by the window, thoughtfully picking her nose. A mower hummed by, ridden by one of the groundsmen.

"So *that* was why he came to see you. I thought all the other was a bit put on. Poor little worm—I suppose one ought to feel sorry for him. . . . But it's all too neat. Anyone else would have got themselves cured of her long ago. I reckon she's his excuse."

"Have you met her?"

"She's never been to the Colindale. But I've seen her letters, pages and pages of them. He shows them around as if he was proud of them."

Perhaps he was. But, as Maggie said, the whole structure was too neat, too analytically sound.

At about five o'clock Abigail was called by the guard at the gate with the surprising news that a man claiming to be her brother was there. Would she please come down and identify him, so that a day pass could be issued.

He was standing where Father Hilliard had been, under the awning outside the guard house. He was shaved and neatly dressed. He might have been anybody's kid brother taking the evening off to visit his married sister. Too neatly dressed, too much like anybody's kid brother. She greeted him cautiously.

"Paul, this is a surprise."

"Hi, sis."

The guard came out of his kiosk and stood between them, Paul outside the Institute confines and Abigail on the inside.

"This your brother, Mrs. Oliver?"

"Of course it is."

She signed the guarantee form for him and the guard made out a pass. As Paul crossed the scanner it emitted an ugly rasping buzz. He pulled a camera with a flash attachment out of his pocket and handed it cheerfully to the guard.

"Sorry. I forgot."

The guard accepted the camera without comment. "Your property will be returned to you on your way out, sir."

He gave Paul a numbered disk and returned to his glass cubicle. Paul walked up the tree-lined avenue behind his sister, whistling Beethoven, leaving her to start whatever conversation there was to be.

"You might have known you wouldn't get away with it."

"No harm in trying." He grinned. "A few feet of film would've been very useful."

"Is that what you came here for? Use me to get you in so that you could take photographs? Your group must be very simpleminded to think you could get away with that."

He shrugged his shoulders. "Talk about it later, shall we?"

"No, Paul, we'll talk about it now. If you're here to make trouble I shan't allow it. This is too important—if necessary I'll hand you over to the guards."

She looked up, noticed Dr. Mozart standing outside one of the laboratories they were passing, and smiled at him. To her relief he made no move, but simply acknowledged her greeting with a formal bow. At that moment a pretty young lab assistant came out of the door behind him and they went off together arm in arm.

"You must be mad, Paul, breezing in like this when you're supposed to be in Africa."

"Who knows that except you and Matthew?"

"Andrew Scarfe does."

"Andy? Any old story'll do to keep him happy."

"And what about Matthew? What are we to say to Matthew?"

"We'll sort that out when we get to it."

"No, Paul, we'll sort it out now."

She guided him into a courtyard surrounded with low residential blocks. There were flower beds and a fountain, pigeons standing around in the cool air of its lee. She sat down on a seat close to the fountain and pulled him down beside her. Water pattered agreeably on the stones close to their feet, running away down the cracks between.

"Paul, what are you doing here?"

"Can't a brother visit his big sister?"

"Don't be childish. We both know there has to be a reason."

"And you're talking to me here because your house is bugged? Is that it? Do they really force you to live like that?"

"Just answer my question."

He stretched his legs in his permaprest trousers and stared at his permabrite shoes. She had never seen him so outwardly respectable.

"The fact is, Abby, I've come here to warn you. I shouldn't be doing it, and if it ever gets out I'm as good as dead." It sickened her that she couldn't immediately trust what he said. "You see, I swung it on the boss that an onsite inspection would be useful. Up to now our plans have been based on hearsay. So here I am."

"Warn me? What against?"

"Against getting yourself killed this coming Sunday night."

"But, Paul—"

221

"I'm not saying any more. Just stay in your house and you'll be safe. Just stay indoors—don't come out, whatever happens."

She was silent, watching the water splash on the ground in front of her. A pigeon came too near, and wet its feathers.

"You must be mad if you think your people can break in here, Paul. There's the fence to get past, and—"

"Just stay in your house. And Matthew too, if you can make him."

"What are you planning?"

"A short sharp bang. Nothing more. Nobody injured even—just a short sharp bang."

"I warned you, Paul. If necessary I'll—"

"Listen, Abby. You won't turn me in; I think you've been here long enough to know just how rotten this place is. Our plans are simple: the night porter at the computer center leaves his desk at one o'clock for a walk around the block. At that time of night the place will be deserted—the maintenance staff doesn't come on till two. So an explosive charge timed to—"

A couple came out of one of the apartment blocks and passed close by. Abigail lit herself a cigarette, passed one to her brother, tried to appear normal.

"You can forget all these plans, Paul. I've been in touch with the C.L.C. Within a week the whole Colindale project will be public property. It won't continue after that. It can't. You know it can't."

"You have touching faith in the power of public opinion, sis. Me, I don't share it."

He couldn't be allowed to wreck everything. There must be some way of convincing him. She didn't ask him how he knew so much about the organization of the Colindale—she wasn't interested. She just had to stop him wrecking everything she had risked so much to achieve.

"Anyway," he went on, "how the hell did you manage to contact that happy band? House bugged, phone tapped, followed everywhere you go—how the hell did you manage it?"

"Let's say I managed it. I'm not a complete fool, Paul. I got to see you without much difficulty."

"I don't believe it. Tell me who you met. I don't believe it."

"A member of the Committee."

"Who, Abby? We have a list of every lousy member. Tell me who."

She hesitated. To convince him she would have to trust him. As he was trusting her.

"Sir William Beeston."

He stared at her. Then he began to laugh. He laughed till the walls around rang with it. He slapped his leg. He took out a handkerchief and mopped his face.

"Billy B.? You can't mean it. You went and told *him* what a naughty place the Colindale was?" He saw her face, and was suddenly serious. "Abby love, Billy B. is a monster. A genuine, twenty-two carat monster. He's no more a member of the C.L.C. than I am. Whoever put you on to him was conning you all the way. Believe me. I *know*."

"But of course he'd pretend to be a monster. If he didn't, then . . ."

But her voice was losing confidence with every word.

"Look, love"—his kindness didn't help—"who told you he was a Committee member?"

The answer was that nobody had, not even Sir Wil-

liam himself. She must have been marked down by
Security as a poor risk—perhaps they'd listened to her
conversations with Matthew—so they'd offered her a
bait, a chance to betray herself. Which she had taken.
The exact progression of her thoughts must have shown
in her face. Paul took her hand.

"You should have known it wasn't possible, love. All
of you here, they have you just where they want you.
You can't move a finger without them knowing. It has
to be like that; without it this place wouldn't have lasted
a day. It's taken us three years to set up this plan of
ours. And even then—"

"What will they do to me, Paul?"

He looked away. She sensed that he was going to lie.

"Do to you, Abby? What can they do? They need
Matthew, so they'll just have to put up with you. Keep
a very sharp eye on you, of course. But I don't see what
else they can do."

She wanted to believe him. If Matthew stood by her,
perhaps he was right. But Matthew was a Colindale
man. And there was so little time. She stood up. The
doctor's visit that morning now made sense.

"Are you coming up to the house, Paul?" She didn't
want to be left alone. "I'm not expecting Matthew back
for another half-hour or so."

"I'd love to. Besides, it'll look better if you invite me
in."

She threw away her half-smoked cigarette, watching
it quench and darken on the damp paving stones. She
disliked women who smoked while walking in the street.
Paul and she went up together past the library.

As they entered the quadrangle she saw Andrew
Scarfe standing uncertainly in the vivid shadow of the

cloisters outside her house. She tried to pull her brother back out of sight, but it was too late. Scarfe had spotted them.

"Paul—how very nice to see you."

"Andy—how are you?"

"Mustn't grumble. But I thought you were in Africa."

"I had some things to see to. I'm joining the others next week."

Paul was very smooth, and Scarfe seemed satisfied. Abigail reminded herself that he had no reason not to be. He turned to her.

"I'm very sorry to trouble you, Mrs. Oliver, but I wonder if you could dig out that Astran primer I leant your husband. I went for the one in the library, but it seems to be out. As I was just around the corner, I thought—"

"Of course." She had no alternative. "Come in. I'll get it for you."

The house was empty, full of ears. Closing the front door did nothing to shut the Colindale out. She sat the two men down in the sitting room she had so quickly come to hate, and offered them drinks. Paul said he'd like something long, with ice in it. Although air-conditioned, the bus journey out had been cramped and stuffy. While she was at the refrigerator in the kitchen she heard them talking behind her, friendly, easy talk about the University. She delayed her return to them, dreading the social forms. Everything was unreal to her; even the cubes of ice that stuck in their coldness to her fingers were dreamlike, at a great distance. She returned to the sitting room, the floor surprising her at each step.

They chatted for a few minutes. Incredibly Scarfe

seemed to notice nothing wrong with her. When he had finished his drink he excused himself and left, taking with him the book he had come for. She returned from the front door and sat down, aware of Paul's eyes following everything she did. There was a quality of sadness in his gaze that she didn't understand. And the microphones waited.

"Well, Paul?"

"Well, Abigail?"

"Matthew will be home soon."

"It would be simpler if I didn't meet him."

"I suppose you're right."

"I'll wait in one of your spare rooms."

"Wait?"

In a way everything that he said was expected, part of the spiral process of her life. Yet he must not be allowed to hide from Matthew in Matthew's house. There was no reason.

"Just till he goes out again. He works late at the center most evenings, doesn't he?"

"No, Paul. There's no reason."

"I could keep you company. We might go for a walk. Surely you don't object?"

"I'd rather not have to pretend you weren't here, Paul."

Inadequate words, admitting their own futility. She had deceived Matthew before, and she would do so again if Paul told her to.

"Well, then, Abby, don't pretend. I've no objection to seeing Matthew. I was thinking of you." He paused before giving her the explanation she didn't want to hear. "You see, there might be things I'd tell him that you didn't want me to. You know how tactless I am."

Blackmail. Between Paul and her, blackmail. He met her incredulity with a regretful smile. She shrank into her chair, sickened.

"After all," he said, "I've nothing to hide. It's as I told Andy: at the last minute I had to put off my African trip for a week. I'm going next Monday instead."

Gryphon dead, Matthew stolen, Sir William a trap, her parents powerless, Paul newly menacing. And the Colindale a cell.

"Don't worry, Abby. I'll look after you. Isn't that what brothers are for?"

"Paul, I've been thinking about what you told me down by the fountain . . ."

"I had to get you to invite me up here somehow, Abby."

"Then what—"

He silenced her, pointing at the microphones. Anyway, her question was unnecessary. His story of coming to the Colindale to warn her was so transparent: she would never have believed it had she not wanted to. There could be only one reason for his presence. She had told him his group would never get through the fence, past the guards, and there he was. She could do no more than hope he would fail. For she, who at that moment had the power to betray, to shout into the microphones what she knew, would do nothing, would decide nothing, would be confused, insufficient. She had cultivated subjection according to the canons of her faith. She would be passed over, would pass herself over, in what still had to be a man's world. Ultimately responsibility, even for herself, was not hers.

Matthew came home as usual, shortly after six. He found the house unusually neat, glasses and plates and cutlery drying in the machine, his food ready on the table. Abigail moved calmly around him, made sure he had everything he needed. He felt she was using her attentiveness as a barrier. He couldn't let her.

"Come and sit down, Abigail. I want to talk to you."

She sat. Composed herself to listen. The things he had to say weren't for an obedient child.

"Abigail, love, look at me."

She looked at him. She looked at him for no more than a moment. She could feel him reaching out to her, and she couldn't bear it. Events were not hers. She inhabited a timeless gap. If life slipped back a cog and started in a new direction, why, then she would be different, able to—

"Abigail, I know this is a mess." Seeing her agony, forcing himself not to recoil from it. "We're both stuck in attitudes. We can't get out of them, and they're driving us further and further apart. The issues are big. I expect we're both willing to die for them. But are we willing to kill? To kill each other?"

She didn't know what he was asking of her. Neither did he. He was simply talking as truthfully as he could, waiting for something to happen between them. Words.

"We make a habit of trying to understand things, my darling. Motives, purposes . . . No, that's not right. It's I who has tried to understand. You have tried to *know*. But—"

She could stand his pressing in on her no longer. She could not be raped, not even she.

"I had a visit from your Mr. Scarfe this afternoon, Matthew."

"Please don't do this, Abigail."

"He wanted the Astran primer back. I gave it to him."

"I love you."

Not that.

"We had a little chat. He seems nicer than he did the other night. Perhaps you overawed him, Matthew." She actually smiled.

"Abigail, I do not want to talk about Andrew Scarfe." And she, she did not want to talk. "Our whole lives are in an awful bloody mess, and all you can do is evade, prattle on about the first thing that comes into your head." She continued to smile. Against such a stretching of the lips he had no weapon. "We must not be torn apart, my love. We're all we have."

Weak generalities, all he had left. She didn't move.

"Stay with me this evening, Matthew."

"Abigail, I can't."

"Of course you can." It had been a sudden idea, a test.

"The director is expecting me." On what other occasions had he not scrapped everything, knowing she would not ask without need? "No, Abigail, I just can't."

"Please, Matthew. Don't leave me."

"Only a very few more evenings, love." So she closed her face to him, let him run on. "I wouldn't go if it wasn't really important. But I'll try to get back as early as I can. . . ."

"Your food's getting cold, Matthew. It's not like you to let your food get cold."

There was nothing more he could do or say. Not then. The next day, perhaps. Or later that night, when he got back from the center. Meanwhile, needing words, avoiding silence as he ate his supper, he played her game and told her about Andrew Scarfe. About the phone call Scarfe had asked him to make to his mother. Oedipus complexes were common territory, a refuge for them both.

She leaned against the front door, listening to Matthew's footsteps fade. She had not asked him again to stay—at heart she was glad of his refusal. For him to stay would have complicated a situation already beyond her. By the time she got back to the kitchen Paul was sitting in Matthew's place, clean cutlery in front of him, waiting to be fed. She did so without comment.

"It's a pity you didn't get Matthew to stay," he said. "I'd have enjoyed a chat."

His crude irony was slightly pathetic.

"Paul, what do you want with me?"

"Want with you?" He held up a finger to remind her they were overheard. "Just to talk quietly for a couple of hours or so. I don't often get over to see you. And when I go to Africa I'll be away for a long time."

So they talked. Quietly. For a couple of hours or so. Discussions about Dad's hobbies, about Mum's back, about what could be done for Aunt Nora. Abigail felt she was going quite mad.

When she could stand it no longer she suggested they go for a walk. It was, she said, a beautiful evening. And Paul had amused himself at her expense for long enough. She took him out, away from the microphones, across the quadrangle, up to the open ground by the white wall to the director's house. They sat down, as if to watch the sunset.

"What are you really doing here, Paul?"

"That's a difficult question, Abby. On one level I'm

sitting beside you, watching a sunset. On another level I'm battling with a disease called life. On another—"

"You're not sixteen any more, Paul. Do try to grow up."

"You grow up too, then, Abby. Stop asking questions when you know the answers."

"It won't do any good, Paul, destroying the computer. They'll only build another. You must fight it with ideas, not bombs."

"I'm not here to argue. Anyway, it's too late. I've done my job now, and—"

He stopped. She was on to him quickly. Away from the house, with the sky over her and grass under her feet—even a Colindale sky and Colindale grass—she could think again.

"Done your job, Paul? What job was that?"

"It doesn't matter."

"What job have you done, Paul? You've been with me ever since you arrived. Not out of my sight for a single minute. How could you possibly have . . ."

Then she remembered. He had asked for ice and she had gone into the kitchen to fetch it. He had been alone in the sitting room with Andrew Scarfe.

"Scarfe? Is he one of your group?"

"Catholics stick together. Always have."

"I'm a Catholic. And—"

"And look at you sitting here with me, a traitorous saboteur swine."

"You gave Scarfe something. What was it?"

"Explosives are very compact nowadays."

And Scarfe had access to any part of the computer at any time. And Scarfe was thorough. She saw now why the book had been forced on Matthew—so that there would be an excuse to call reclaiming it at a time when Scarfe knew Paul would be in the house. The delivery couldn't have taken place anywhere safer. And the talk, the smooth talk about why Paul wasn't in Africa had been simply to fool her. To keep her quiet, to keep her in ignorance for as long as possible. They had used her, her home, her loyalty. And Paul was speaking to her now so gently, so reasonably.

"You see now why it had to be me, Abby. Some newcomer whose right to enter wouldn't be questioned. Somebody making a first visit: no regular would have got away with using that camera to cover him through the scanner at the gate. Andy managed the same trick the day he came here, brought in an incendiary under the cover of a pocket tape recorder. And even then he was damn nearly caught."

"Then it was Scarfe who killed Henderson." No longer disgusted, simply dulled and weary, weary of the words.

"Bloody fool, he was told to go for the machine, not the man. He'd have been withdrawn and punished if his cover here hadn't been so perfect. Killing is not our way, Abigail. It won't be our way tonight. I promise you."

It was a promise he was in no position to make. She distrusted him and she feared him. The sky was darkening as they watched, cloudless and pale to the jagged roof horizon.

"You tricked me, Paul. You used me to—"

"It's up to you then." He sounded bored, lay back on the grass, his hands behind his head. "It's up to you. I'm unarmed. The director's wife is in the house behind us. If you called for help she'd be bound to hear. I couldn't stop you. So it's up to you, Abby."

ELEVEN

IMPATIENCE. Matthew could feel it gathering like electricity in the air. It showed in controlled voices, in sudden pointless getting up and sitting down, in vain attempts to attract the attention of the Japanese fantails behind their wall of glass. It beat the air-conditioning, made the basement room profoundly uncomfortable.

But the members of the group, even Mallalieu, contained it, bore with the director's desperate persistence out of compassion if nothing else. They checked the data he asked them to check. They sat with him, one by one, going over each associative complex. They even showed enthusiasm, followed by disappointment, in each new half-hour run of the program. Only Scarfe didn't bother to hide his disenchantment. The checks he made for Professor Billon were cursory, the results tossed insultingly onto his desk, merely humoring an obstinate old fool. It was an unpleasant exhibition which the director chose, with effort, to ignore.

FINDEF SM 101
POINSTOP FINDEF SM 101

And the output never varied.

Abigail hugged her knees and stared down at the neat, sophisticated buildings of the Colindale. Mist was beginning to gather in the hollows. It was merciless of Paul to make the responsibility hers. Merciless but just. She remembered Matthew on decision-making: however much you weighed the advantages and disadvantages, the decision you finally made was intuitive, emotional, the one you had secretly known about all along.

"I shan't interfere," she said.

Paul rolled on his side and broke off a long stalk of grass to chew.

"Good for you." He spat pith. "Not that it matters, of course. The question was academic. I mean, it had no practical application. You see, the charge has a failsafe device. Andy's setting it to go off at five past one, when the porter's out on his rounds. But there's an acoustic trap so that any interference with it before one five will make it detonate there and then. So your gracious permission was hardly needed." He patted her shoulder. "Still, it's nice to know where we stand."

She didn't flinch away. She also was glad to know where they stood.

"Paul—you promised no killing. But Matthew's down at the center now, and he didn't get home last night till after two. There's bound to be others with him."

"Andy's dealing with that. He's there, and it's part of his job to get everybody out. I meant it, Abby, when I said we want no killing. All I'm here for is to help him get away if it's necessary."

"But why does it have to be tonight? Why not some other night when there wasn't the same risk?"

"I don't know why. That's Andy's decision. He sent the message to come, so I came."

"Message? I thought this place was supposed to be proof against messages."

"We fixed a very simple code. Just a message to his mother saying he would be busy for the next few nights and couldn't get to see her. His mother's been invaluable —she writes interminable letters to him, the sort of personal code that's just about unbreakable."

A message to his mother, sent by Matthew. And for some good reason. She didn't mind if Matthew was being set up; it would make Scarfe want to keep him alive. She was at a stage where situations could only be dealt with one by one, as they arrived. And she wanted Matthew alive.

The Colindale was dusting over into night, windows losing the buildings around them and existing simply as yellow squares of light. With the sun gone Abigail felt cold, and shivered. Paul helped her up, leaning back with outstretched undergraduate arms, and they walked slowly back together, down to the house.

Paul played Matthew's harpsichord for an hour or more, simple pieces, very badly. Abigail sat in Matthew's corner of the sofa and smoked and watched the clock. When it struck eleven Paul stopped playing.

"If I don't go now I shall miss the last bus."

"You can't go." Thinking he meant it. "You can't leave me alone here."

"I'll stay the night, sis, if you really want me to. If you're sure Matthew won't mind."

And then she remembered the microphones.

About an hour later there were footsteps in the quadrangle, and quiet voices. She recognized Zacharie Mallalieu's. She listened as they passed, expecting to hear Matthew's key in the door. When he didn't come she ran out into the cloisters, called after the small group of men, not caring.

"Your husband, Mrs. Oliver?" Their voices came back along the tunnel of no moonlight. "Your husband, Mrs. Oliver? He's stayed behind with the director. He and Scarfe. They looked to be settling in. No point in waiting up for him, Mrs. Oliver. I'd go to bed, Mrs. Oliver."

They had no reason to be mocking. It was her imagination. She shut them out, slamming the door.

"There's no need to panic, Abby. Andy'll get him out. There's plenty of time; you really mustn't worry."

At twelve forty there were more footsteps, and then a sudden loud knocking on the door. She hurried to answer it. Paul came after her, caught her arm.

"Don't open. Find out first who's there."

"Who is it?" she called.

"Dr. Mozart. May I have a word with you, Mrs. Oliver?"

"What do you want?"

"Just a word with you, Mrs. Oliver."

His voice was compounded of soothing reassurance. Paul drew her nearer to him.

"Security?" She nodded. "I thought so. Don't let him in. I'll handle this. Where does Matthew keep his laser?"

He noticed the movement of her eyes toward the bedroom even as her brain was refusing to tell him.

"Mrs. Oliver? Let me in, Mrs. Oliver. There are things we must talk about."

"It's nearly one o'clock, Dr. Mozart. My husband's not here. Can't we talk in the morning?"

"I'm afraid not. It's a matter of the greatest urgency."

"Tell me what it is. I'm not letting you in till I know what it is."

There was a pause, confused muttering on the other side of the door. Paul returned from the bedroom, Matthew's laser in his hand.

"Mrs. Oliver, please be sensible. I have guards with me. If you do not open the door we will simply have to burn out the lock. Please be sensible."

"What do you want with me? How dare you come threatening to break down the door."

"We have an order for your committal, Mrs. Oliver. The doctor's report and the evidence of Sir William Beeston. It will be much better for all concerned if you agree to come peacefully."

She stared at Paul, suddenly terrified. He moved quickly to the door and turned the light out at the switch there.

"You're early," he said loudly. "Storm troopers usually make these raids at two or three. The effect is supposed to be more demoralizing."

"You must be Mrs. Oliver's brother. Talk to her, please. Tell her to be sensible. Resisting committal will only worsen her situation. Tell her—"

"I'll tell her nothing. If you want her, you'll have to come and get her. And I warn you, I'm armed."

Dimly Abigail watched him take a stool to the door and stand on it, so that he could see through the narrow strip of window above. Outside in the cloisters there was careful movement, and the sound of orders being given. More than anything else, Abigail felt incredulity. Suddenly she was judged insane, fit for reformative custody. The transition from her Kensington life to this had been too abrupt. She was the same person, yet she couldn't be. Paul was whispering at her in the dark.

". . . Half an hour. That's all we need. When the charge goes up in the computer center that'll draw them off. We may be able to get you out in the confusion."

"I don't want to be got out, Paul. What's the use?"

"Once in that lot's hands and you'll sink without a trace, Abby. If you don't care for yourself, then think of Matthew."

Matthew . . . he was still at the computer center. She no longer trusted Scarfe to get him away in time. She no longer trusted anybody.

"Paul—I'm going to ring Matthew and warn him."

"But, Abby—"

"Don't try to stop me. This may be the last chance I'll ever have of speaking to him."

"All right. But if you tell him about the charge, for God's sake tell him it's no use trying to defuse it. If he does try, he'll only—"

The cloisters were suddenly illuminated with brilliant greenish light, throwing Paul's head into sharp silhouette against the narrow window. At the same moment the guards moved in quickly to the door. Paul fired down at them, shattering the glass. Return fire cut brief rods of light around him. The guards retreated, one of them wounded. The hall filled with the smell of scorched plaster and brickwork. Paul tried with his gun for the light source, but it was out of range.

In the hush that followed, Abigail stumbled to the telephone in the sitting room and dialed the computer center. The bell at reception rang and continued to ring. The room she was in was strange and hideous. She moved from the phone to switch off the lights, preferring darkness. As she waited there was a further attack on the front door. The hiss of the lasers cracked like whips and there was a brief muffled scream from one of the guards. No killing. Her brother had promised no killing. Events would take control, push her back from stand to stand.

At last the night porter answered. Calmly she asked to be connected with the director's office. Another bell began to ring. From the cloisters silence, and then the clicks of an amplifier being tested.

"Listen in there." Dr. Mozart, his voice huge. "Mrs. Oliver, talk to your brother. Make him see sense. We can get you out with gas any time we want to. Make him see sense."

The phone rang in the director's office. The time was ten to one. For Abigail life had moved away into fantasy, into classic nightmare. The phone bell rang on steadily in the creeping dark.

"Coffee, Oliver. D'you mind?"

The director did not look up, his belled reflection motionless in the black glass of the dome. Scarfe fussed beside him, urging him on, screwing him tighter. Matthew had tried several times to intervene and each time had been repulsed by tormentor and victim alike. They were locked together, satisfying complimentary needs. Matthew went down the steps and through the double doors into the main part of the building. He was glad to get away.

Data. Data analysis, data response, data association, data looping, data definition, data compensation, data redefinition. Round and round into insanity. And back always to the same conclusion, the output that was wrong and could not be and was and could not be. Matthew cursed himself for being there, for staying when the others had left. The director had not asked him to. But when he and Scarfe had gone up from the basement to the Bohn desk under the blank glass cupola, Matthew had tagged along. He was sure that somehow that night, out of the mutual suffering of the two men—for Scarfe suffered while making the director suffer—a solution to the problem would come. FINDEF SM 101: with repetition even the symbols' meaninglessness sometimes took on meaning. Could that be the point, the whole thing a bad joke? Had the Bohn acquired a tortuous sense of humor? FINDEF SM 101. And Matthew had stayed, gooseberry to a sophisticated coupling, obscenely needed.

As Matthew passed the director's office he heard the telephone ringing. He went in to answer it. In the darkened room moonlight flashed off the slowly revolving sculpture, scattering random flakes. He crossed to the desk and had his hand on the telephone switch when the ringing stopped. It left the room painfully quiet. Against the moon-white grass outside he saw the huge pupils of the three eye windows. Suddenly they were more than a harmless eccentricity. He returned quickly to the corridor and made his way to Data Reception.

He collected three cups of coffee from the machine. The late shift had been gone for nearly three hours, leaving the room unpeopled, falsely still, its unreality heightened by the uncompromising neon. The tables were everywhere littered with blue data sheets. Some of them would be on his desk in the morning, part of an endless process larger than human. The three plastic cups began to burn his fingers.

Professor Billon stared at the coffee as if he didn't

recognize it, had forgotten that he had ever asked for it. The pad in front of him was covered with minute, obsessive calculations. He scrubbed the lot and began again.

"Substitution, Scarfe. There's a relationship we're missing somewhere. A progression that the Bohn accepts—but on what level? Suppose we assume faulty conditioning?"

They had assumed faulty conditioning before and before. The words were meaningless scurryings to and fro. The telephone began to ring, a receiver unit without amplifier. The dome was a place for concentration, not to be interrupted. Billon picked up the receiver and laid it down on the desk, taking no further notice of it. A faint rasping sound came from the earpiece, possibly female. He had not looked up from his pad, from his assumption of faulty conditioning.

Scarfe sighed. "It's five to one," he said.

Matthew checked, agreed pointlessly that it was five to one. Scarfe got up slowly from the desk and crossed to a low bookshelf by the door. He stooped in front of it, searching. When he straightened and turned back toward them, a plastic-bound manual in his hand, his whole manner had changed. He stood straighter, his deformity more noticeable. Gently, almost caressingly, he spoke the director's name.

The older man didn't respond, continued to draw flow diagrams, boxes with phase numbers neatly printed in each. Scarfe repeated the name, slightly more loudly.

"I'm trying an address substitution, Scarfe. Help me. Don't stand there."

"But you're wasting your time, Professor." A long silence. "I said, you're wasting your time. I have the solution. I have it here in my hand."

"Go home, Scarfe. You've been at it too long. I can get on quite well without you. Just go home."

Angry, Scarfe strode across to the desk. Matthew was about to intervene, Scarfe's manner so threatening that he might have struck the professor. Instead he flung the manual he was carrying down on the desk.

"There's your answer."

Billon touched it uncertainly, straightened it. Matthew edged around behind him, read the title of the manual over his shoulder: *Manual of Basic Control Circuits on the Bohn 507. Confidential.*

"Control circuits, Scarfe? There's nothing wrong with the control circuits. Anyway, we're neither of us electronics engineers. What possible good is this to us?"

"We can read, Professor."

"Far too late for games, man. Just tell us what you're getting at."

Scarfe leaned forward and pointed with sarcastic patience at the index number on the top right-hand corner of the service manual.

"You see," he said. "Paranoia is catching."

The index number was SM 101.

Matthew refused the implications, looked away at the distorted reflections above them in the curved black glass. Hardest to bear was Scarfe's perverse humanity. Now he was explaining, his arms swelling and dwindling as he gestured, not because explanations were necessary, but because he enjoyed making them.

"You see, Professor, the Bohn has never been given a word for itself. To itself it has no name. Not even a number. Its existence has been so complete that one was never needed. Then we offered it a program for which itself was the only answer. Undefeated, it decided it was the sum of its own circuitry—as expressed in Service Manual 101. Asked to redefine, it resorted to its party tricks, under the impression that a thing *is* what it *does*. . . ."

He lowered his voice, stooped, spoke close in the director's ear, his words a mocking incantation.

"Bow down, Professor. Worship the Cathode Printout, the Random Access, the Loops and Ten-tier Processing. Bow down and worship. And if you are sickened, just remember that the Bohn is what you made it. You and the others, you taught it the basic connections. So if you are sickened—and I believe you are—just remember what it is that sickens you. As I said before, paranoia is catching."

Matthew drew his attention back from the looming presences all around them. He looked at Scarfe, flushed, triumphant. Then at the bleak figure of Professor Billon, motionless but for the scar twitching on his forehead and his eyelids blinking steadily over the one real and the one plastic eye. He needed a shave. His hair had fallen sideways, disclosing a small bald patch. But he still commanded. He ceded none of his dignity to the up-start, grasping Scarfe. The triumph could offer no glory. Above all, he was not pitiable.

"You've known this for some time," he said.

"It came to me this afternoon."

"Playing an unseemly game with me."

"Waiting for the right moment."

"No doubt you enjoyed it." Professor Billon at last turned his head to look at the other man. "Of course,

Scarfe, you hate me. You envy me and you hate me. No doubt it was you who killed John Henderson."

"Does it matter?"

"It matters to me. Matters to his wife and children."

"I like your order of priorities. Consistent to the end."

The director saw his cup of coffee, picked it up and drank it. Matthew wanted to speak, but had nothing to say. He was essentially outside. Scarfe looked at his watch, narrowed his eyes.

"I'm going home."

"You're a man without responsibilities, Scarfe. Simply a systems analyst. It is I who ought to envy you."

"If you've any sense, Dr. Oliver, you'll come with me. While there's still time."

To Matthew the threat in his words was meaningless. He stayed by the desk while Scarfe went to the head of the stairs.

"Are you coming?"

"Go on, Oliver." Billon swirled the last of his coffee around and around in the bottom of his cup. "Go on, man. There's nothing to be done. Just leave me. Moment of truth and all that. Just leave me."

Matthew did as he was told. Scarfe was so far ahead that he had to run to catch up. He didn't want the man's company, but neither did he at that moment want to be alone. The computer inhabited the place, the air tasted of it. Their footsteps were louder than was suitable.

"Hang on, Scarfe. What's the blasted rush?"

"I want to get out of here. Don't you?"

Matthew didn't answer. They hurried on down interminable corridors. At last they reached the reception hall. The big clock there showed a minute past one and the porter was getting ready to make his round of the outside of the building.

"Signing out, gentlemen?" A chatty man. "Glad to see it's not quite as late as it's been the last few nights. You gentlemen work too hard, in my opinion. Enough's enough, that's what I say. . . ."

He registered the time and they signed alongside. He looked slowly down the column, still keeping them.

"Most of the other gentlemen left at midnight, I see. Who's left now, then?"

"Only the director."

The porter confirmed this carefully.

"That's all right then. He pleases himself when he comes and goes. Fine gentleman . . . Well, I'm trotting along now, gentlemen, so I'll see you out."

The three of them walked together across the dimmed glass floor to the entrance.

"By the way, sir, you're Dr. Oliver, aren't you?"

"That's right."

The man had seen the signatures but it made him warm all over to be told he was right. Matthew paused, resisting Scarfe, who was dragging him on.

"Anything the matter?"

"Only a phone call for you, sir. I rang around, but I couldn't find you. Rang your office, rang the director's office, rang the basement, rang the computer room, even rang the upper level desk, sir. Couldn't seem to find you."

"Who was it? Was it important?"

"I'm trying to remember who it was, sir. . . . Got it wrote down back at the desk. Shall I take a trot back and have a look?"

The desk seemed very far behind them.

"No, don't bother. I expect it was my wife."

"There you are, sir. Right first time. At first she said it was important, then when I told her I couldn't find you she said not to worry. Said it didn't matter." They pottered on, arrived at the doors. "Still, you're going home now, sir, so I expect you'll hear all about it. . . ."

They went through the doors and down the steps. On the path they parted from the porter and walked away, slowing, their eyes becoming accustomed to the moonlight. Behind them the computer center was in darkness, except for the foyer. As they moved further away they were able to see the glow from the glass dome and to make out the figure of Professor Billon. He was sitting exactly as Matthew had seen him last. Something, possibly this sight, started Scarfe talking.

"You know, I nearly didn't tell him. If his favorite word hadn't been humbleness I don't think I ever would have. . . . I suppose you think I'm just another sadistic cripple."

Matthew thought nothing. There was a bigger conclusion he needed to find.

"He had to be told, of course. You'll see why in a couple of minutes."

He wasn't yet certain, he couldn't yet see for sure if the mistake was inevitable. The edge between necessary pride and outright delusions of grandeur was narrow. Scarfe caught at his arm.

"Honestly, Dr. Oliver, doesn't it terrify you to think of society in the hands of people like yourself?"

Matthew wouldn't argue. It was suddenly possible that his wife had been right.

"At least the rest of the project is sound enough," he said, hoping to be left that much.

"Do you really think so? The director doesn't. Not now. He's shrewder than you, even if he is madder."

Matthew stared up at the dome against the sky. It contained whatever trust in himself he could ever have.

"I'm going back," he said.

"I wouldn't, Dr. Oliver."

"I'm not asking for your advice."

"But I'm giving it. Just wait another two or three minutes."

Matthew shook him off and ran back the way they had come. Scarfe stared after him till he came into the light from the foyer and vanished inside the building. Perhaps he was better dead. Andrew Scarfe had done his best. And Dr. Oliver would make a far more useful scapegoat *in absentio.*

The house was silent. After Dr. Mozart's warning about gas they were left to think it over. She waited by the telephone, listening to bells ringing in various parts of the computer center. The clock in the sitting room said five to one—if she kept the porter much longer he would be late going out on his rounds. She would not for anything have his death her doing. She told him it didn't matter. She said it wasn't important.

When she had rung off she stood for a moment in the dark, undecided. Then she went through to where her brother was still standing, watching through the broken window above the door.

"Paul, I can't contact Matthew. I must get out. I must try to get to him."

"You haven't time. Leave it to Andy."

"No, Paul. No—I must do what I can."

"You'll never make it."

"I will. I can get up onto the roof from the garden. If I'm careful I can drop down the outside wall."

"It's up to you, then. Just be quick. If I hear them going after you I'll create a diversion out the front here."

She stood for a second staring up at him, grateful for his unexpected sympathy.

"If you're going, then go."

She crept away, out into the garden. Under the brilliant moon it was a tiny landscape of extremes, the shadow of the roof lying across it, one side silvered dew and the other side dead, not there. She had never seen how total was the darkness cast by moonlight. She could use that darkness, slip down the shadowed outside wall and not be seen. And there was still time.

Even for her the climb onto the flat-pitched roof was not difficult, window frames and ledges providing ample footholds. Once on the roof she crawled up to its outer edge, using the tall mass of the fir tree to prevent herself from being outlined against the sky. She sat on the edge of the roof and looked down. Everything was still and quiet. From the cloisters Dr. Mozart's voice came to her clearly, his English as disdainful as ever.

"Have you not yet made up your mind, Mrs. Oliver? You and your brother must know there is nothing to be done. We cannot wait all night, Mrs. Oliver. Please come out now, and avoid further trouble. I promise you will both be treated well."

She turned onto her stomach, her legs hanging over, toes scrabbling at the wall, and let herself slip slowly backward. Her skirt was up around her waist. The edge of the roof hurt her breasts. Then she was hanging by her hands, gathering the courage to drop. She released her hold awkwardly, one hand before the other, twisting her shoulder.

As she fell into the wedge of shadow she was clutched at, surrounded at once by people, by men, by men whose uniforms she could smell. They held her tight. She screamed like a rabbit in a net, and continued to scream till one of the guards got a damp sweating hand over her mouth. She tasted his sweat.

From the front of the house there were confused sounds, banging, shouts, the quick indrawn breath of laser guns, then silence.

The guards led her, surprisingly gentle, around into the brightly lit cloisters. Green light, and a smell of burning wood and brick and flesh. Dr. Mozart met her, tried to block her path; but she looked past him to the small group close outside the front door. Two guards, Paul on the ground between them. The scene was like a smart photograph, underexposed, crudely black and white.

"He came out firing, Mrs. Oliver. What could we do?"

The diversion he had promised. Because she had screamed. . . . She stepped around the German—he made no real effort to stop her—and went to Paul, experienced a quick flush of hope when she saw he was not dead. But his eyes were. When he turned his head to face her, his eyes were.

"Abby? I want to tell you—"

"I'll fetch a priest."

"There's not time." He groped for her hand and held it, his grip very strong. "I remember learning the act of Resignation at school. But it's gone. . . . Pray for me, Abby."

"It's not the words that matter, Paul."

"You'd be surprised, you'd be surprised how much it is the words that matter."

Then he was still for so long, his eyes so empty, that he might have died. One of the guards walked away, examined scorch marks on the wall around the door. Lights were on around the quadrangle, doors open, people roused and curious. She prayed for him.

". . . There are things I want to tell you, Abby."

"Not me. There's no need to tell me anything."

"I want to. I want you to forgive me."

"My forgiveness isn't important."

"You loved Gryphon and I murdered him."

"I loved him once. . . ." She was past surprise. "Not to me, Paul. You don't need my forgiveness."

"Did the guard hear me? Might as well put the record straight."

She looked up at the guard high above her. He nodded.

"He heard you."

"I believed it was right. He knew about us, about the group. I believed it was necessary." He shuddered briefly. "I was mistaken."

The searchlight was turned off. Slowly the moon established squares of gentler light between the pillars. Dr. Mozart approached.

"The ambulance is waiting, Mrs. Oliver."

"It won't be necessary. My brother is dying."

"Not for your brother, Mrs. Oliver. The ambulance is not here for your brother."

Paul released her hand.

"The computer center—you must go while there's still time."

She shook her head. There could be no time at all.

Professor Billon had risen from the desk and was carefully replacing the service manual in the bookcase. He made no comment on Matthew's return. The air under the dome possessed a curiously dead quality; it was the only part of the building where the incessant activity of the Bohn was inaudible.

"Interesting fellow, Scarfe. Devious, but no fool." He kept his head down, looked at Matthew from under his eyebrows. "Strange it should need somebody like that. No way of reckoning the harm we've done, Oliver. The harm I've done."

"I'm involved, Professor." Eager for a place. "If you're throwing guilt around, it's mine as well."

"You think that's what I'm doing?"

"Aren't you?"

"Self-knowledge, perhaps. I've dealt with enough paranoids. Ought to know the signs."

His thought processes, rendered even more obscure by truncation, were beyond Matthew, who was there for reassurance.

"Scarfe was saying the whole project was finished. The Colindale project—all of it."

"Indulge me, Oliver. Will you? Just for a moment?"

He returned to the desk, sat down. He pulled a pad toward himself and started writing. Suddenly he scrubbed the lot.

"Of course the project is finished. Paranoia implicit in every stage. Fed by the tainted, blinkered minds of brilliant lunatics. That sort of thing rubs off, Oliver."

"I think you're exaggerating, Professor. I—"

"For God's sake, man, if you must be loyal, be loyal to people. Not to ideas. Be loyal to me. Sit down. Help me. Listen to me. Indulge me."

Matthew sat down beside him, in the chair that had been occupied by Andrew Scarfe. If everything was not to fall about him he needed to find the break, the fault in his line of reasoning, the jump that had made it possible for his work at the Colindale to be the logical extension of his career and beliefs. Where he had gone wrong. Without that break in continuity he was left with nothing.

"We're left with nothing, Oliver. Except our natural resilience. Our inquiring minds. Nothing more." He turned suddenly sideways in his chair, looked at Matthew as if for the first time. Then he relaxed and leaned back. "Time I told you about my dud eye," he said.

Paul was struggling to look at his watch. Abigail eased back his sleeve and read it for him. Beside them Dr. Mozart's feet shuffled irritably on the smooth mosaic. The waiting guards were beginning to talk in whispers. The time was five past one.

In the seconds of waiting Paul died. His sister, feeling no difference, seeing no difference, was as aware of the event as if his soul had risen like a white dove from his body and flown away across the slanting moonlight. He was dead, his hand no colder in hers, his head no heavier on her arm. She prayed for God's mercy on him and on Matthew, on herself and on all sinners. She lowered his head to the paving.

When the explosion came, it was disappointing. She had hoped for something more sensational. Dr. Mozart was dragging her to her feet. Around them alarm bells were ringing, car engines being started. She stood up slowly.

"It is clear now, Mrs. Oliver, why your brother was here. You have a lot to answer for, the three of you."

"Three of us?"

"Your husband was a part of the plot. I misjudged him. If your brother brought the explosives in, then it was Dr. Oliver who took them to the computer center."

And all she could think of was to tell him that *misjudge* wasn't used like that: you misjudged a man if you thought evil of him when he was really good.

"Where is he now, your husband? You know of course that he cannot possibly escape."

She knew that Matthew was dead. That he had been in the computer center and that he was now dead. She knew this beyond any possible doubt. Toward Andrew Scarfe she felt nothing. He was unimportant. He would go free, perhaps live to blow up the second Colindale and the third. . . . Dr. Mozart was speaking to her, but she couldn't hear. Firelight began to overpower the livid city glow above the roof of the library. The sky became red and full of smoke. Matthew was dead.

"Will you come this way please, Mrs. Oliver?"

Guards came and went, making reports. The fire was under control, would not spread beyond the center itself. No one was able to find the director. He had last been seen by some systems analyst at the upper level Bohn desk.

"Will you come this way please, Mrs. Oliver?"

"If I'm to be charged with something I demand"—why not?—"that my solicitor be present."

"No charge is necessary. The doctor's report is more than adequate. You're a sick woman, Mrs. Oliver."

They would tell her this. Every day they would tell her she was sick, and she must not believe them. For the rest of her time with them she must resist believing them. She was not sick. She did not believe them. She was not sick.

"My solicitor—"

"This is not a legal matter, Mrs. Oliver. You're not a criminal. You have a schizoid personality. Please come this way, Mrs. Oliver."

"I am not sick."

"Please come this way, Mrs. Oliver."

Mrs. Oliver. Wife of Matthew, widow of Matthew. She began to cry. Grief that was long overdue, an inward bleeding, secret. But God loved her and she'd survive. Nobody was tested beyond what he could endure. She let herself be led away down the moonlit cloisters to her novitiate.

Don't miss these

ACE SCIENCE FICTION SPECIALS

A distinctive new series of quality science fiction

88600 — 60¢
WHY CALL THEM BACK FROM HEAVEN?
  by Clifford D. Simak

89850 — 75¢
THE WITCHES OF KARRES by James H. Schmitz

65300 — 60¢
PAST MASTER by R. A. Lafferty

71860 — 60¢
THE REVOLVING BOY by Gertrude Friedberg

66200 — 60¢
PICNIC ON PARADISE by Joanna Russ

83550 — 60¢
THE TWO-TIMERS by Bob Shaw

79450 — 60¢
SYNTHAJOY by D. G. Compton

72600 — 75¢
THE RING by Piers Anthony & Robert E. Margroff

81780 — 75¢
A TORRENT OF FACES by James Blish & Norman L. Knight

14245 — 60¢
THE DEMON BREED by James H. Schmitz

Ask your newsdealer, or order directly from Ace Books
(Dept. MM), 1120 Avenue of the Americas, New York,
N.Y. 10036. Please send price indicated, plus 10¢ hand-
ling fee for each copy.

More

ACE SCIENCE FICTION SPECIALS

37465 — 60¢
ISLE OF THE DEAD by Roger Zelazny

38120 — 95¢
THE JAGGED ORBIT by John Brunner

47800 — 95¢
THE LEFT HAND OF DARKNESS by Ursula K. LeGuin

67800 — 95¢
THE PRESERVING MACHINE by Philip K. Dick

37425 — 75¢
THE ISLAND UNDER THE EARTH by Avram Davidson

71435 — 75¢
MECHASM by John T. Sladek

76385 — 75¢
THE SILENT MULTITUDE by D. G. Compton

65050 — 75¢
THE PALACE OF ETERNITY by Bob Shaw

65430 — 95¢
PAVANE by Keith Roberts

06530 — 75¢
THE BLACK CORRIDOR by Michael Moorcock

72781 — 75¢
RITE OF PASSAGE by Alexei Panshin

24590 — 75¢
FOURTH MANSIONS by R. A. Lafferty

Ask your newsdealer, or order directly from Ace Books
(Dept. MM), 1120 Avenue of the Americas, New York,
N.Y. 10036. Please send price indicated, plus 10¢ hand-
ling fee for each copy.